LIMBO

KENNETH ROYCE

LIMBO

Hodder & Stoughton
LONDON SYDNEY AUCKLAND

British Library Cataloguing in Publication Data
Royce, Kenneth
  Limbo.
  I. Title
  823.914 [F]

ISBN 0-340-57729-0

Published by Hodder and Stoughton,
a division of Hodder and Stoughton Ltd,
Mill Road, Dunton Green, Sevenoaks, Kent TN13 2YA
Editorial Office: 47 Bedford Square, London WC1B 3DP

Typeset by Hewer Text Composition Services, Edinburgh
Printed in Great Britain by Biddles Ltd

TO STELLA

1

For a split second the emotion was almost overwhelming. Then it was gone and the emptiness returned and it was as if he had never even experienced the fleeting fear. It had been enough to make him want to walk away. Yet he remained rooted, standing in a grocer's shop doorway, moving aside as people entered and left, but keeping his gaze on the terraced house across the street, his vision broken at times by some of the heavier traffic.

It was what some estate agents might refer to as a decaying area. This South London suburb had been fashionable once and beyond the means of most. The shabbiness probably encroached after the war when the bombs had taken their toll and nothing was ever the same again.

Someone jostled him and he moved. A man said, "You're blocking the bloody doorway, mate. Why don't you move out?"

Reg Dine, for the first time, took his gaze from the house across the street and bleakly stared at the man. He said nothing but there was something about his gaze which made the man falter and then turn away. Dine moved his gaze back to the house.

Dine's features were drawn as if he was suffering, but the wiry body beneath the expensive clothes was rock hard. His expression could be so intense that he appeared to be transmitting energy like a power pack. At other times he appeared empty and lifeless. He was sixty-one years old and in some respects like his lined features, looked older, and in others much younger, like his quick reflexes and sharp mind. He was well groomed and obviously well-off. He did not belong to this part of South London.

Across the street a door opened and a grey-haired woman emerged with a man who appeared to be elderly, in his late sixties or early seventies. Both were poorly dressed and, as they closed the street door behind them and trundled away, they appeared to be bickering.

Dine felt empty as he watched them, and his vision clouded as though he was peering through a heavy veil. His mind scrambled and he was almost beyond any feeling. Could forty years do that to a lovely, laughing young girl who had been full of fun and vitality? Could it turn her into a near-shuffling, shapeless old woman? It was like watching his own mother as he had remembered her: work-worn, tired, and getting through life day by day without knowing why. Had he made a dreadful mistake? He left the doorway and followed the couple up the street until they stopped at a bus shelter. Not sure of what to do next he continued towards the bus queue, taking in as much as he could as he passed them. He rounded the corner and quickened his pace to the spot where he had parked his car. He had some distance to go.

He unlocked the Mercedes, climbed in and for some moments just sat there thinking. There was nothing to show the nature of his thoughts; there was no-one better at hiding his feelings than Dine; he had had considerable practice. But he finally gave way and gazed upwards to utter an inaudible curse. He dialled a number on the car phone and for a few moments conversed in fluent Cantonese. He drove back towards central London, his driving subdued like so much about him on public view. He was disturbed, but perhaps it was mixed with a peculiar kind of relief. When a degree of shame crept in he dismissed it quickly, there was no room for it, and its intrusion was unjust. Perhaps he should have stayed away, for nothing could come of the visit.

When he reached the London Road and turned towards Brixton his eyes started to water and he wiped them quickly. His cheeks were wet; it must be the cold October air cutting through so he closed the electric windows and switched on the air-conditioning, not really deceiving himself.

* * *

Lonnie Dine walked along the rows of glass-topped vitrines and viewed the objets d'art. Along the walls tall display cabinets contained most of the larger pieces. The room, about forty feet by thirty, was a veritable treasure trove and the alarm system was comprehensive with back-up batteries if the power failed.

There was only one door to the room and that was steel plated with three security locks. There were also contact points between door and frame connected with the main system, as were the sensors buried in the plaster along the door frames should anyone have the wild idea of by-passing the contacts by taking the whole frame out with the door. There were no windows, but the room was on the main air-conditioning circuit, so it was cool, the temperature constant. And there were humidifiers so that the veneer on the antique cabinets did not lift. Recessed spotlights covered the ceiling and were controlled by a battery of switches by the door. No-one was allowed in this room without invitation, a fact which annoyed Lonnie very much. The room was a rich man's playground but, in Lonnie's view such treasures should be shared.

Lonnie liked London. They had moved from Hong Kong to England in 1981 when he was twelve. He was sent to a good private school and was now at Oxford. He often argued with his father. But he cared for him, and worried about him, too. It was a concern he never understood. For his father was rich and had been before he left Hong Kong, but that was merely about money. There were sides to his father he had never understood and sometimes thought it best not to. There were even times when he was afraid for him; really afraid.

He had never known his mother. It was as though she had not existed, and his father had always been too reticent to talk about her. In his father's absence he had searched for, but had never found, anything relating to her. There were no letters, photographs, nothing. He had always assumed that they had not been married; that did not worry him, but he often wondered what had happened to her. When the subject arose his father gave the impression that it was

9

all too painful to talk about. They had quarrelled about his mother more than anything else, sometimes quite violently. At such times Lonnie had seen a side to his father he would have preferred not to have seen, and it had frightened him. He had not raised the matter for years.

The only certainty about his mother was that she had been Chinese. Lonnie had only to look in a mirror to realise that. Although he was taller than most Chinese, almost six feet like his father, he had the olive smooth skin and the dark hair of the Chinese. His eyes, too, were a giveaway, deep brown and slightly slanted and attractive to most women.

Lonnie was twenty-two, an age to find a few things out about himself. He was sure his father needed him although he had never said as much. It was a strange bond, born of uncertainties, the unknown, and yet somehow the sometimes uneasy ambiguity provided the stimulation and the will to see it through. It was as if he was still searching for answers and not sure whether he really wanted to find them.

Lonnie left the room, careful to lock it and to switch on the room alarm which remained on day and night unless one of them was in there. He went to his own study on the top floor and looked out of the tall windows which faced the Thames, and beyond that, Battersea Park. It was a pleasant, untroubled view but why did just the two of them need a four-storey Georgian house on the Chelsea Embankment? They did little entertaining and friends seldom stayed with them. Lonnie himself brought friends home but he had his own apartment in the house; that was useful, of course. And his father had a huge study on the ground floor which was a very private place, even to Lonnie.

Why was he thinking like this? Why now? It was old hat. Perhaps because he had noticed his father was acting rather strangely over the last few days, which had driven him into the shell he could so easily erect to protect him even from his own son. It meant a crisis of some sort.

He did not hear his father arrive but heard him call out. He left the study and ran down the rich carpeted stairs until he reached the first landing. He gazed down the magnificent cantilever staircase which half-circled to the main hall. His

10

father, taking his time, had almost reached the top. He thought his father looked pale. "Are you okay, Pop?"

"Of course I'm all right. And stop calling me Pop; I'm not a bloody American, nor are you."

Lonnie did not reply; his father had too many American friends for that to be taken seriously. Instead he said, "I want to bring a friend of mine round to look at your collection."

Dine reached the main landing showing no sign of being out of breath. "What sort of friend?"

Lonnie grinned. "The usual kind."

"Is she British?"

"What the hell has that got to do with it?" They were walking together towards the main first floor drawing-room. "Actually she's French."

They went into the beautiful room, Dine moving towards the drinks cabinet. He made no hurry to reply which annoyed Lonnie who added, "She's quite honest. She won't steal anything. She's simply hooked on art, whatever its form."

Dine poured out two malts and added ice. He did not ask what his son wanted to drink but handed over one of the charged glasses. They sat down, almost at opposite ends of the huge room, which meant raising their voices to be properly heard. They each had their favourite chairs but nobody had ever suggested placing them closer together.

"What's her name?"

Lonnie was irritated. "Does it matter?" It was not the first time his father had asked the names of visiting friends as though he carried a directory in his head.

Dine gazed across at his son and realised how abrupt he must have sounded. He was too preoccupied with the shock he had received in South London. "I'm sorry, Lonnie. I have something on my mind. But I was only trying to show interest."

Lonnie was not convinced. "Jeanne Darbot. Speaks English better than you do." Immediately he saw his father stiffen, the glass in his hand held rigidly. His father did not like any reference to his early days, it was a closed book, and it was obvious that he had not enjoyed the same standard of education his father had provided for him. "Sorry, Dad,"

11

he added quickly. "I didn't mean that the way it came out. I merely meant that her English is impeccable, as it should be, considering the money her father must have spent on her."

Dine showed no sign of relaxing; a raw nerve had been struck and it still hurt. He raised his drink slowly and sipped it with considerable control. "Of course you can bring her round. There are no secrets in there but most items are valuable and people do talk." And after a short pause, "When are you going to settle on one girlfriend?"

Lonnie grinned. "I'm too young, Dad. It will happen." They were back to normal. His father would work in his study for a while, they would eat together about 7.30 unless either had made a previous arrangement. Lonnie, due to return to Oxford after the weekend, then went his own way while his father largely stayed in to watch television or to read his international newspapers and tinker with the computer in his study. Sometimes his father went abroad for long periods, often at a moment's notice; he kept a suitcase packed for such emergencies and his passport was always up to date.

She was a beautiful girl and wore a simple designer dress beneath a short jacket. Her hair was dark and attractively bobbed and her eyes were full of mischief. She gave Lonnie a ready, wide smile of welcome as he opened the door. To Lonnie's surprise she had a man with her, much older and rather diffident.

"This is my father," explained Jeanne Darbot in English. "He flew over last night. May he see your treasures, too?"

There was little Lonnie could do that would not appear churlish. Surely she had not brought her father as chaperon? Lonnie smiled in defeat and led the way in. Her father would cramp his style completely. Perhaps that was why Jeanne appeared so impish; she had cut off any possible line of attack.

Claude Darbot was dressed formally as if he was going to an important luncheon, but he was pleasant and knowledgeable about art, and grateful that Lonnie had taken such a charitable view of his surprise arrival. He spoke English formally too, with a pronounced accent.

12

Lonnie made coffee, and afterwards took them to the display room, with Jeanne giving him a wicked smile as she stepped ahead of him. He unlocked the door and they stepped through, Lonnie closing the door behind them. He switched on the lights, adjusted a few of the directional beams, and led them round.

None of the items was described. Dine himself knew what each one was and where it had come from, but Lonnie was not so well informed. The objets d'art came from all over the world. It would be natural for jade carvings from Hong Kong to be included, but there was beautiful Shibayama inlay in lacquer and ivory from Japan and treasures from all round Europe, including a Fabergé egg mounted on an elaborate gold tripod. There were also miniature paintings on tiny easels in some of the larger cabinets.

From the start it was clear that Claude Darbot had a deep knowledge of objets d'art in general and was able to supply some of the background to various pieces. He was quickly absorbed and went his own way, fascinated at what he saw. He looked up once, while Lonnie was trying to hold Jeanne's hand behind a cabinet across the room, and expressed his sincere appreciation at being allowed to see the collection.

At the far end of the room Darbot leaned forward, peering through the glass at some Sèvres figures. Suddenly he froze and felt rather faint. He put his hand against the cabinet to steady himself and turned his head so that the others would not see his expression.

Slowly he re-focused, to stare at the figure that had caught his attention. His stomach churned. He would never forget that night in Paris. Never. Nor could he ever forget the beautiful, white biscuit group of mid-eighteenth century Sèvres porcelain standing proud behind the glass. Were there others? But how had this one got here? He glanced quickly across the room but the two youngsters seemed to be happily engaged with each other. Thank God, for he knew he was not hiding his shock too well.

He had last seen the Sèvres piece at the Hôtel Marigny opposite the Elysée Palace in Paris. The Marigny was where foreign dignitaries were housed during official visits. It was

13

early summer 1978 and Nicolae Ceauşescu, the Romanian dictator, and his wife Elena had made a State visit.

It was long ago but he would never forget it. When the Presidential rooms were checked after the Ceauşescus had left they were found to have been plundered. Everything of value had gone. Ornaments, lamps, vases, ashtrays, even bathroom fittings had been removed. It was as though a whole team of thieves had spent several days there. To make it worse, the walls of the rooms had been gouged out as Romanian security men had searched for listening bugs.

The then French President, Valéry Giscard d'Estaing, having received this horrifying news was distraught enough to telephone Queen Elizabeth at Buckingham Palace to warn her as the Ceauşescus were due to arrive in England on a similar State visit. She passed instructions to ensure that what happened in Paris would not happen in London. Nor did it, thanks to the French warning.

Nobody involved in the unhappy affair would ever forget it, but Claude Darbot was unprepared to see one of the stolen items staring him in the face in a private collection in London. He felt he had not the nerve to look for more. Not now. He did not want to give himself away, not in front of the collector's son. He needed time to think.

Could he be mistaken? He smiled grimly to himself. There could be no possibility of that; he carried a mental image of virtually every item that had been stolen. But the one before him was special, rare and modelled by Falconet. It was flawless, a superb piece of craftsmanship.

His mouth felt dry and he needed a glass of water. He must have appeared ill for Jeanne called out, "Papa, are you all right?"

"I feel a little faint," he said. "Perhaps I'd better sit down."

They took him to the drawing-room and Lonnie gave him a glass of water, noticing the paleness and puzzled because the display room was anything but claustrophobic.

Claude Darbot drank the water and wondered how he should deal with the discovery. He could not leave matters like this. He gazed up at Lonnie, the young, concerned face,

14

and wondered about his father. How could a piece of Sèvres stolen in Paris by a Romanian dictator, be in this house in London, thirteen years later? He had to know. And he could see that he might hurt people while finding out. That was too bad, but the splendid piece belonged in Paris. And where were the others?

2

Thomas Ewing took 'Glasshouse' Willie Jackson, and 'Jacko's' lawyer girlfriend, Georgette Roberts, out to dinner. The fact that Ewing's wife was not there suggested to Jacko that the dinner was not simply out of friendship, although that left him puzzling over why Georgie was invited. The restaurant being one of the most expensive in London bore out his suspicion. Much as he liked Ewing he had the feeling that their host was not footing the bill. Perhaps the thought was uncharitable, but although Jacko trusted Ewing as a person, he did not trust what he represented: politics, a personal dogsbody to the Prime Minister. "How is Liz?" he asked pointedly.

Ewing, unruffled, turned smilingly to Georgie. "That means he does not trust the purpose of this meeting. Suspicious devil."

Georgie, a stunning girl who preferred law to modelling, winked but added seriously, "That's how he has survived."

Ewing turned back to Jacko. "Liz is in New York. She'll be back tomorrow. But you're right. There is something on offer which might interest you."

"Dangerous? Like the last time?" Georgie was Jacko's great protector.

"Would I have invited you along, Georgie, if it was anything like that?" Ewing called for more wine. "A simple enquiry job, that's all."

"Then why don't your simple wooden-tops deal with it?"

"It's delicate. We would rather the police not be involved. A private detective agency could do it, but it is something we would rather keep under wraps. We trust you, and there are few we can say that to."

"And you don't trust your Security Service to take it on?"

Ewing poured the wine. "It's not big enough for them, Jacko. Don't take it as an insult, you should know better than that."

"Is this a request to you from the PM? I mean you still have your old job?"

"Just about. But with a change of Prime Minister I'm not sure how long I'll be there. The source of the request is nearer to the Home Secretary."

"I am no friend of that toe-rag. We've had words in the past."

"You know very well it is not the same man. He's trying to do a favour for the French."

"The French?" It was as if someone had just died. "I don't do favours for the French. Why can't they use their own services?"

"Because the problem seems to be on our soil. I need not have mentioned the French. I'm trying to be honest with you."

Jacko gazed across the table. "There was a time you didn't have to try." Jacko pushed his coffee away in exasperation. "Look I'm tired of sorting out the leftovers from the police, the Security Services, or PIs you'd rather not trust. I'm just a plain cockney kid who lives on a different planet from your crowd, and always will."

"Thanks very much," said Georgie in her most cutting, cultured tone.

Jacko put a hand out to her. "You know what I mean, love. These toffee-nosed sods are only using me. I'm expendable."

"Not to me, you're not," said Ewing, with feeling. "I thought we had quite a friendship, and with the sum I managed to squeeze out of Government for you the last time, I was hardly using you."

"I don't need the money."

"I know you don't."

"So you've nothing to offer?"

"Only more money. And thanks and appreciation from HM Government."

"You can stuff that."

"When you were in the SAS it was Government money that trained you. When you outlined a fellow soldier with bullets as he sat in a chair, who paid for the ammunition? Who paid for the whole experience that has made you what you are?"

"I'm not sure I like what I am. If I did I would have married Georgie by now."

Georgie smiled. Her feeling for him always heightened when he became introspective; it was the only time he was not sure of himself.

Jacko looked miserable, his stocky figure hunched over the table as if he had stomach ache. "Fill me in," he said, "I'll listen."

"A porcelain figure that was stolen from the Hôtel Marigny in Paris in 1978 has pitched up in a private collection in London."

"That's supposed to excite me?"

"The Marigny is opposite the Elysée Palace. They use it for foreign dignitaries." Ewing brushed back his hair, looking his most serious. "It was stolen by Nicolae Ceauşescu."

Jacko stared, his lips twitching with amusement. "Go on."

"He and his wife stayed there. They cleaned out the Presidential Suite."

Jacko tried to take it in. After a while he said, "It didn't do him much good, did it?" And then, "If you know where it is why don't you simply ask the bloke who has it where he got it from?"

"We don't want to upset him. He has excellent contacts in China and Eastern Europe and the trade he generates is valuable to the country. We would rather avoid any form of official enquiry."

Jacko sat back, looked at Georgie who appeared as puzzled as he, and said, "Why the hell should he tell me?"

Ewing lowered his glass. "You're being deliberately obtuse. You have contacts you could use without confrontation. You know all sorts of people."

"Bent people. Villains. Fences. Isn't that what you mean?

18

You know I'm going straight but you have no objection to me digging up the past for your benefit."

"You make it sound far worse than it is. Anyway, it's not for my benefit."

"I wouldn't do it for the bloody French. You've got a nerve, Thomas."

"Supposing it benefits the person who has the thing? Gets him off the hook of suspicion? He's British. He might need help."

"Is this thing valuable? I mean, is it worth all the hassle?"

"It's valuable but hardly worth a fortune. It's not the value that matters but who stole it and how did it reach London. What else might there be?"

Georgie sat back resigned. She knew what would happen and it would have nothing to do with Ewing, the French, a Sèvres figure, money, or any of these things. Jacko always tried to talk his way out of this type of situation, but Ewing knew, as she did, that it would be Jacko's own insatiable curiosity that would decide. It would merely be a question of how he rated the matter. Her presence indicated that the issue was not too serious and could easily be cleared up. She wished her sudden anxiety indicated the same.

"If you're as keen as you say you are to marry me, why don't you take elocution lessons and move to my planet. Then we can do it?"

They were sitting in the back of a cab with their arms round each other and were returning to Jacko's place. "It wouldn't be me, though, would it, love? I mean, every time I rang you'd think it was one of your upper-class friends. They all sound the same. You'd be calling them all darling, thinking it was me. I couldn't take that risk."

"So we'll never make it? We'll live like this for ever. I don't want that, Jacko. Your place or mine; what about *our* place for a change?"

"It's just that I'm afraid of letting you down."

"You've never let anyone else down so why should I be the first one?"

19

"Because you are the only one who matters. I wouldn't want to lose you, Georgie."

"Then you know what to do."

"Let's get this thing out of the way first. Let's detour down to the Chelsea Embankment to see where this bloke hangs out."

Jacko studied the information Ewing had handed to him after dinner. He was sitting alone in the drawing-room of his house in Notting Hill. Since he had got to know and respect Thomas Ewing, he had dropped a lot of his flashy act. His clothes were more sober, and the furniture throughout the house had been replaced by more classical styles. Georgie had at last managed to get him hooked on antiques, and now he studied books on them and visited the V&A with her. It was all much more exciting than he had realised, and with her help he was beginning to buy things.

His dark hair, once shoulder length, was now much shorter. There was little he could do with his tough, granite face, but it was cracked around the mouth because he laughed a lot. The little finger of his left hand remained crooked; it had been broken in training when he was still a serving soldier.

Jacko owned a café in Soho, and a costume clothes warehouse in the East End which theatre and film people often used. He was not short of money, but going straight, part of a bargain he had earlier struck with Ewing in exchange for glossing over certain activities, had deprived him of various incomes.

He went off the rails when his younger brother had died and he had served six months in a military, 'glasshouse', prison, and after that had been discharged from the service. The army had been his life; he had lost that and his friends in one effort. Nobody understood why he had taken the death of his brother so badly, and he sometimes wondered if he understood it either.

There was still quite a wildness about him but it was much more controlled. Getting back with Georgie had made a tremendous difference to his attitude.

It was still quite early although Georgie had gone off to

her office in Highbury. He rose to make coffee and took it back to the settee where he had left Ewing's papers, and went through them again.

It was obvious that the man who at present had the Sèvres group was extremely wealthy. Anyone who lived where he did had to be. The Sèvres was apparently only part of a magnificent collection. Jacko did not need to view the place to accept that it would be comprehensively alarmed. There was no way he could break in even if he wanted to. Although he knew others who might be tempted.

Reginald Dine had started life in Hong Kong. He was born there in 1930, and subsequently made his fortune by trading in a variety of things, but it was property speculation that made his real money. So the dossier proclaimed. He had strong trading links with China and traded quite a lot also in Europe, including Eastern Europe. Jacko pondered; did that tell him anything? Was Eastern European trade all that profitable?

Credentials had been checked at the time, 1981, when Dine came to Britain. Immigration was cautious of anyone even wanting to live in Britain and, perhaps especially, of those who had been born in the British Colonies and claimed British nationality. The authorities were already sensitive to the number of people who might want to come to live in Britain. Some kind of pruning was inevitable to avoid a massive influx once Red China took over Hong Kong.

Dine was only a boy when the Japanese invaded and because of it escaped the worst. His British parents were less fortunate. They were killed during the Occupation and nothing was seen of them again. It was on record, as was Dine's birth certificate. He had been born in Kowloon. His parents' business was crushed by the Japanese and he was placed in a camp for displaced persons. But Dine learned a great deal about survival, and on his eventual release, now in his early teens, he started where his parents left off. But he was still only a boy and too young to cope and made many mistakes. It was not until the early 1960s that he began to emerge as a financial success in a high-density, small colony where huge success was not unknown. Some very wealthy people lived in Hong Kong and, in his thirties, Dine had become one of them.

Dine, however, kept a low profile. He did not mix a lot outside business and this still seemed to be the case. He was virtually a loner, unlike his half-Chinese son who appeared to be a likeable lad. The report did not suggest anything as strong as love between them but the son had shown concern about his father.

Jacko found it strange that Lonnie Dine was concerned for a father who was clearly immensely capable of coping on his own. Lonnie's mother was not mentioned except on his birth certificate. Her name was given as Mae Li Seng. There was no further information and no mention of a marriage. It looked as if it had been a very brief affair and Dine had taken on the responsibility from the resulting birth of Lonnie. Such things happened all the time and, as seemed to be usual, Dine had kept his counsel and just carried on. It was nobody's business but his and Lonnie's, and Immigration's, who were clearly satisfied.

Jacko put the report back in the buff envelope and was not impressed with any of it. The only certainty was that Dine was floating on a sea of cash. Background was something different. Jacko and Ewing had already been down that road with a man called Ashton, now dead, who had an unbelievably obscured background. The difference was that it had not come under official scrutiny until far too late, whereas Dine's had, in order for him to stay in England.

Jacko tried his coffee and found it cold. He pulled a face and put it down. He sprawled on the settee, mulling over the whole business. He was not keen on taking this job but had been unable to refuse. But he did not intend to spend time on it. Ewing would be furious with what he was about to do but it was a quick way out and should have been tackled directly in the first place.

He looked up Dine's number, surprised to find it was not ex-directory. Perhaps it had to be readily accessible for business purposes. He dialled.

"Mr Dine's residence."

A woman; his secretary? "May I speak to Mr Dine, please."

"Who is calling?"

"Detective Sergeant Willis, New Scotland Yard. It's just a quick query, Miss." Jacko hoped he still had the false warrant card handy should he need it.

"Dine. How can I help you Detective-Sergeant?"

"Probably not at all, sir. This is about something that was reported to us some time ago and somehow got lost in the system. Probably because someone saw it as unimportant, and that is probably right. I understand you have a valuable collection and included in it," Jacko scrutinised the piece of paper Ewing had given him with the file, "is a Sèvres biscuit group, whatever that means, modelled by a man called E.M. Falconet, dated about 1760."

"That's correct. It is pronounced bisk, by the way. At its simplest, Sergeant, it means plain white. The paste is unglazed."

"We have reason to believe it was stolen."

A faint sigh came down the line. "That wouldn't surprise me. Collecting is a hazardous business. I do my best to check the background of items I buy. It's not always easy. In the end I have to trust my suppliers and I've been very careful in selecting them. Have you some detail of the theft?"

"Oh, yes. It was stolen from a place called the Hôtel Marigny in Paris in 1978 by the Ceauşescus."

"The Ceauşescus?"

"The Romanians; yes."

"That comes as something of a shock. I bought it much later than that; early 1990. How can you be sure it is the same piece?"

"We are simply acting on information received. We would have to get an expert in to be sure; someone from Paris who knows the piece would have to come over. I was hoping it would not come to that. Did you buy it in Romania, sir?"

"Austria. The documentation is in order; it has been through customs, all the proper channels. You have me worried."

"I'm sure there is no need for that. Did you pick up other pieces from the same source while you were in Austria?"

"I am sure I would have done, but I would have to check."

"Let's leave it at that for the moment, sir. If we want to take it further I'll come back to you. You've been extremely helpful."

"Detective Sergeant, I would like to make it clear that while this group is valuable, and rare, we are talking of relative values. This is a piece of early porcelain, not a masterpiece of a painting. It is something that makes very little difference to me financially and is not something I would take any kind of risk for in order to possess. You understand? I have done everything by the book."

"I'm sure you have, sir. It would not be the first stolen item to be bought legitimately. Don't worry about it. We'll be in touch."

"Thank you. But if I can help further, do contact me. May I have your name again?"

"Detective Sergeant Willis. Goodbye, sir."

Jacko put the phone down and thought he had got nowhere. But where else could he expect to obtain information? At least Dine was not dodging the issue. Jacko smiled. How did he know?

He got up and crossed to the window to view the house opposite through the sweeping net curtains. A West Indian was sitting on the steps with arms bared. Born in Trinidad and taking to the British weather better than the Brits. Jacko pulled the curtain aside and waved.

Ewing was going to do his nut when he found out the short cut Jacko had taken. That evening, when Georgie returned, and while he cooked her a meal, he told her what he had done.

She was astounded. "I thought the whole object of the exercise was to do it surreptitiously, so no hackles would rise. You've warned Dine and offended him at the same time. Thomas will be delighted. Have you told him yet?"

"I didn't want it to appear too easy. I'll hang on for a bit."

24

"Jacko, you sweet idiot, you've blown it. Dine will soon find out it was not the police who called."

"I'm banking on it, Georgie. I've stirred it up if there is anything to stir. I wasn't going to get anywhere by standard enquiry. Let's see what happens."

"You're mad. Anyone could have rung him up."

"But anyone didn't. He thought he was dealing with a copper and acted accordingly. Had it been Willie Jackson he'd have told me to get stuffed and would have threatened me with the police. Come and eat this; I've been working on it for most of the day; it's Italian, delicious."

As Georgie sat down he said, "Have you washed your hands?" She almost threw the plate at him but she knew he was trying to take her mind off what he had done. All she could see was stalemate, and that was not like Jacko at all. Normally he had some plan in mind but when it was as nebulous as this it always worried her.

Reginald Dine ate alone that evening, as he often did. Loneliness was something he could cope with. Isolation could have its advantages. After Jacko's call he had telephoned New Scotland Yard to discover that they did in fact have a Detective-Sergeant Willis, but that he was on a course and would not be back for another week.

He sat at the dining-table long after his live-in cook, Mrs Morris, had cleared it. He had no drink before him and he did not smoke. He just sat there feeling the chill of uncertainty. He had aroused someone's interest and that was something he had managed to avoid for many years. Whoever had phoned was a professional and had handled it very well. But what sort of professional was he and who employed him?

He went to bed and did not draw the curtains. Suddenly he wanted to avoid complete darkness. As he lay gazing up at the misty shadows on the ceiling he suffered a feeling he had not felt for many years. It turned the clock back. He had always looked forward, looking back was the road to disaster and he was not sure he could cope with it.

The strain set up a confusion in his mind and drew a veil

over reality. His thoughts became jumbled until he was not even certain who he was, and sweat began to break out all over his body. He went to the bathroom and gazed at himself in a mirror, appalled at what he saw; an old, grey-faced man full of fear. What had happened to the fighter, the man who took on the world and made it pay?

Dine could feel the tremors creeping over him and he had never been nearer to giving up as then. He could move away but would his fears remain behind? He went to the kitchen and made himself some cocoa, and sat at the table with all the lights on.

Two things had happened that day to unnerve him. One had been self-inflicted, yet he knew he would do it again until satisfied; the other had come out of thin air; he was being investigated. He did not know by whom or why but it had to be stopped.

He was beginning to recover from the shock, think positively as he always had, tackle the problem head on and then remove it, once and for all.

3

Jacko took a cab to the Chelsea Embankment and stood on the nearest corner to keep watch on Dine's house. It was not easy to keep out of sight, but he was not sure he wanted to do that. If Dine was straight he would forget the whole thing, but if he was not he would probably take steps to find out who was harassing him.

Jacko had enough underworld contacts to set up a team to watch Dine's movements but first he wanted to see what he was up against.

It was half-past eight in the morning, there was a chill wind coming off the Thames and it started to drizzle. Jacko suddenly realised that someone in one of the other houses had seen him, as he caught the flick of a curtain on his peripheral vision. In an area like this any suspicious-looking character would be reported to the police and suddenly it seemed a bad idea to hang around.

He walked along the Embankment but realised he was making things worse and was being watched all the way. Not a good moment to discover he was out of practice. And then he saw someone leaning out of a first-floor window of Dine's house. The man appeared to be in his sixties, thinning grey hair and taut face. Jacko kept his head down as a voice called out, "Are you looking for a particular house?"

Dine. Jacko recognised the voice at once, but he had to say something or police would be called.

"I was thinking of buying one of them."

"I don't think there are any up for sale. And I doubt that you could afford one on a policeman's pay."

So Dine had recognised his voice as easily as he had Dine's. He should have attempted to disguise his, but he had set out

27

to stir and could not complain if he had succeeded. "I can dream," he called back.

"Then do it over a coffee. Why don't you come in, you've been dying to."

The invitation was pleasant enough but Dine was not inviting him in to discuss the weather. What the hell? What could happen to him on the Chelsea Embankment?

Jacko crossed over and the door had been released by the time he reached the steps. A plump, grey-haired woman wearing a butcher's apron, who turned out to be Mrs Morris the cook, lingered in the back of the hall. She had obviously hastily been told to tell him to go to the first floor.

Jacko closed the door and mounted the magnificent sweep of stairs to find a dressing-gowned Dine waiting for him on the landing.

"I've been expecting you. I didn't think you would leave it at a phone call," said Dine who led the way into the drawing room. You're a fast worker but this morning's effort was really clumsy for a pro."

"I agree," said Jacko sitting in a proffered chair facing the windows. "It's too early in the morning for me. Either that or I've lost my touch." He had to take his cue from this man who now sat opposite him. He had thrown himself in the deep end and, at the moment, was floundering.

"It will never be too early in the morning for a man like you. Although even good pros slip up. What's your name and who employs you?"

There had been a subtle change of tone. It was still friendly but the equality had disappeared. Dine was now treating Jacko more as an employee. By the slightest change of emphasis he was now talking down to him.

Before Jacko replied Mrs Morris brought in a tray of coffee and put it down near Dine. "Black or white?" asked Dine.

"Black, please." Jacko noticed that the coffee jug was a plain pot; not the silver service for him.

Dine handed over a cup not asking whether or not Jacko wanted sugar. There was no spoon in the cup, so it was black and bitter.

"You haven't answered my question," said Dine.

28

"I didn't think you expected me to. And anyway, you already know my name." He produced his forged warrant card and held it forward.

"Bullshit," said Dine without raising his voice. "You knew I would check with the Yard. What game are you playing?" Jacko had the impression that he was nearer to the real Dine, a no-nonsense Dine, battle-hardened. "I'm doing a private job. My client's name is unavailable and I could give you any name you want so you give me one."

"How about Liar?"

Jacko was not put out; he was fencing and so was Dine. "I don't think we're going to get anywhere," said Jacko. "What about telling me all about the Sèvres group?"

"I've already told you. But when you've finished your coffee I'll take you to see it. Could that be fairer?"

Jacko was finding Dine an interesting man, not because he was rich, he had met too many of those to be impressed, but because there was something totally different about him. He did not seem to be upset by the harassment, yet he would not have invited Jacko in if he had not been worried, otherwise he would simply have called the police, something he could still do if he wanted.

As he finished his coffee, Jacko said, "My name is Jackson."

Dine rose. "I suppose that's as good as any. Have you a first name?"

"Willie. A good old English name. Solid."

Dine smiled and led the way to the door. "Almost original. Willie? That's good. Well, it's a step but if you ever feel inclined to give your real name, please feel free."

The display room made an immediate impact on Jacko. He had been studying hard but he was not prepared for this.

"You can look at the other stuff later, but this is what you rang about. Beautiful, isn't it?"

"Oh, yes. I thought that was what was called Parian ware."

"There is a technical difference between Parian and biscuit. Basically it is unglazed porcelain, but that is not what you have come about."

29

"No wonder Ceauşescu nicked it."

"I have only your assertion that he did. It probably passed through several hands before reaching me. Who is this person who claims it was stolen?"

"I don't know and that's the truth. He's not my boss. I'm beginning to wonder if any of it means a toss. It seems to be in good hands so far as I am concerned. I think I'm wasting my time."

"I'm certainly wasting mine. My only excuse for bringing you in here is because I never tire of looking at such beauty. Do you know anything at all about such treasures?"

"Very little. I'm learning but there is such a lot to grasp. It's easy to get hooked on it."

"So what do you intend to do now?"

Dine voiced the question softly, as if it did not really matter, but Jacko felt the tingle of old; it mattered a great deal. To them both. Dine had thrown down the gauntlet and would deal with it either way.

Jacko gazed slowly round the room. "I report back. I'm no further forward. I don't really see that it matters where it came from. Better here than in Romania."

"It matters to whoever sent you. Was he a Frenchman?"

"No. Not the person who asked me to look into it. Who asked him I have no idea."

"You're not listed as a private detective?"

"Definitely not."

"Yet you are acting for someone of influence. So you must be known to that person and the way you handled it yesterday, and are handling it even now, suggests you are well used to enquiry. You must be someone special and that puts a different complexion on things."

"It's not my usual work," said Jacko. "I'm simply doing someone a favour."

"Well, I have you on record, I'll see if I can run you down."

Jacko grinned. "I noticed the camera. Tidy job." He took one last look round and headed for the door. "I don't know why you're bothered."

"Because I don't like people interfering in my affairs. You

may have found a novel way to case the place; I noticed you weighing up the alarms."

"Too difficult for me." And then, as he reached the door, "You must do what you feel you must, Mr Dine. But I do appreciate your inviting me in. An education."

"You'll get another one if I see or hear of you again. I've been straight with you, and open. This had better end here and now."

They reached the landing and Jacko went to the head of the stairs. "That sounds like a threat, Mr Dine."

"A promise, Mr Jackson."

Jacko noticed the change of tone again. Once more he felt nearer to the real Dine, but immediately wondered why he should think that. Was Dine putting on an act all through? In a strange way he felt a sudden affinity with him, as though they had something in common.

Then he saw something in Dine's expression that warned him, and it was a warning he chose to heed. He wasn't dealing with a wealthy man with a fabulous collection; there was much more to Dine than that.

"Why don't you call the police?" he prompted.

"Is that what you want?"

"If I was as innocent as you seem to be, that's what I would do."

"I don't think you would. I think you would take care of it yourself which is exactly what I intend to do. It's what I've always done."

They reached the hall and stood behind the impressive door to face each other. "I quite like you, Willie. There was a time in my life when I could have done with a friend like you. But I had to look after myself. I still do. I'm very good at it, so let's go our own ways, shall we? I hope we don't meet again."

Ewing did not know what to say. He sat in Jacko's drawing room, drinking whisky rather than his usual Campari, now that the weather was colder. Eventually, he said, "It was a bit of a bulldozing approach, wasn't it? Not exactly subtle. I mean, you've cut off your tail." He sounded bitterly disappointed.

31

Jacko replied touchily, "I don't know what you expected me to find. He's willing to admit the Sèvres could be stolen and might have changed hands several times before it reached him. He has made no denial at all. What more do you want? If the French want it back let them go through the courts. I don't suppose they will get anywhere. And, anyway, doing it this way has kept your expenses down."

"So there is nothing to the man?"

Jacko looked surprised. "I thought you wanted me to find out about the Sèvres, not the man. He's an enigma."

"In what way?"

Jacko looked disgusted. "If I knew that he would not be one, would he? There's my bill." He handed over a type-written sheet and Ewing whistled as he saw the amount.

"You're not that good," observed Ewing. "This is a bit steep."

"If you don't like it use somebody else. If you want the best then you pay for it."

Ewing threw the bill down on the low marble table between them. "Anyone could have telephoned."

Jacko grinned wickedly. "But not as Detective-Sergeant Willis of New Scotland Yard. That takes class and nerve. That's what you pay for. If you are going to challenge my charges then that's the last time I do anything for you."

Ewing pulled a face and produced his cheque book.

"Cash," said Jacko. "Tomorrow will do. And I take it you don't want me to proceed any further?"

Ewing got up and poured himself another drink. Whatever their differences Ewing always felt at home in Jacko's house; it was one place he could be himself and speak without having to worry whether it would go beyond these walls. "I think you should go to Hong Kong," he said quietly as he returned to his seat.

Jacko heard the front door unlock and a moment later Georgie put her head round the door. Seeing Ewing she said, "Hello, Thomas. Don't get up, I'm not coming in. Things to do." She was about to close the door when Jacko called out, "He wants me to go to Hong Kong."

Georgie looked from one to the other. Still half-hidden

behind the door, she said, "I don't think much of that. I can't get away." She closed the door and they could hear her footsteps going towards the rear of the house.

"That's your answer," said Jacko.

"A pity." Ewing glanced at his watch. "I must get back. I promised Liz I'd take her out this evening." He rose and drained his drink as if it was lemonade.

"You aren't interested in the Sèvres at all, are you? Well, maybe a little. You are interested in the man and thought I'd continue on because he intrigued me."

"Well, doesn't he?" Ewing put his empty glass down.

"Not enough to go to Hong Kong without Georgie. Sorry, Thomas."

"Oh, well. I'll be off then. If you change your mind, let me know."

The telephone rang when they were halfway to the door. Jacko took the call on the hall phone as Ewing lingered by the front door. "Willie Jackson."

"Yes, I know. You really did give me your own name. Wasn't that careless?"

Jacko mouthed 'Dine' silently to Ewing over the mouthpiece. "Why should it be careless? I thought we were both being honest with each other. You've got me on camera; you'd have traced me sooner or later. I'm surprised you bothered."

"I just wanted to let you see how quickly you could be run down. I now know where you live."

"Bully for you. And I don't intend to move in the near future. Was there something else you wanted to say?"

"I've already said it. I just wanted you to know that I know where you are."

"I hope you sleep better for it, Mr Dine."

"Oh, I will. But will you? Think about it. Good evening."

4

Ewing collected his raincoat from the hall stand, noticed Georgie further down the hall, and refrained from asking Jacko the obvious question.

"It makes no difference," said Jacko, reading him correctly but keeping his voice down. "I tried a frontal attack and he's counter-attacked the same way. With a man like that it's inevitable. Maybe another good reason for my not going to Hong Kong. This guy just warned me off. And I take it seriously."

Georgie called from the back of the house, "Give my love to Liz."

"Of course, Georgie. I'll fix something up for the four of us. See you."

Jacko went out of the door with Ewing and they stood on top of the steps. From the direction of the house opposite came a low whistle. They looked across the street. Ewing's white Daimler Sovereign was parked outside the house of the West Indian who, initially on Jacko's request, kept an eye on the car when it was there. The West Indian was seated on the top step, now with a jacket on. It was not easy to see him for it was already quite dark and he used the shadows well.

Jacko knew the whistle was to attract his attention but he had to strain to see the almost imperceptible signal, an index finger indicating somewhere further down the street. Jacko squeezed Ewing's arm in warning and escorted him to his car.

Ewing unlocked the car door, knowing something was wrong, and taking his cue from Jacko. Jacko gazed up at the shadow as he held the door open while a frustrated Ewing climbed in.

34

"Four doors down this side," a voice whispered.

"Thanks, Sam." Jacko leaned down and said to Ewing, "Bring another thirty quid for Sam. It's about time you paid him for looking after the car."

"Yes, of course." Ewing was peering up hoping Jacko would give some idea of what was going on, but all Jacko added was, "Drive away slowly on full beams after I've backed off a few paces." He patted the roof of the car and stepped back against the railings lining the street. The car moved off and Jacko ran quickly and silently in its wake.

Ewing turned the corner as Jacko reached the foot of the steps Sam had indicated. He raced up them as someone started to go down, and thumped the figure in the midriff as he tried to go past. As the figure bent double with a rasping gasp, he side-handed him on the back of the neck. By this time Sam was at the foot of the steps keeping watch.

Jacko knew he had to work quickly; the house comprised several apartments and someone might appear. He dragged the body under the porch, propped it against a wall and went through the man's pockets. He found a detective agency identity card, and felt a little sorry for the man; he slapped the face gently until he slowly came round and he kept repeating the question, "Who sent you?"

When the answer finally came from the still bemused detective it was no more than Jacko expected; he had merely been assigned to watch Jacko's house by his employers, and to report on any callers. Jacko removed a notebook and miniature tape recorder and slipped them in his pocket. He gazed down at the man who was still not steady enough to climb to his feet, and reckoned that, if he was only half a detective, he would remember Ewing's car number.

Jacko managed to extract the location of the man's car and fortunately it was just down the street. With Sam's help he got the detective to the car. Jacko found the car keys and they bundled him into the driver's seat and left him there to drive off when he felt up to it.

As they walked back to Sam's place Jacko passed across some bank notes which Sam immediately tried to give back. "I don't need paying for that, Jacko."

"I know you don't. But that's from the boyo in the Daimler and there's no way I'm handing it back to him. Take it."

Jacko crossed the street to find Georgie outside on the top step. "What's going on?" she asked. "You've been so long."

"I had to clear up a few things with Thomas and then had a few words with Sam. Come on, it's chilly out here."

He was dying to look at the notebook and listen to the tape recorder, but he did not want to worry Georgie so had to wait until they had eaten. He explained he had a few things to do and went to his study while Georgie read through a brief in the drawing-room.

The detective was Lawrence Reed and he worked for the Dalton Enquiry Agency. 'Nobby' Dalton was an ex-Scotland Yard Flying Squad officer and ran a highly respected agency. It was the kind of agency whose books were always full and Dine must have waved a fat cheque to get taken on so quickly.

As Jacko expected the notebook contained the time Reed had taken up observation, the times of Ewing's and Georgie's arrivals, and, of course, their car numbers. There was a good deal of abbreviated material on other cases. He tore out the relative page and then ran back the tape and played it. It took some time to run through but there was nothing relating to his affairs.

He placed both notebook and tape recorder in a small jiffy bag and clipped it. He then addressed it to the Dalton Enquiry Agency. He checked a number in the directory and rang 'Nobby' Dalton at home.

"Willie Jackson. We met briefly a couple of times. I think we know more about each other than those brief meetings suggest."

"Oh, I know all about you. Look, I'm in the middle of dinner; is this important?"

"I have Lawrence Reed's notebook and tape recorder. He's the operator you designated to watch my house. I'll let you have them back in exchange for the name of the person who hired you."

"Don't be stupid. You've committed theft, probably with

assault. You're a common mugger, Jacko. And as all my calls are monitored, you've confessed for the record."

"As you have to invasion of privacy, and out-and-out harassment, mate. Take me to court, Nobby. It will sound good for your bloke to confess publicly that his notebook and recorder were taken from him while in the line of duty. And details for your other clients on tape and paper will make a few people furious. You'll lose quite a few clients, Nobby, not to mention your reputation."

"That's blackmail."

"And so was yours. What about it? A fair exchange?"

"You know I can't do that. Apart from ethics, I'd be committing commercial suicide. Just send the stuff back and let's both forget it."

"Let me put it another way. I know who hired you, I just want to be sure."

"Don't be daft."

"Okay. If I give you a name, just say nothing if I'm right. Reginald Dine."

There was silence but Jacko knew that Nobby was still there. After a few seconds, Jacko said, "Thanks, Nobby. I'll send the stuff back."

"Thanks for what? I wouldn't have said anything whatever name you gave or how many. Don't grasp at straws, Jacko. Be a good boy and return the stuff, and I hope you haven't done my boy any serious injury, or you're in trouble."

Jacko cut off then rang Dine. Mrs Morris answered the phone and Jacko had to wait.

"Yes? You're interrupting a meal."

"Everybody eats so late. That was clumsy putting a PI on to me. He retired injured."

"I don't know what you are talking about."

Jacko found himself cut off but was satisfied. Dine had sounded shaken. And that was how he wanted him to be. As he joined Georgie in the drawing-room he worried about her and Ewing. If Reed had remembered the car numbers Dine would quickly trace them. He could protect Georgie to a large extent and did not think she was at risk. But Ewing would be traced back to his political connections and Dine

37

might arrive at the right conclusion the wrong way; as far as Jacko knew this was not a political issue. Ewing was not capable of looking after himself in any physical way and he wondered if he should warn him.

Georgie put her papers away as Jacko sat beside her. She quickly saw his preoccupation. "What's on your mind?"

"I think Dine has managed to get Thomas's car number. I think he will connect him with this enquiry. Should I tell Thomas?"

"Is he in some sort of danger?"

"Well, for an innocent man, Dine seems to have taken some strange steps. More and more he's showing he has something to hide and if he thinks Thomas has instigated an enquiry against him there might be a development. I don't know. Thomas has never been in the front line before."

Georgie tucked her long legs under her. "If he has Thomas's number then he has mine."

"I think our association will be taken for what it is. Why should you be involved? Thomas has connections that might worry Dine."

"I thought you had given this up when you refused to go to Hong Kong. You make it sound like some kind of war."

"That depends on whether Dine is protecting his privacy or something else. I had given it up, Georgie. That was the idea. But it might not be willing to let me go. Dine may not believe I've given it up. I think I'd better warn Thomas." He went out to the hall telephone.

When Jacko went down to make coffee next morning he checked that the post and newspapers had arrived. He took them in to the kitchen and started to open the mail while the coffee was percolating. Amongst the usual circulars was a small, brown-paper parcel sealed with sellotape. As he tore away at the tape he suddenly saw a thin wire along the wrapping underneath.

He tore no more off. He carefully placed the parcel in a bowl of water and carried it out, pushing it under a bench at the far end of the small walled garden.

He had to curb his impatience and hide his anxiety until

Georgie had left for her office. When finally she had gone he went out and pulled the bowl from under the bench. He lifted the package out and used scissors to snip away at the paper.

Jacko was lying flat. It had been a long time since he had defused any kind of bomb and he took his time. Long before he had finished he was convinced it was a hoax but had to be sure. Eventually he finished up with a pile of soaked brown paper, a large wad of cotton wool, a cardboard box now cut open and a piece of wire running round it and crudely held on with glue.

Dine had moved fast. If there was any lesson to be learned it was that. In a very short time he had hired a detective agency and posted a dummy bomb as a graphic warning.

Jacko threw the mock parcel bomb into the outside bin and went back into the house. He was worried, puzzled and angry. All this because of a stolen group of Sèvres figures? It was overkill.

He sat in his study and wondered what to do. He had deliberately provoked Dine and so could not complain at what had followed. It was the extent to which Dine had gone that concerned him most. There was something crude about it yet, at the same time, ruthless. It did not add up. A gangster would have been more specific if believing himself in real danger. His warning would have been more directly brutal, like a threat to Georgie, or an attack in the dark and most certainly he would not have used a detective agency, he would have used his own men. It was this sort of reasoning that had made him believe Georgie was in no kind of danger. Now he was uncomfortably unsure.

Jacko drove his Ferrari to his costume warehouse in London's East End. The area was just one more due for redevelopment. He pulled up in a narrow stretch of dilapidated buildings, no longer in use except for his own business. He knew he would eventually have to move but meanwhile it suited him well. He did not need a plush district or a grand shop window for what he hired out. He had a good selection and was well known. Behind the narrow, virtually unused street, almost an alley, the high-rise buildings rose from the dock area like a bizarre backcloth on a film set.

The padlock was off the big double doors and one was slightly ajar. He went in and passed between the rows of costumes, dresses, and uniforms, towards the admin section at the rear. Two women sat in a glass-fronted office and greeted him as if he had come for a job.

"Show a little respect," he said, "I own the place."

"Then drum up more business; we're dying of boredom here." Molly McCann was fat, jolly, and in spite of her name, Welsh. Nobody knew how it came about.

"It's the recession," said Jacko. "Nobody in this country can afford to make films or run big parties these days. It'll come back." He smiled at the younger girl. "Take no notice of her; she was born miserable." He turned to Molly. "Keep those doors closed. Let them ring the outside bell and look through the letter-box before letting anyone in. You're asking to be mugged."

Jacko went round the rails and selected a military uniform and a dark suit. From another section he took an array of wigs, false beards and moustaches.

"Doing a job, are you?" asked Molly who had accompanied him.

"You'll definitely be mugged," said Jacko and telephoned Georgie from his own small office opposite the girls', to ask her to check on any companies owned by Dine or of any directorships he might hold. He hung up before she could argue. From a row of shelves he produced the latest copy of *Who's Who* and found nothing under Dine's name. He then took down the *Institute of Directors Directory* and again found no entry.

Jacko drove home, parked and carried his bundle into the house, dumping it in a spare room in case Georgie saw it. He went round the house inspecting the window locks, and he tested the alarm. He was getting jumpy, which annoyed him.

He did some work in his study – he usually checked the café accounts at home – and in the early evening started to prepare a meal for Georgie and himself; it was something he always enjoyed doing.

40

When Georgie came home they embraced as they always did, and then went into the drawing-room for a drink. He had barely sat down opposite her when she said, "Dine telephoned me today; well, someone on his behalf".

Jacko almost choked on his drink. Before he recovered, Georgie added, "He, through his intermediary, wanted to know if I could handle some work for him."

Jacko was speechless for a while. And then he asked, "And what did you say?"

Georgie laughed. "You are really thrown, aren't you? Has he beaten you at your own game, Willie?" She never called him Jacko. "The element of surprise you are always telling me about?"

"Don't touch it. Don't touch anything he wants you to handle. He'll compromise you. You know damn well why he's done this."

"I need the work. And what has been mentioned is something I can do. And the fee is far better than I could get elsewhere for the same kind of work."

Jacko was irritated. "I thought you had a scale of fees?"

"Oh, yes, but when someone wants a favour there is nothing to stop him offering more."

"So you are going to do it? Georgie, don't be a fool."

"It seems straightforward. He's got to use someone."

"But why should he use you? He doesn't even know you. You're being stubborn, Georgie. You're not thinking it through."

Georgie spread her arms along the back of the chair, looking her most provocative. "It's you who's not thinking it through. I've no reason to refuse. It's work. I am told I have been recommended by another company. Don't you think it will look very odd if I don't accept?"

"But Dine must know you are very close to me. He's attacking me from all possible angles and all at the same time. I've never known anything quite like this. And all over a piece of Sèvres nicked from the French fourteen years ago? Gertcha. He's trying to stop me looking closer, and setting out to impress just how quickly he can move. And he can. Keep out of it, Georgie, before you're in up to your neck."

"If I say no he'll know you've warned me. And who knows how a man like that will react? If you are worried about me I would guess that I'll be safer accepting than refusing."

"What a bloody mess." Jacko felt he was losing all control of the situation. "I wonder what else he'll come up with." But he was speaking to himself. He said to Georgie, "I suppose it's too early for you to have come up with anything about his holdings?"

"I've had to farm it out to a friend. It should not take too long to run him down; if there is anything to find."

Jacko was inclined to think the same and it came as little surprise two days later to hear that Dine did not seem to be listed anywhere about anything. Yet surely he must hold shares in something; he would not keep his money under the floorboards, or totally in objets d'art.

The following day Georgie discovered, through an intermediary, that Dine had held an account with a commercial bank under investigation for alleged money laundering and other indiscretions. But the trail stopped there. Dine had closed his account.

During the three days covering these enquiries nothing else had happened to disturb Jacko. Georgie had taken on some work introduced by Dine but was not dealing directly with him. She confirmed that the work she was doing was perfectly straightforward and above board. Perhaps that had been Dine's aim, to show that his affairs were prosaic.

So here was an obviously wealthy man, active, yet not listed as a company director and not known as a big investor. He had to do something with his money. To check off-shore holdings would be difficult and could take a long time. As at least some of these would probably be shady they would be well guarded by a mass of confusing companies, holding companies, false names, and Jacko accepted that he did not have the resources to look into them. Even with official help it could take months, even years for a full account.

The early impetus died down. Jacko received no more threats and Georgie continued with her work, pleased by now with the extra business. It seemed that Dine was a man who made his point forcefully and speedily, and once sure his message had come across, left well alone.

Jacko, having decided to give up the enquiry, mainly because he was afraid for Georgie, drove to the costume warehouse, and went in to return the uniform and suit he had taken out. He had a chat with the girls and was on his way back to the car when an enormous explosion blew the double doors in and threw him backwards.

5

As Jacko was blown off his feet he heard the girls scream behind him and the crash of glass. There was a terrible rending of metal as the racks nearest to the door were hurled back and the wheels screeched.

The rack wheels needed oiling. It was a ridiculous thought as he lay among a pile of assorted costumes, pinned by some of the racks. He must have hit his head on the hard floor for it felt as if it was bursting and his mind was scrambled. He tried to move but the effort was solely in his head.

Then there was confusing movement and women's voices, one half-sobbing, and someone was trying to pull the racks away. Jacko made a stronger effort and managed to move a little. It was Molly's voice that penetrated his mind and made him strive further.

"He moved. Oh, God, he's not dead."

Good, caring Molly. Jacko heard himself say, and it sounded as if he had been drinking heavily, "It's okay, Molly, it was the blast." What blast? Jacko really struggled now, pushing away the piles of clothes and metal. His memory returned as he managed to sit up with the help of the two girls.

He gazed blearily around. "What a bloody mess. It must have been a gas main. Has someone phoned the gas board?"

But they were still trying to sort out the mess around him and there was no smell of gas. His vision seemed impaired as he tried to gaze round, and then in panic, he made a final effort and stood unsteadily, the girls holding him by each arm. "Jesus, what the bloody hell happened?" Through a clearing haze he saw the two big double doors, one blown completely off, the other hanging at an angle, the hinges ripped off. "Get

on to that chippie we know. Get him to fix those doors quick."
But as Molly moved away Jacko almost collapsed again and
they helped him to a chair in his office.

It was some minutes before he was ready to walk unaided.
He again told Molly to get on to the chippie; he wanted
the doors fixed quickly otherwise it would mean moving
all the stock out. He stepped out of the office to assess the
damage. The front glass of the girls' office had been blown
out; somehow the blast had channelled down the main aisle
and the racks on each side were worst affected.

Apart from the doors, which could easily be fixed, and
the general mess caused by the overturning racks and the
scattered clothes, things were not nearly as bad as they
seemed. As he went towards the door the younger girl
followed, repeatedly asking if she should call the police.
Jacko ignored her. He did not want the police here. "Stay
there," he instructed, and then carefully stepped past the door
out into the narrow street.

He could feel the heat even as he stepped through. The
smell of burning rubber turned his stomach, and flame and
smoke still spiralled from several piles of smouldering metal
scattered all the way along for some distance. One section
of metal had hit the opposite wall and had torn a great hole
from it.

As he stood there in despair and disbelief he realised that
the piles of smouldering scrap had once been his beautiful
Ferrari. He stepped away from the doors and leaned against
the wall. He slowly sank to his haunches as he began to take
it in. This had been no gas mains explosion but a bomb in
his car.

Jacko realised he would have to call the police. The sound
of the explosion would have been heard some distance away,
even over the noise of distant traffic. He gazed along the
narrow street at the separate piles of twisted metal and
debris, and realised that the bomb was much bigger than
even the IRA used. This was no gutted car, but one that had
literally been blown to bits.

For a while he did not move; he was confused and bitter
and was having trouble controlling a slowly rising anger. He

eventually rose and went back inside to learn that the chippie was on his way. The girls were looking at him strangely, knowing that the police should be called.

Without explaining to them what had happened outside, Jacko picked up the phone and dialled a special number Ewing had given him some time ago in case of emergency. He prayed that Ewing would be there and was relieved when he answered. "Jacko," he announced. He glanced over the phone at the two girls, knowing they were about to be further shocked. "My car has just been blown to bits outside my warehouse. I might have been in it. Now just listen, Thomas. I will have to call the police. Have you anything to advise before I do?"

The question had no sooner been asked when they heard a police siren; a patrol car probably trying to locate the area of the explosion.

"You don't think it was Dine, surely?"

"Who the hell else do you think it was? Give me some advice quick; they're on their way, you can probably hear the siren."

"Just tell them what happened. Don't mention Dine. I'll have a word first with some people I know and will advise you further. I'm terribly sorry to hear this, Jacko. Are you absolutely all right? Do you need a doctor?"

"Is that the best you can do, Thomas? The police are going to want some answers."

"Just give them the facts. You have no enemies and no idea of why this should happen. Obviously, it is mistaken identity."

"I've worked that out for myself. Thanks for nothing."

When Jacko looked across the desk he noticed that the younger girl was shivering and scared out of her mind. He should not have called in front of them, but even now he could not think straight. "You go home, love. Take tomorrow off. And the next day if you don't feel up to it."

The girl made a dash for the door and called back over her shoulder, "I'm not coming back to this bloody place. I don't want to be blown up." Jacko gave a signal to Molly who hastened after the girl in an effort to calm her down.

46

When Molly had gone he dialled 999 and asked for the police; they would have to take the stuff away for forensic, anyway. When he went outside again there were people each end of the street. One or two had ventured nearer. Before putting a handkerchief over his mouth, Jacko called out, "There's some gas about. Be careful. There might be further explosions."

It cleared the onlookers to the ends of the street again and there they hovered until the siren preceded the flashing blue light and the small crowd opened up to let the police car through.

"Jesus!" exclaimed the first policeman to climb out. He gazed at the main bulk of twisted metal and asked, as though it was a routine matter, "Is that your car, sir?"

"It was," said Jacko. "There was nobody in it at the time."

Jacko met Ewing at the Hot Pot, a club frequented by dubious characters, which snuggled under a film agency and was squashed between a wine bar and a strip club. Ewing totally out of place, sat with Jacko in the furthest corner of the bar realising from the glances cast at him that he was cramping a few styles.

The wine list was surprisingly good and so was the coffee; even some villains have good taste. Jacko said, "Don't be so uneasy. They know me so you'll be okay. You won't be mugged on the way out."

"Thanks very much. Couldn't we have met somewhere else?"

"I couldn't meet you at home; I don't want Georgie to know anything about this. She would be scared out of her wits. She thinks I'm putting in a little late work."

Ewing nodded in understanding; he would have the same problem with Liz. "How did it finish with the police?"

"I've got form, albeit only military, so they don't believe a word I say. They won't get anywhere with it because they decided it was the IRA. I'm ex-SAS, and served under-cover in Northern Ireland, so they are happy to follow that line. They'll hand it over to C13, the Anti-Terrorist Squad, and I'll probably get a visit from them which is a pity because I don't like those boys wasting time."

Ewing sipped his wine and then said, "Couldn't it be true?"

"You just don't like the idea that it could be Dine. The IRA fit better and no-one is surprised if it is not solved. Don't mess about with my life, Thomas. It was not the IRA, they make mistakes but would be more likely to get the quantity of explosive right. I'm willing to bet that it was not Semtex that was used, but something more old-fashioned like gun-cotton and Aminol. The explosion was wild; too much was used."

"Thank God you were not killed."

"That's the big question, isn't it? Was I meant to be? I'll never know. If it was a timed explosion there is no way anyone could know whether I would be in the car or not. If it was command-operated it means someone was around the warehouse and probably detonated deliberately as soon as the car was empty. I would have noticed if I'd been followed. Unless I'm losing my touch. It could not have been connected to the ignition or I would have gone up the moment I switched on."

"So you think it was a warning?"

"Well, I've had enough of them these last few days. If it was it was pretty extreme and you owe me a new Ferrari. Maybe excessive explosive was used so that forensic would have their work cut out finding clues."

"I cannot sanction a new Ferrari. Surely your insurance will cover it. Anyway it was several years old."

Jacko showed his feelings as he glared at Ewing. "And who covers the loss of my 'no-claims' bonus? You bloody well pay, Thomas, one way or the other."

Ewing looked awkward. "I'll never be able to convince them that it was the result of something you were doing for me, thereby for HM Government. I'll do my best, but it will be all uphill. Meanwhile, hire a car and I'll pick up the tag." He was unable to meet Jacko's gaze as he added, "If it were down to me I would not hesitate. I'm sorry, Jacko." And then quietly, "I suppose you'll drop out of the enquiry?"

"I don't think this guy will let me. I think what triggered

this off was that he must have got wind of our enquiries into his commercial background and didn't like it. But we didn't discover a thing."

Ewing reached for the ice bucket. "It does rather indicate that there is something quite interesting to find, though, doesn't it?"

They went to the opera. It was Jacko's turn to compromise; he would rather have gone to Ronnie Scott's Jazz Club. But he was developing a slow taste for Georgie's preferences particularly since Pavarotti had entered everybody's home by singing the theme music for the Soccer World Cup in Italy.

"Where's the Ferrari?" asked Georgie as she swung her long legs into a dark blue Jensen.

"Brake and shock absorber trouble. She'll be in for some time. Difficult to get spare parts." Jacko switched on. "I've hired this from a friend of mine." And that was it. There had been a report in the daily newspapers but as nobody was killed or injured it was not an item Georgie would have picked out.

"What's the name of the bloke you deal with for Reginald Dine?" asked Jacko as he eased into the heavy evening traffic. It was the day after the explosion and he had done a lot of hard thinking.

"Walter Kwang. Why?"

"Chinese? I suppose that's not surprising as Dine made his fortune in Hong Kong."

"I didn't say he was Chinese. He doesn't sound Chinese; more like Eton."

"Where does he hang out?" Jacko ghosted past a taxi.

Georgie turned to look at Jacko and realised she should have more sense. Jacko never took his gaze from the road when driving. He had a special contempt for films where the driver of a car held long conversations with a passenger while never looking at the road, but she also knew it was the perfect foil for hiding his thoughts.

"He has an office in Lisle Street."

"That doesn't sound like Eton, more like Chinatown. Anyway, how do you know? Have you been there?"

49

"Why would I want to do that?"

"To make sure he's there, of course. What sort of set-up he has. Don't you check on your clients?"

"I can't call on every client to see if they live or work where they say they do." She laughed. "Some of them wouldn't even know; they have convenient blackouts."

"I'll check for you. When we get home you can give me his address."

"You're scratching, Willie. Dine has you sealed up and you don't like it. You've met your match. Just call it a day, darling."

What would she say if she knew about the phoney bomb, and the Ferrari? He was tempted to tell her for she had a right to know if she was at risk. He wavered, but when they stopped at traffic lights, he said, "The Ferrari was blown up outside the warehouse. I think it was a warning. That's why we have the Jensen."

He did not know what to expect. He did not turn or even glance at her. She would have found out about the Ferrari sooner or later; he could not fob her off for ever, but she need never know about the hoax parcel bomb. She was silent for so long that he began to worry.

"Are you sure it was a warning?" She was a little breathless.

"Everything adds up to it. The police think it was the IRA taking a late swipe at me, but it wasn't. I'm not a big enough name." He could feel her moving beside him and caught a brief glimpse of her ankles as she twisted in her seat.

"Can we go home, Willie?"

"What for? We're almost there and I've fiddled some parking."

"So that I can give you that address."

Oh, God, she was really worried. She was going on the attack to protect him. "It can wait. We do the opera first. I'll probably forget the whole thing."

"If he'll let you. You said that yourself."

The last time he had been to Lisle Street was in search of some cheap reel-to-reel recording tapes. Almost anything could be bought there in the electrical line, and yet the flavour was completely Chinese. Betting shops, restaurants, oriental food stores, and an abundance of Chinese on the streets.

He went as far as Wardour Street and turned back. He had yet to contact Kwang Bros. (Exports, Imports). Georgie had given him a telephone number, which he had checked with the directory, but he had decided not to ring.

He found it at last. A board beside a green door badly in need of paint listed four concerns; the bottom one was Kwang and his offices were on the third floor. Surprisingly, the street door was open but above it was a camera fixed to record anyone who entered.

That made it difficult. Jacko was reluctant to show Dine he was still active. The camera could belong to any of the four concerns in the old building but Jacko was willing to gamble that it belonged to Kwang Bros. Georgie was right, Dine had sealed him up or, rather, built an effective barrier around himself.

Jacko moved away from the camera angle. Next door was a café and he went in and bought two chicken rolls. When he left the shop he walked away from the Kwang Bros. entrance and headed towards Leicester Square where he found space on a bench in the gardens. He sat down and slowly ate his rolls, not knowing what to do next.

The gardens were bronze and saffron with fallen leaves which rustled around him in spirals. It was chill so few people sat out. He had rarely felt so frustrated. His only surprise was that Dine had taken such extreme measures to warn him off. Why bother? He could get nowhere near him. Dine was a sealed unit and sight of the Sèvres piece did nothing to prise him open.

He almost gave it up then, not for the first time. But there was always something that annoyed or intrigued him and made him think again. The Ferrari. He had loved that car, it had been a personal friend and had helped him out of many a scrape and reminded him of a country he loved. Apart from the sheer delight of driving it, there had been a bond between man and car, something that Georgie had not understood but which Ewing had. When he thought about that his adrenalin

51

rose and he knew what was clear to Georgie all along, that it was not in his nature to give up.

He finished his rolls and decided to cross the square to get a drink. He screwed up the paper looking for a rubbish bin, when someone sat down beside him. A voice said in the broken, sing-song English of the Chinese, "A velly cold day."

"Not all that cold," Jacko responded. He threw the rolled-up paper into a bin near the seat, was about to rise when he noticed the man beside him wore a dark suit, no topcoat, and white gloves.

White gloves! The gloved hands were resting on the knees so that they could not be missed. The stocky Chinese was looking straight ahead as though fixed, but knew he was being scrutinised. Satisfied that his message had been delivered, he rose slowly, white-gloved hands now hanging loosely at his sides. Without looking at Jacko he said in his atrocious accent, "Have a nice day, Mr Jackson".

"Hold on," said Jacko, rising quickly. "Who gave you my name?" But he knew. Dine had warned Kwang to expect him some time and he had not been quick enough to avoid the camera.

The stocky figure strode on, ignoring Jacko even as he drew up beside him. He gazed straight ahead even when he crossed the street, and Jacko guessed that he must have incredible peripheral vision, or be totally reckless.

It was as though Jacko did not exist. Several inches shorter than Jacko the man strode on, unhurried and ignoring everything Jacko said to him. Jacko once grabbed his arm but his grip was broken with a sudden movement and Jacko felt the strength of the man. It would be ludicrous to pick a fight in a crowded London street and he was not sure how he would come out of it; he had already glimpsed a gun butt as the wind caught the jacket but he would not put it past the man that the revelation was deliberate.

They walked on together, heading towards Lisle Street with Jacko saying nothing further. He wanted to be satisfied that the Chinese was returning to Kwang Bros.

They walked straight past Kwang's and continued on until Jacko realised that they were retracing their steps and heading again for Leicester Square. This man would walk all day and at the end of it Jacko would have learned no more. Jacko headed back towards Lisle Street, taking the short cuts. He stayed some distance from Kwang Bros. but was able to keep the door in sight. It took the Chinese longer than he expected to reach Kwang's but when he did he turned in and Jacko was satisfied.

He picked Georgie up from her office that evening; she usually travelled by underground and taxis. As soon as she was seated beside him he said, "Drop the Kwang Bros. business first thing tomorrow."

"I didn't think you came out here for myself." She smoothed back her long hair and used the passenger vanity mirror on the reverse of the sun shield. "What's happened?"

"They are using Triads." He told her what happened, and added, "I don't think this is about Triads at all. They might be in there somewhere and the whole thing reeks of the oriental, but I don't think they are the real issue."

The evening traffic was at its worst and they were making scant progress. "How do you know he is a Triad? Just because he came from Kwang?"

"Because he wore white gloves. It's a warning of impending violence. They just stand near someone they want to intimidate and the white gloves are the emblem of intimidation and fear."

"He couldn't know you knew that."

Jacko chuckled. "Dine would know that I would. Dine will know quite a lot about me by now. Get rid of them, Georgie, I'm serious."

"I know you are and I will. But it seems so pointless. They know where I work."

"Take a few days off. If you were suddenly ill you would have to. Can't one of your associates help you out?"

"Only at cost to themselves. There would be no notice. I must go in."

Jacko shook his head, gaze still on the road. "No. If I have to chain you up you are not going in. You ring Kwang's from anywhere but the office and you tell them you can't act for them any more. It was a mistake in the first place. Your

53

colleagues can help you out for a while. You'd do the same for them; in fact you've done it." He suddenly struck the steering wheel in a burst of anger. "Bugger this traffic."

Georgie gazed at him. "But they know where we live. What's the point? We can't hide from them."

"Oh, yes we can. I'm going underground, Georgie. I'm on open view as I am. Every time I wag my big toe they know. Dine has beaten me to the punch every time I've thrown one. A mate of mine will stay in the house, and I'll be in his. Right now I'm taking you to your friend Suzie what's-her-name." He passed over the car phone and told her to ring her friend.

Georgie sat holding the phone with a mixture of anger and fear. She resented her life being disorganised like this. She stared at Jacko again, trying to break his concentration.

"Dial," he said. "Dine is going to try to get me out of the way one way or another. And if he can't get at me he'll get at you. Believe me."

"I've no clothes at Suzie's. Nothing."

"I'll fund you for some more. You can spend your time buying. That can't be too bad, can it?"

She lifted the heavy phone and before dialling, said, "When am I going to see you again?"

"I'll make contact. Don't worry."

She wanted to say she wished he had a nine-to-five job but if he had she doubted she would be sitting beside him now; he would not be the same person. But she would never get used to moments like these and they terrified her.

"Willie, has it really come to this?"

"Yes it has." For a split second he turned to face her and she saw his expression. "Yes it has," he repeated.

More than his grim expression, it was the fact that he had broken his own golden rule and taken his gaze from the road. He had never done that before. It gave her an empty, sick feeling. And Willie never exaggerated, he always kept something back. She made the call then tossed the phone back at him, distressed and fearful.

6

"Come up, Mr Jackson. I have your drink ready."

Mrs Morris gave him a motherly smile and closed the front door as Jacko went up the curved stairs. Dine approached the head of the stairs as he had before, but was now dressed in a quiet, charcoal grey suit, silk shirt and red tie. "You know the way." Dine stood aside for Jacko to enter the drawing-room, crossed to a drinks trolley and handed Jacko a large Scotch and water.

Jacko sat down with the drink, facing the door. "You must have an army doing research on me; and a lot of friends in important places." He raised the glass, "Cheers."

Dine was smiling quietly as he sat at an angle from Jacko. "I see you don't like sitting with your back to the door. Your wisdom comes late."

"You must have a lot of video footage of me by now. What a waste."

"And sound recording. Not a waste, I think. Now what's on your mind? It is rather late for a social call, although you did telephone me first."

"You move very fast, Reginald. Faster than any man I can recall. Too fast for me. I can't keep up so would like to call a truce. I'm not getting anywhere, anyway."

"You've called to tell me that? I already knew. How can you get anywhere when there is nowhere to get?"

Jacko had the feeling of perpetually marking time. He had made no progress at all. "If I'm wasting my time why see me?"

Jacko gazed at Dine who wore that secret smile of his, barely a twitch of the lips yet managing to convey that whatever Jacko said, he could have said it for him. Jacko thought it was not anticipation but bloody knowledge. It began to get under his skin and that was a loser's attitude.

"I like to see confirmation of my beliefs. You bring nothing new."

"I'd better go," said Jacko in exasperation, putting his drink down. "This is a mistake." He was halfway to his feet when Dine said:

"For goodness sake sit down, Jacko. Let's get rid of the bullshit. You came here to tell me that you are willing to drop your enquiries into my affairs in exchange for me letting you get back to a normal life. Isn't that it?"

Jacko nodded. "Yes. That's about it. What's wrong with that?"

"Nothing if it were genuine. We don't have to beat around the bush any more, do we? You know what I've done to you and you know why. You've had a broadside of warnings in double-quick time and they have shaken you up. Suddenly I'm too hot to handle. Well, you've at least found that out."

"Okay. I agree. Let's leave it at that."

"I can't, Jacko. It is not what I've got to hide that I am afraid of you finding, I've nothing worth a mention and what there is is all on record. It is the fact that you are prying at all. I won't tolerate that sort of thing. It's a bloody nuisance and it spoils the quiet life which is all I want."

"And you'd kill to protect that?"

"If I had set out to kill you you'd be dead. Why did you say that?"

"I thought we weren't beating around the bush? How else can you stop me unless, as I now want to do, we call it a day?"

Dine laughed. He was drinking beer and now took a long swig, wiping his lips afterwards.

Jacko picked up a fleeting image and decided everything about this man was fleeting. He wondered if Dine sometimes confused himself, like questioning killing when he had left it as an only course if he continued in the same way. As Dine lowered his glass his eyes were glazed and he suddenly looked very old beneath the straight grey hair. For a moment Jacko would have sworn that Dine did not know what was going on

56

about him or even where he was; there was a sudden panic in his eyes. And then it was gone and although he appeared weary, his eyes were suddenly alert as he saw Jacko gazing at him across the room.

"Where were we? Oh, yes," said Dine, "You want to throw it in and I don't believe you."

"Are you calling me a liar?"

"No, no." Dine waved a dismissive hand. "At base you are a very honest man, Jacko. Which is the point, isn't it? You want to give up to keep the lovely Georgie Roberts out of the firing line. But you are unable to give up. It simply is not in you. And even if, by some freak, you did, sooner or later your interest would be aroused again. You might despise yourself for even thinking of giving up. That is the problem. That is why I agreed to see you, to explain my thoughts on the subject. I am really sorry for I like you a great deal but I never let feelings stand in the way of practical appraisal. It's a hard life."

Jacko gazed at his empty glass. There was no getting past this man. He had not let Georgie know he was calling in a final attempt to come to an understanding. It disturbed him that Dine seemed to know more about him than he did himself.

"Speechless? Don't be hard on yourself, Jacko. We all meet our match sooner or later." Dine intertwined his fingers, relaxed and sure of himself. "You're kidding yourself. You came here in a last desperate attempt to learn some more about me. You are scratching."

Jacko slowly rose. "Oh, I've learned some more about you all right. More than you think." As he crossed the room, he said, "Thanks for the drink. That's a good malt." Almost at the door he added, "I believe your son is at Oxford?"

Dine's features became set, his eyes hardened. "My son doesn't come into any of this. You had better remember."

"And nor does Georgie Roberts. So had you. If anything happens to her I'll get you one way or another."

Dine quickly recovered. "You don't impress me, and neither does the Browning you carry in your waistband. You would not try it here."

"Don't be so bloody sure."

57

"You would harm me but not Mrs Morris. That you would find impossible to do. So I am safe. Why do you think I let you keep the gun. But you had to make sure I saw it, didn't you? You're becoming pathetic, Jacko."

Jacko grinned, "I liked the way your tame Triad showed me his. I thought I'd try the same."

By now they had reached the hall. Jacko said, "But I'll bet you one thing, Reginald; I bet I'm a bloody sight better shot than either of you. Did your research dig that up?"

When Jacko drove off he expected a tail and got one; a brown Ford Granada. As he wove through the traffic he made no attempt to lose his follower. He kept driving, taking turn-offs at a whim and not increasing speed. He took such an erratic route that he guessed that the following driver would by now have decided that his presence was known. It was always disconcerting when a tail knew that; they did not know whether to pull back, keep going or call it a day. This one stuck with Jacko until Jacko decided to lose him.

Jacko knew his London as well as the best taxi driver, and many more places where a cabbie would not expect to go. He chose his area, a complication of one-way streets. He tied the traffic up in knots with a sudden burst of speed, accepted the curses and horn-blowing with a grin, and a few minutes later sat on the Granada's tail. He could see the silhouette of the driver's head turning this way and that as he tried to locate Jacko's car in one of the turn-offs.

Jacko made a note of the car number and fell back, eventually to take a long route round to his friend's address in Chelsea. Jacko had moved upmarket but in area only; the house was not as big or as expensively furnished as his own but it had the luxury of a garage and was not too far from the Chelsea Embankment, and Reginald Dine.

He put the car away, went into the darkened house, switched most of the lights on, and then telephoned Ewing at his home. Liz answered and they gossiped for a while. There was a bond between them. Jacko had done Liz an enormous favour, one which had enabled her to marry Ewing and had saved her from prison. It was something which was never mentioned or even acknowledged as existing, but Liz knew

58

what he had done for her and would never forget it. She took down the number he gave her and assured him that Ewing would contact the police immediately.

It was better than contacting Ewing direct because he would have hedged; Liz would not allow him to try. Jacko made some coffee and switched on for the ten o'clock news. The telephone rang during the interval and Jacko made a note of the name and address Ewing gave him.

Jacko switched off the television, unlocked the garage, and backed the Jensen into the street. He drove to North Kensington and turned into one of the squares off the Portobello Road. The Granada was parked almost outside the address he had been given. He tried the car doors, not surprised to find them locked, mounted the railinged steps, and rang the bell for the ground floor apartment.

An attractive woman in her mid-thirties opened the door and Jacko produced his false warrant card and asked if he could see Mr David Thomas.

"He's only just in; having his supper. Can't it wait?"

"It can if you let me in. I don't mind waiting till he finishes his meal."

Jacko was shown into a clean, chintzy lounge where the television belted out and a seedy youth suddenly left his chair and disappeared. "Thinks I've come to nick him," said Jacko with good humour, but the woman did not find it funny.

"You'd better sit there," she shouted above the noise of the television. "And I suppose I'd better turn this off."

The silence was a relief as Jacko sat down. He could hear the clink of crockery from the next room and supposed that was where Thomas was eating.

The woman went into the room and when she returned she said, "I'm his wife, Lottie. Anything I can do to help? I mean what would the law want with him?"

"Not a lot. Is there somewhere where I can speak to him privately?"

"Oh, I'll buzz off when he comes in here."

Thomas took his time, which suggested he had dealt with the police before; innocent people wanted to find out quickly. When he did come in it was in cocky fashion until he saw

Jacko seated there, smiling up at him, and a strange, almost sick expression changed his features.

He was quite smart, trousers pressed, tie still on and straight. He was fair-haired, blue-eyed, and nearing forty. "What are you doing here?" But his tone was truculent with a strong undercurrent of uncertainty. By this time Lottie had left the room.

Jacko dangled his warrant card. "Didn't he tell you you were following a copper?"

"What are you on about? I haven't followed anyone anywhere."

"Yet you were just surprised to see me. Come on, Dave, you can do better."

"I'm surprised to see any copper." Thomas wiped his hands on a handkerchief and then wiped his lips. He did not sit down, hoping Jacko would get up and go.

Jacko produced a notebook, turning the blank pages as if they were full. "Your car, your number. I checked with DVLC. You picked me up outside Dine's house on the Chelsea Embankment. Have you told Dine that you lost me? He wouldn't have been pleased. Why would you follow a policeman, Dave? What were your precise instructions?"

Thomas was looking more confident. He came further into the room, sat down and hooked a leg over the arm of the chair. "I don't know anyone called Dine and I was not following you. If we followed the same route it was coincidence. That's no crime."

"I'm afraid it is, Dave. Harassment. My word against yours and me a police officer. You followed me all right which is why I took your number. Now, are you working for Dine direct or for an agency? Perhaps the Dalton Enquiry Agency?"

Some of the earlier cockiness was reappearing in Thomas's attitude. He knew that nothing could be proved and saw no merit in answering questions.

The door behind Thomas was slightly open and Jacko wondered if Lottie was listening further down the passage. He got up, closed the door, and returned to his seat while Thomas watched with amusement.

"Going to start the heavy stuff, are we?" said Thomas

with a sneer. "Why don't you just piss off and leave us alone."

Jacko pulled out the Browning and pointed it at Thomas's stomach. With his free hand he produced a silencer and screwed it on. If Thomas was going to make a move it had to be then, but the man was rooted to his chair, eyes slightly bulging with fear. "You're right," said Jacko, "it's heavy stuff time. Don't move or I'll blow your guts out." He waited for Thomas to adjust to the shock and added, "I can see you've arrived at it and you're right. I'm not a copper. Now did you hear the questions or do you want me to repeat them?"

"I've never heard of Dine until you mentioned him. I was told the house and given a photo of you, and was told to follow you when you came out. I couldn't give a toss what this bloke Dine thinks; he's not my boss."

"Who is?"

"Pete Selby. I do odd jobs for him."

"This one was certainly odd." Jacko had heard of Pete Selby. He was a middle-of-the-road crook who did not really deal in the heavy stuff, so largely kept out of trouble. From what Jacko had heard he seemed to prosper. "Have you told him you lost me?"

"That's none of your bloody business."

"Did you?" Jacko repeated, raising the Browning slightly.

"Yes. As soon as I got in."

"Okay. Give me his address and phone number."

Thomas was scared, his eyes moving shiftily. "I can't do that."

"For God's sake, I can get it from the telephone directory. I'm simply trying to save time. Anyway, Pete isn't the recriminating type. He'll be narked but he won't blow your head off. Some would for far less than failure. Write it down and I'll get out of your hair."

Thomas crossed to a bureau and scribbled on a pad, tearing the sheet out and passing it over.

"Thanks," said Jacko, rising. "You're not likely to tell Pete, but don't tell anyone you've had a visitor. You followed me, you failed, that's an end of it. You wouldn't want anyone to know you've given out Pete's ex-directory number, would you?"

"You bastard."

"You're probably right, Dave," said Jacko with a grin. "But it's too late to be brave. I'll let myself out."

Pete Selby lived in Islington which is a fair drive from North Kensington. It was now not far off midnight and the traffic was light. Jacko was in no hurry, but had trouble finding a parking slot for at night the streets became one big car park. He had to park fifty yards away and walk back to Selby's house, a tall, thin, three-floor upright, squeezed between others and just as anonymous.

There were still a number of house lights on but Pete's was in darkness. The street lamps were poor and there was an eerie touch about the place at this hour. The street was understandably empty except, perhaps, of hidden predators. Jacko strode quite casually and perhaps emitted his own warning signals to the foolish. He rang the bell for a good long period.

He stood back and saw a light come on upstairs but as nothing further happened he rang the bell again. A window rose noisily and a blond halo of woman's hair appeared above him.

"Was that you ringing the bell?" She spoke in a fierce, grating whisper.

"It was. I want to see Pete."

"Well, sod off and come back some other time, we were asleep, you stupid bugger."

"Of course you were." Jacko kept his voice down. "But it's either now or crack of dawn." He held up his card. "Police. The neighbours will start talking if you don't let me in."

The window closed, more lights came on as she descended the stairs finally to face Jacko at the front door and swear continuously for several moments.

"That's impressive," said Jacko when she had finished. "Ever considered entering for the *Guinness Book of Records*? Where's Pete?"

"Where's your warrant card, you bloody wooden-top? And what do you want to see him for?"

Jacko produced the card thinking he should get one in another name. As she scrutinised it, he took stock of her. She could be any one of the many hard-faced hookers he had seen in his life, and, like so many of them, protective of her man. "Are you his wife?" he asked politely.

She ignored his question and said, "You're dirtying the doorstep; you'd better come in. Go to the room at the end of the hall. He squeezed past her, her dressing-gown held loosely in front. There was a faint trace of perfume and then he was heading for the rear of the hall.

The light was on in the end room and he went in to find it was a small television room, spotlessly clean and tidy, and seemingly comfortable. It was a corner room with no windows but had an air-conditioner unit mounted high in one wall.

He turned to face her. Her hard face had relaxed a little. As her features softened he could see that she had once been beautiful and would still turn a few heads. He had an impression that she would put up a far better fight for her man than Lottie would for Dave Thomas. He suddenly developed a soft spot for her; she really was worried. "I'm not going to nick him," he said. "Do you think you could get him for me?"

"You're not bad for a copper. I'll see if he's awake."

As she turned for the door a big man entered the room, dark hair dishevelled, pyjama jacket gaping to show part of a flabby body. He had a disconcertingly honest, plumpish face, wide eyes and a ready smile. He put an arm round the woman and gave her a big hug. "Luverly, ain't she? Our Sandra would do anything for anybody."

"Would she make a cup of tea while we talk?"

Sandra flounced off as Pete gave her a hefty pat on the behind to help her on her way.

"Could you close the door?" asked Jacko.

"Sure. What can I do for the police? Funny time to call."

Jacko drew close and hit Pete hard under the ribs. Pete gave a gasp like a ruptured tyre and doubled up in agony. Jacko helped him on to a chair.

63

"Sorry, Pete, but I'm running out of time. Just relax and answer a few questions and then I'll go. Can you hear me?"

Pete managed to nod his head.

"You set one of your men to tail me tonight. Don't ask me how I know because I won't tell you. Was it a guy called Dine who hired you?"

Before Pete could answer Sandra came back with the tea leaving Jacko thinking that she must have made instant. She put the tray down and immediately went to the suffering Pete.

"What did you do to him, you filthy pig?"

"It's your cooking; he suddenly got guts ache."

Pete made an effort for Sandra's sake. "It's all right, love, nothing to worry about. Leave us for a while."

Sandra went out shooting venom at Jacko who did his best to appear innocent. "Police brutality," she said before closing the door, "I'll report this."

"Who hired you, Pete?"

Pete managed to straighten. "There was no need for that. Dine didn't hire me. I'd never heard of him, but when I took on the job I looked the address up and found out the name." He rubbed his stomach and his jacket slipped wide open. He gazed up at Jacko who was still standing, and said, "Dine may have nothing to do with it; somebody knew you were visiting that house and we had to tail you from there."

"Then who did hire you?"

"You're asking me to get topped." The fear in Pete's eyes was genuine and it was not because of Jacko. "Just you calling here could do that."

"You're guilty of having a policeman followed, for God's sake. You're in trouble."

"You think that's trouble?" Pete had almost recovered.

"I just want a name. You'll never be involved."

"You do some funny thinking for a copper. Of course I'd be involved. I'm the only one who knows who hired me. And I ain't talking."

"So it wasn't Dine?"

"It wasn't Dine, not who hired me, it wasn't."

Jacko sat on the arm of a chair and stared down at Pete.

64

He pushed one of the cups across. "We'd better drink this or we'll upset Sandra."

"Don't do that for chrissake." Pete reached for his tea.

"Look, copper, it's not ethics or any of that crap that stops me telling you, it's sheer bloody fear. I'd rather go to jail."

"I understand." Jacko sipped his tea and noticed that the door key was on the inside; whoever used this room wanted no interruptions. He put his cup down and went to the door. Opening it he bawled out, "Sandra, can you spare a minute?"

Pete looked surprised. "What do you want her for?"

"I have an idea," replied Jacko, relieved that he could hear her footsteps approaching. He stood by the door, and opened it wider for her as she came in. She crossed straight to Pete to make sure he was all right, heard the door close, and did not panic until she heard the key turn. When she spun round Jacko had gone and the key was the other side of the door.

She was about to hammer on the door when Jacko called through, "If you kick up a racket you'll wake the neighbours and then you'll have some explaining to do."

"You stinking bastard, what are you up to?"

"Just keep cool, Sandra. When I've finished looking around I'll unlock the door, okay? You look after Pete."

Jacko moved quickly from room to room. He did not know how strong the television room door and lock was. Pete might even have another key. He found the room most likely to contain what he wanted, a study with a copying machine and electric typewriter, desk and filing cabinets. He worked as fast as he could.

In the TV room Pete did his best to calm Sandra. She wanted to break the door down with anything she could find but Pete struggled to restrain her. "You're not thinking," he bawled. "We can't afford to attract attention." He struggled to hold her but she squirmed and broke away and started to hammer the door again.

"If you're doing it for me, Sandra, you'll have me inside in no time."

She turned and stood with her back to the door, almost on the point of tears. "He's getting away with it? And you don't seem to mind."

"There's nothing for him to find. He's wasting his time."

She was sometimes distressed by his apparent lack of courage. "Will you report this? He has no warrant; you could get him off the force."

Pete smiled and held her. "Of course I'm not going to report him. For two good reasons: one, I don't want to be persecuted by coppers for the rest of my life; and two, I very much doubt he's a copper anyway. He wouldn't come at this time of night on his own and armed."

"Armed?" suddenly she was scared. "Armed?"

Pete smiled. "He let me see it on purpose. He was trying to get something out of me."

Sandra was scared now. "He'll come back and kill us."

"He could have done that already. Don't worry, gal. Just stay put."

Neither of them heard the key turn in the lock and Jacko had been gone some few minutes before Pete tried the door again. It was open and they went out into the hall with some relief.

The telephone rang near the front door and they were both startled. "What the bloody hell next?" Pete strode to the phone and picked it up. "Yes?"

His face and tone changed in a flash and Sandra could see it was trouble. "No," he said. "Nobody has been here. At this time of night? You're kidding."

"Then what the hell are you doing up?" asked the voice.

"Watching telly. What else? Who's stirring it up?"

"Okay. It's a false alarm. Get back to bed."

At 3.30 that same morning two men parked their car in the next street and took their time walking to Pete's house. They expertly sprang the two locks, cut the door chain with bolt cutters and crept up the stairs. With silenced pistols they emptied their magazines into the two bodies lying together in the bed. After the first two shots Sandra opened her eyes and placed an arm across Pete, protective to the last. It was a futile token of love. There were no screams.

Pete, who had betrayed no-one and had never carried a gun in his life, was dead. And so was Sandra who had little idea what a silencer looked like.

66

7

Jacko did not go straight home once he left Pete's house. He had found some information which might be useful and his urge was to wait awhile. He was uneasy, recalling Pete's fear when he said that Jacko's visit alone could get him topped. Pete was a small-time crook, and was what the police call an "honest villain", he was not the sort of man to let anyone down and Jacko felt a certain affinity. People like Pete usually finished up losers simply because they were not sufficiently ruthless.

Dave Thomas was different and something worried Jacko about the connection between the two. Pete would not have given out Thomas's name, but the reverse was not true.

Jacko stayed in the porch of a house opposite Pete's and after a while, as the cold crept in, wondered just what the hell had induced him to hang about. When the lights went out progressively from ground floor to bedroom, he knew that Pete and Sandra had belatedly found the TV room door unlocked and had finally gone upstairs. Just prior to that Jacko thought he heard the faint sound of a telephone; he knew there was one near the front door of Pete's house. It stopped and he thought he had probably imagined it; it was a strange time to call anybody.

When the upstairs light went out he left the porch and strolled slowly back to his car, still wondering why he had stayed at all. He reached the Jensen, unlocked it, and as he was about to climb in, saw the reflections of headlights in the next street. He could hear the faint purr of the car engine, and then it stopped and the lights disappeared.

Jacko quietly closed the Jensen car door and walked to the street corner. At first he could not locate the car, there were so many nose-to-tail, revealed, in the poor light, by the dull sheen of their tops.

He suddenly saw the faint outline of two men appear much further down, and start to walk away from him. Jacko followed, keeping a good distance between them. They turned left at the bottom and entered the street Pete lived in.

Jacko quickened his pace but it was dead of night and the slightest sound carried. He rounded the corner just as they mounted the steps to Pete's house. By the time he was halfway down the street they had disappeared. He sprinted then and took up position opposite in the porch of the house he had used before.

He could guess what was happening but by the time he could get across the street and up the stairs in Pete's house the job would be over. Only seconds later the two men reappeared and went back the way they had come.

Jacko ran in the opposite direction to approach the Jensen from the other end of the street. It was longer but he could hurry. He was breathless by the time he switched on and eased the car out from the line. He drove without lights but there was light enough. The Jensen crept to the corner purring like a cheetah and he stopped at the junction.

He could not distinguish the men's car but had it placed when the beams came on and it drew out. He followed, holding back as far as he dared.

In the back streets of Islington, driving without lights and following another car was not too much of a problem, but once they hit the main roads it became too risky even though they were virtually empty at nearly four o'clock in the morning. But it was a time when those in police patrol cars looked for something to do to ease their boredom. Jacko was forced to switch on his sidelights although he could see sufficiently well without them.

Even hanging back he knew he would be seen sooner or later and he was sure the two men were pros. He simply kept going. When the route became erratic and they started using tactics he himself would have used in a reverse situation, he knew for certain he had been seen.

He took a gamble on the general direction they were taking

and detoured to pick up the main route at another point. It worked the first time for he saw the tail-lights in the distance and closed up just enough to make sure it was the same car. Then he detoured again.

When he joined the main street this time he saw no sign of them. Just a well-lit London street, heading in the general direction of the Thames to suggest the other car might be going south of the river. It was strange to see shops in utter darkness yet the street itself canopied with effective light. A taxi came drifting towards him with its flag down but as it passed Jacko saw no sign of a passenger.

It was tempting to speed to see if they were following the same direction, but that would bring another kind of risk, and to confirm it a patrol car coasted out of one of the side turnings and Jacko was well scrutinised as it went past. For a moment, as he saw the brake lights come on in his mirror, he thought they were going to stop him but the patrol car picked up speed again and was gone.

Jacko decided it was time to go home and greet the dawn and the milkman. His thoughts reverted to Pete and Sandra and he wondered whether he could have done anything to save them. A shoot-out on the stairs against two men in the dark would not have gone his way and it would still have been too late. But he felt badly about it. His thoughts were drifting and he was now very tired. He enjoyed doing a U-turn in a street which would soon be teeming with traffic and, as he straightened, the car he had followed turned out of a side street and cut straight across him.

Jacko slammed on the brakes and skidded into an uncontrollable arc. He was fighting with the wheel when he saw someone lean out of the other car with a silenced pistol pointing straight at him. He ducked and drove blind, braced for a crash. Glass spattered over him as his windscreen shattered and he heard a ripping noise in the empty seat behind him.

The car rocked and swayed and he was forced to raise his head to see what was happening. He was hurtling towards a blank sheet glass shop window, was about to mount the kerb when he desperately spun the wheel, hit the brake to swing into another skid, and the movement was so violent he thought he was going to roll over. The Jensen rocked from one pair of wheels to the other, its low-slung body enabling it to avoid a capsize. But the car was still skidding, swaying this way and that and he just had to ride it out. When he managed to stop Jacko was in the middle of the street, realising he had to get to a side street quickly. When he gazed behind him he saw that the rear window had spider-webbed.

He climbed halfway out of the car. It was a bizarre scene; a well-lit London street with his damaged car almost dead centre and nothing in sight moving. He climbed back in. It would be pointless to try to pick up a trail now. He drove off, the cold early morning air biting hard through the gaping hole in front of him, making his eyes stream. He took the first turning and after a while pulled in.

He was covered with glass and his neck was bleeding from slivers that had struck him like icicles; it was everywhere. He sat there with lights off. He had been caught flat and it annoyed him. He swivelled in his seat to see that shots had ripped into the rear seat and padding was puffing out like bubble gum. It was not his car, which added to his anger.

He switched on. The warnings were over. The action was now for real and he had not come out of it too well. He drove off intent on avoiding the main streets, and using them only when he had to cross them. It was difficult to see with streaming eyes so he donned a pair of dark glasses.

It had been a long time since he had felt so defeated and it depressed him. By the time he reached his temporary home in Chelsea he was tired out, but satisfied he had made the journey alone.

There was little of the night left. He took off his jacket and shirt to shake out the glass and decided the cuts on his chest and neck were superficial. It was not worth going to bed so he made strong coffee and drank it at the kitchen bar. He had already made a note of the gunmen's car number and now he went through the bits and pieces he had picked up at Pete's house.

They were mainly names and addresses jotted down on odd pieces of paper and in different coloured inks. Some were almost illegible and he had to search for a magnifying glass to help him. Most were unknown names but there were three that he recognised and two of those were of men not to be played with. The third name was the same as that of a back-bench politician but that could be coincidence. The pieces of paper were swimming under his gaze by the time he had finished trying to make sense of them. But nowhere was there any semblance of a connection with Reginald Dine.

He paced up and down to keep himself awake for he knew if he fell asleep it might be for hours and he wanted to make an early round of phone calls. And he was anxious about Georgie; he had not contacted her since she had moved in with her friend Suzie.

In spite of himself he fell asleep in an armchair and woke with a throbbing headache. It was 9.30. He shaved then, and showered to clean off the congealed blood. He rang Ewing for a trace on the car number and lost his temper when Ewing complained that he was abusing his privileges. He asked Ewing if he could give a run-down on an MP named Simon Wherewell. Ewing knew him but Jacko wanted fuller information than he could give off the cuff. He rang Georgie to assure her he was all right but could not see her for a while and to tell her not to worry if she did not hear from him for a day or two. He hated doing this but could see no option.

He then rang a garage contact who would ask no questions to have the Jensen collected and repaired. He checked the other two addresses with the telephone directory and they remained the same. One of them, Sonny Rollins, was probably the most dangerous gangster in the country, up to his hairline in rackets.

Jacko had indirectly crossed Rollins before. Rollins was involved with certain ostensibly respectable businessmen, one of whom had had more rackets going than Rollins himself and had been killed a couple of years ago. Amongst other things, Rollins was involved in money laundering and had important connections in America. Proving it was another matter. Jacko began to think that it made some sense if Dine was involved with Rollins.

The other man was more difficult to assess. Charles Jason

71

was outgoing and charismatic. He controlled a variety of businesses, mostly in leisure; it was rumoured he was involved in arms deals but was not a registered arms dealer. Whether he was an agent or actually bought and sold, Jacko had no idea. It was hearsay, information grapevined through the underworld with which Jacko had occasional contact. Jason also owned a couple of night clubs and gaming houses in the north of England, and one in South London. He was what Jacko called a fringe man, seeming always to be on the edge of things rather than completely involved. But that was only an impression.

Jason had some questionable friends in the upper hierarchy of crime. From time to time his photograph would appear in the Sunday magazine sections at this party or that, sometimes grouped with people the police would probably have on file. Yet, so far as Jacko knew, Jason had no actual record. There were types of businessmen who for some strange reason obtained satisfaction from mixing with the shady, preferably the upper-bracket shady, like groupies with pop stars. So it was difficult to believe that they were not used from time to time, to boost their sense of importance.

The other side of the coin was that some top villains enjoyed mixing with legitimate big names: politicians, entertainers, anybody who superficially placed them in an important bracket. Criminal history was littered with such cases much to the embarrassment even of members of society and Prime Ministers. Jason, extremely wealthy, well spoken, fitted into this category, where Sonny Rollins had more than the odd whisper against him.

The two names were a strange combination. Jacko could not see Charles Jason going quite so far as to mix with Sonny Rollins, who sent fear through most of those who knew him and was rarely seen in any photograph, or in public. Rollins did not seek publicity of any kind. It was difficult too, to imagine Pete Selby having anything to do with either of these men; they were both way out of his league. But he had recorded their names and addresses, rather carelessly, and, true enough, big wheels often needed the services of small wheels.

It was well over an hour before Ewing rang back. They had another argument during which Ewing explained that he did have his real work to do, mainly for the PM, but Jacko shot that down by blaming Ewing for getting him into a life or death situation.

The car had been reported stolen and had been found abandoned near Waterloo Station. This confirmed Jacko's surmise that the gunmen had been heading south of the Thames but that really meant nothing except to suggest where they had left their own car to continue on.

The news on Simon Wherewell was more interesting. Although not a very well-known Member of Parliament, he was thought to be wealthy. He was a 'name' at Lloyd's, the insurance brokers, and had a range of investments though no directorships that could be found. He had an interest in China, had been there, and had money in the Bank of Hong Kong. It was believed that he had lost a good deal of money through Lloyd's, as many of the 'names' had in recent years, but had expressed no hardship resulting from it.

"Where did you get this stuff?" asked Jacko.

"Never you mind. You are always complaining that I don't help. You've put me well behind in my work and I will have to stay late. So be grateful."

"I am, Thomas. Tell Liz it's my fault. You must have got this either from the police or MI5. Is he being watched?"

"Goodbye, Jacko. Try to give me better warning next time."

Jacko realised his headache had gone and his adrenalin had risen. Suddenly he was not tired any more. But he was still frustrated. A driver called for the Jensen and drove it away after removing the rest of the front glass out and inserting a temporary windscreen.

He rang Georgie again but she was out and he was reluctant to leave a message on somebody else's answering machine. But he really needed more information, which he hoped Georgie might dig up for him. He checked Charles Jason's address again and set out for Eaton Square. He was reduced to using public transport and that would slow him down.

8

Reginald Dine had put Willie Jackson out of his mind the moment he left the house. The problem was no longer directly his. He went to bed that night, alone in the big house except for Mrs Morris who slept in a back room which had once been the study.

Dine sat up, sweat oozing from him. It had not been as bad as this for years. He thought his head was breaking open, his thoughts crammed and pulling against each other as if no single thought had a right to be there and he could not separate them. He was trembling and his pyjamas were wet through.

He climbed slowly out of bed and stripped off in the adjacent bathroom. In spite of the time – it was now after 1.30 a.m. – he showered, the water hammering at his head but his agonising confusion remained. He ran the water cold for several minutes and this torture calmed his jumbled thoughts. By the time he finished he was shivering rather than trembling but his head was clearer. He dried off, put on fresh pyjamas and returned to the bedroom.

Instead of going to bed he went over to the big window and pulled on the cord to open the drapes a little. He looked down into the empty street and to the ghostly mist building up over the grey waters of the Thames. He sat on a straight-backed chair to look out and stayed there for several minutes. Only then did Jacko return to his thoughts.

Yet it had really started when his son had allowed his girlfriend's father to see the collection without first asking him. He could understand, however, and no-one could know that the Frenchman would be acquainted with some of the history of the Sèvres group. Dine did not know himself, not

74

the full context, so it was difficult to blame his son or anybody. Yet the repercussions had already been enormous.

If he could solve the problem by giving the Sèvres piece back to the French he would do so readily. But that would only invite more speculation on how he had obtained it in the first place. Whatever he did the damage was already done and somebody's interest was sufficiently aroused to employ someone like Willie Jackson. Why not the police? Or even the Security Service if it was thought that it was sufficiently political as the French probably would? He thought he knew why and felt sorry for Jacko.

This sort of thinking put the clock back too far, but he was already hooked to a time warp he could not escape. He dozed for a while in the chair but the problem would not leave him alone. His only relief was that there was now only one subject in his mind and not the crammed information of other years.

Dine felt lonelier then than he could remember. There was no-one with whom he could talk over old times because no-one would understand. But that was not the only reason. The past was dead and yet in one respect he was resurrecting it.

He did not return to bed and seemed little the worse for wear when he took another shower and shaved, and went down to breakfast in his dressing-gown. He was feeling much better but was being pulled away at a time when he knew he should be stronger willed.

Mrs Morris always insisted he had a full breakfast but this morning he really did not feel up to it. He did his best for her sake but had to leave most of it and left the house about mid-morning, driving the Mercedes.

He was well south of the river before he realised he should be paying far more attention to his rear. It was instinctive for him to watch out for cars who stayed behind him for too long. In tailbacks it was unavoidable but he had been vigilant for so long that he believed he could pick out the innocent from the guilty, like a police patrol who spot some almost indefinable difference of road behaviour, and know with some certainty that it will be the fifth car ahead of them which will pull out to speed.

Dine slipped back into normal routine and watched his

back, satisfied that he was travelling alone. He reached the outskirts, drove round to find a parking space, and walked slowly back to the place where he had learned that Thursday was the usual shopping morning and that they invariably both went together.

These strange excursions achieved nothing but more confusion, yet he was unable to avoid them. This time he took up position to one side of the grocer's doorway so that he obstructed no-one. While he waited he wondered, as he had before, just why he was doing it.

He was no wiser when the couple appeared, as they almost always did about this time on this day of the week. The woman still appeared dowdy, wearing the same coat as before, and now she wore a hat which largely covered her grey hair. She seemed to be happier than the last time, and the man too. He took her arm and they trundled up the street with Dine following on the other side. When they reached the bus stop they joined the queue as before and chatted with people they obviously knew.

Dine crossed over and this time joined the queue behind a young woman who had slipped in before him. He wanted to get near to the man to slip a wad of notes into his well-worn top-coat pocket and tried to ease past the young woman.

The woman thought he was queue-jumping and gave him a glare and a nudge which Dine barely noticed as he realised that putting something into someone's pocket was as difficult as taking something out. The act could also be misconstrued.

The young woman, already annoyed at Dine's tactics, suddenly saw what she thought he was up to and said loudly, "He's trying to pick your pocket." She grabbed Dine who shook her off and hurried away, to shouts of 'thief'. He broke into a run and turned round the nearest corner and hurried as fast as he could.

It was fortunate for him that nobody in the bus queue was willing to lose their place, particularly as he had been stopped in the act. He took another corner and leaned against the nearest wall to get his breath back.

He felt dreadful, tearful, childish, amateurish, all these

things and realised he could have put himself in a silly position. Even had he succeeded in passing the money, what sort of mystery would he create for the couple? They would try to puzzle it out. As he stood there, passers-by giving him strange glances, he accepted that he had acted totally stupidly. A woman came up to ask him if he felt all right. He thanked her, dried his eyes and walked in the direction of where he had parked the car. The possibilities of what might have gone wrong at the bus stop were still running through his mind and shattered his confidence. He was shaken and scared when he reached the car. By the time he was halfway back home he had recovered and was forcing his thoughts ahead rather than behind. There was no future in dwelling on what might have been. His only reaction now was that he should never forget it again. It had been a foolish lapse which would never be repeated.

Then his mind clouded again and he lost co-ordination and began to drift to the wrong side of the road. He was lucky he was not yet on the main road, for he missed having an accident by inches. Horns blared and fists were waved at him as he pulled on the wheel at the last moment. He should have pulled in at the first opportunity but he somehow kept going, still shaky, but trying to be careful. The shock had pulled him round and his head cleared enough to see him through.

What was happening to him? He knew but was reluctant to face it. His mind was being triggered into confusion to a point where he did not know which day or even which year it was. It was a terrifying situation. Past events came tumbling back to mix with the present and they all attacked him at once until there were times when he thought he was going mad. It was made worse because he had believed that those days were long over.

He knew what had triggered it as it had before, and arising from it, other problems had arisen. Destiny was in his own hands; there was a point in life when he had firmly believed that to be true and he had proved it to be so. It was still true if he obeyed the simple rules he had created for himself, but he was beginning to ignore them. He would conquer the problem, though, he always had. But he was reluctant to admit that this time it was different and largely self-created.

9

Charles Jason lived in a penthouse in a block of flats off Eaton Square. Jacko called at the Reception desk and asked if he was in. When the porter asked for his name Jacko produced his well-used warrant card and the porter rang through. After a while the porter hung up and said, "I didn't think he was in. Early riser. Goes jogging at 7a.m. and to his office at 8.30."

"Where is his office?"

"I thought you blokes knew all these things." The porter smiled, showing his age through his teeth. "Press a button and it all shows up."

Jacko grinned. "It's only a query about his car. He had one stolen in the country. We've got it back but it's a bit of a mess. We'd like to get it out of the way."

"Ah. Can't help you anyway. Don't keep business addresses here. Not our affair."

"Not even for a tenner out of the slush fund?"

The bald head came up and brown eyes twinkled. "I just don't know. That's worth a tenner."

"I couldn't justify it. A phone number then?"

"You can have this one. Where's me money?"

Jacko laughed. He did not mind having his leg pulled. "What about letting me into his apartment to wait for him?"

The porter shook his head. "More than my job is worth. Anyway, Sergeant, he could be all day." And then with a secret smile, "And sometimes all night."

Jacko gave him a fiver and asked for the nearest pay phone. He met Ronnie Darrell at the Hot Pot for lunch. He had reserved a table, which was made easier by mentioning Darrell's name. Darrell was not as high up the tree of villainy as Sonny Rollins who sat supreme in the London area if not

78

the country. There were those who would dispute this pecking order but never to Rollins' face who, probably, never thought about it.

Darrell was fairly high up the tree, had a police record and had done time but not since his early thirties. He had learned the art of delegation a long time ago so that others took the risks and the penalties while he stayed just ahead of the police and made a lot of money.

Jacko was lucky to be able to meet him so quickly for he was a difficult man to run down, but he had a soft spot for Jacko because he was one of the few men he knew who would not stab him in the back. He trusted Jacko more than he would trust his own brothers and that, by his standards, was a tremendous compliment. He also enjoyed Jacko's company which was free of the sycophancy of some of his cronies.

They sat side by side in the corner Jacko always tried to get and faced the room. They had a few drinks, ordered lunch and wine, and Darrell smiled slowly as he looked round the crowded room. "What is it you want, Jacko? You're taking a bloody long time getting to it."

Darrell was a big man who wore his suits slightly too tight to show the size of his muscles; it was often quite an effective deterrent. He had the mushed-up face of an ex-boxer with a broken nose he had never bothered to have straightened. Yet there was a deceptive pleasantness about him which women liked.

"Ever heard of a bloke called Charles Jason? Has a couple of clubs up north and another south of the river."

Darrell raised his heavy brows. "Not a lot. I heard you were going straight, by the way." Which was Darrell's way of saying 'What do you want to know for'.

Jacko grinned. "I've always been straight. I don't know how I came to know people like you."

No-one else would have dared say that to Darrell who laughed loudly and thumped Jacko on the shoulder.

"I'm trying to establish where he stands in the scheme of things. I have my reasons. I heard he has even been in here on occasion."

"He's been in with me. He sometimes hangs around, gets

himself invited to some of our parties, seems to get a kick out of it. Maybe it's wishful thinking because I don't think he has the guts to be one of us. Anyway, I should think he's loaded enough without doing something silly."

"I heard he was into arms."

"I heard that too. That's not illegal, is it?" Darrell looked surprised.

"It can be. Do you know if he knows Sonny Rollins?"

"You're spoiling my lunch, Jack. Why bring him in? Nobody ever sees him around, anyway. I don't think he's ever been in here. I mean, this place is a club to the fraternity. Sonny is not one of us."

"So you think the answer is no?"

"How can I be sure? Sonny's a hard bastard. I don't see Jason that way."

"Yet he still makes a lot of money, so I'm told."

"Maybe he was born into it. Maybe he hasn't as much as he would have people believe. His clubs aren't up to much; I've been to the South London one: second-rate. It wouldn't stand up in the West End." Darrell stared at Jacko curiously. "You trying to give the guy a testimonial, or something?"

Jacko shook his head. "I'm just trying to find out what I can about him. He might not be what he seems to be."

"You mean he's a nark?" Darrell was suddenly nervous.

"I doubt it. Well, you've done your best. I thought you might know more. Thanks, Ronnie. Let's get some more of that wine."

They ate in silence for a while when Darrell suddenly looked up and said with his mouth full, "You want to see Sharon. She spends some time with Jason. I used to doss with her myself but Jason took a fancy to her and I didn't mind. She might help but you'll have to give her more than a lunch."

"Sharon? Sharon who?"

"That's all I know her by. Sharon whatever-she-likes-to-call-herself. She probably uses a different name weekly. But I can tell you where to find her." Darrell suddenly chuckled. "You might find them both at the same time."

Jacko called for Cognac. "Is Len Tiler still around?"

80

"Haven't seen him. I think he came out about three weeks ago. Some of the boys threw a party for him. Sam at the bar will know. Why?"

"I want him to do a job for me. Just a small one."

"You might have a problem. He suffers from arthritis in the hands. Poor bugger can hardly hold a pen. Len the Pen they called him in his heyday. Now he's being nicked too often as his forgeries aren't so good, and 'pen' has taken on a new meaning. Sad business, though. Nice bloke, Len; you should see his paintings."

They parted about three o'clock. Jacko had obtained an address for Sharon, and Sam the barman had given him the last known address of Len Tiler.

Len Tiler lived over a strip club off Dean Street in London's Soho, in two rooms on the top floor. The climb up the narrow stairs was difficult for Len now the arthritis was playing him up. Consequently he rarely went out, except to shop and occasionally to go round the corner to the pub to see old mates.

Len let Jacko in and they shook hands, but Jacko was appalled at the state of the man and helped him to a chair. The living-room was a shambles and had a small electric cooker in one corner, and the smell of fried eggs and rancid cooking fat was still in the air.

The furniture was torn and shabby and dirty crockery was piled in the sink. But among the jumble and dust and grime, positioned anywhere where there was space, were incredibly beautiful paintings. Some were copies of old masters, others original. It was almost impossible to equate the fine brush-work and artistic flair, the supremely natural talent of a fine artist, with the grot which framed them.

Len was pleased to see Jacko. He did not know him too well, but these days he was glad of the company of anyone willing to climb the stairs. He offered Jacko a cup of tea or coffee, but Jacko took one look at the sink and said he had just had one.

Len carelessly moved a painting off a chair so that Jacko could sit down and Jacko felt the springs sag beneath him.

"Why don't you sell these?" asked Jacko. "You'd make a fortune."

Len smiled sadly. He was a small, thin man, hands bony and gnarled. He sat between two small country scenes, a sorry little figure surrounded by near-squalor and beauty. "I've been inside too much. Sold too many fakes. And for peanuts, old son. It was the agent who made the money and he's still free. Nobody trusts what I've done. They're afraid to buy in case there's a backlash; they can't afford to buy something that might be fake. They are too scared even to buy the genuine ones. One day, those who have bought will make a nice tidy packet. When I'm gone. Now what can I do for you?"

Jacko produced his warrant card and tossed it across. "Can you do another one for me? In a different name?"

Len studied it and shook his head. "Did I do this for you?"

"No. Someone gave it to me for a job I had to do." It was Ewing who had supplied it and Jacko suspected that the Security Service had provided it. He was supposed to have handed it in after the case but claimed that he had burnt it.

"It's very good," observed Len. "But it's too near the mark. I can't take that kind of risk. Anyway, my hands have seized up."

"If you can get blanks and have the official stamp, the actual amount of pen work isn't too much. I'll pay well."

Len still held the warrant card and Jacko could see that he was tempted, so added, "No-one will ever know you did it."

"The last time I heard that I got five with remission. I couldn't face going in again, it's so damp in some of those places."

Jacko almost gave up. He did not want to compromise Len and believed that he could implicate Ewing into protecting him should anything go wrong. But in forgery terms, the card was not a big deal. "I'll buy one of your paintings so there will be no traceable transaction for the card. You can give me a receipt. Charge me for the painting and the card and make it all out for the painting. I'll even give you a cheque, that would be open enough."

Len sat up, eyes bright. Only his real art interested him. "Which painting?"

"The Renoir. How much for that?"

"Including the card? A thousand?"

Jacko smiled. "I never thought I'd get a Renoir for a grand. You're underselling yourself, Len. Don't be beaten down. This is superb stuff. I'll give you a couple of thousand and it's the best deal I've ever had. I'll never get a Renoir for that price again." He moved over to the Impressionist painting. "Make sure it's your bloody signature on the canvas and not a copy of Renoir's."

"Okay, I'll do the card. Collect tomorrow. I've still got one or two blanks."

Jacko handed over a spare photograph and produced his cheque book. "If you're worried then get a special clearance. Give me a receipt when the job is done. What about promoting me to Detective Inspector?"

Len, quite bright now, took a long look at Jacko and shook his head. "Leave it at Sergeant. What name?"

"Michael Stedman. Off the top of the head. If I don't get a new one soon the fuzz will be chasing all over London for the guy who's leaving a trail as Detective Sergeant Willis. It could cause problems in high places. This way nobody knows but you and me. Thanks, Len."

Still in Soho, Jacko was only a block away from Len Tiler's rooms. The sign read, "Photographic model. By appointment only." There was a telephone number on the card which was fixed behind a small glass case along with a few other signs. The house was the usual mixture of shop, in this case delicatessen, and small apartments.

The door to the apartments was at the side of the shop and Jacko rang the appropriate bell to wait for the voice box to crackle a greeting. Nothing happened. He rang twice more and hung on and finally decided that Sharon got out a good deal more than poor old Len. He turned away and almost bumped into an extremely attractive brunette. She was well dressed, held herself well, was slightly heavy on the make-up, and had the clearest blue eyes he had seen. And she was tall, almost as tall as Jacko himself.

"Have you been ringing for Sharon?" The voice spoiled the image but Jacko found it impossible to complain.

"Yes. Is that you?"

"That depends on what you want her for."

"I want to ask her a few questions for which I expect her to charge me."

"Oh, a talker. Haven't had one of those for a long time." She was fiddling in her handbag for a key and finally produced a bunch. "I have to be careful. There are a lot of dangerous kinkies around these days. Judy got murdered only three days ago. It upset us all."

"I wouldn't be hanging around talking to you like this for everyone to see me, if I intended to harm you. Can I come in?"

Sharon was eyeing Jacko shrewdly. "Did someone recommend you?"

It was on the tip of his tongue to say Charles Jason when he stopped in time; Jason was probably not the kind of man who would want to share; he could afford exclusive rights. "Ronnie Darrell. Had lunch with him today. We're old friends."

"You'd better come up, then."

Sharon opened the door and preceded him up the stairs and Jacko was fascinated by the shapely legs in front of him.

When they entered her apartment he was surprised by the tastefulness of everything he saw. The place was spotless, and almost flawless; pastel walls blended well with dove grey carpets and most of the furniture was antique. Sharon either had good taste or good advice. She was obviously not short of money and probably would not need his.

"You may as well give me a name," she said as she sat down and crossed her legs. "If you don't want to give your own any name will do as long as I have something to call you by."

"Like Sharon, you mean?"

She gave Jacko a devastating smile, her blue eyes harder than before. "Yes, but Sharon would sound funny on a man."

"How about Bruce Willis?"

84

"So you're a talker and you fantasise." Her accent was almost cockney but her perception was honed fine. "Besides, you're leaner in the face than Bruce Willis." She clasped her hands round her knees. "Well, Bruce, have you any money for this talk?"

He produced a bundle of notes far in excess of anything she would expect and laid them on an occasional table at his elbow.

"Do you know a guy called Charles Jason?"

He saw her glaze over and stiffen. She was about to try to get rid of him when he added smoothly. "I'm trying to protect his back against a threat he does not yet know about. He went into a certain business rather unwisely and some of us have heard rumbles. We're trying to cover him."

"I don't know anything about his business." She leaned across to the occasional table and just managed to reach the bundle of notes. Jacko did nothing to stop her. She carefully counted and peeled off what she wanted and reached forward again to return what was left of the bundle. "Leave it there. The charge might get higher."

Jacko guessed that she was not in need of money but was greedy for it. Because of her extraordinary good looks she had graduated to being kept by one man at a time, so far as they knew. Hanging around with men like Ronnie Darrell had obviated pimps long since; they would not dare try to muscle in.

Jacko watched her tuck the money away in her handbag and he said, "If you don't know his business you must know something of the people he moves around with. His talk can't always be about sex. Ever heard of a man called Reginald Dine?"

"Doesn't ring a bell, Bruce."

Jacko was patient but put an edge to his voice. "That was a bit too quick. If you go on like this I'll want a refund."

"Well, you won't get one. I can't help it if I don't have the answers to your questions." Something about Jacko's change of expression made her uneasy. "I may have heard of it. I'm not sure."

"Don't take me for a soft touch, Sharon. If I say I'll get a

85

refund then I'll get one. And you won't be working tomorrow. So far I've been more than fair; that can change. Now have you heard the name or not?"

She put her hand on her handbag as if that would protect the money. "It was only pillow talk. He was drunk once and was telling me how rich he was. He told me about his clubs but I already knew about them from Ronnie, and Charlie had already told me himself. He'd had far too much to drink and I don't think he ever knew what he said."

"Just as well, maybe." There was a grimness in Jacko's voice that made her wince. "Never let him know what he told you. But you've still told me nothing."

He had worried her. "Charlie wouldn't hurt me, would . . . he?"

"I wouldn't spend time asking him. For chrissake get on with it."

"He mentioned Dine then. And another man; a big wheel in politics."

"Can you remember his name?" And when she shook her head, "Was it Wherewell?"

But she did not remember and he did not want her agreeing to appease him so he pressed it no further. "Did he say what they were all up to?"

"No. I wouldn't have remembered anyway. I wasn't interested but had to sound as though I was. He was so boozed up that he couldn't finish the job that night and fell asleep."

"He must have said more than just giving you names. Think. You've nowhere near earned your money."

"He kept burbling something that sounded like 'sawed'. He'd say it over and over and fell asleep saying it."

"Sawed? Had he seen something?"

"How would I know? He'd have a fit if he thought I remembered any of it."

"He'd have a fit if he remembered any of it. You may not realise it but you've been a lucky girl, Sharon. Now, if I give you some questions to ask him do you think you could? Only if he gets like that again. Has it happened before?"

"Once or twice. There's no way I'll ask him. You've scared the living daylights out of me."

Jacko knew he had, but realised that if he was to stop Sharon passing any of this back to Jason he had to scare her. "You can name your own price."

"I've said too much already."

"You've said damn all." He was tempted to ask her to ring him should she recall anything else but decided she would be too scared. "I'm hardly likely to tell him we've met and I'm sure you won't. I mean, apart from anything else he might think we jumped in bed together. He wouldn't think too much of that. So we both keep quiet."

He was satisfied that he had made a connection between the men. It was a start. He crossed to the window and looked carefully down into the street. A few doors along Walter Kwang's faithful Triad was talking to another man in a doorway. As Kwang's office was not far away his presence could be coincidence.

He kept his back to Sharon. "Is there another way out?"

"Why?" She shot up in alarm.

Jacko turned casually. "No reason except to make it easier for you. You wouldn't want someone telling Charlie you had another man up here. If there's a back way I'll take it."

"There's only the fire escape. You get to it from the kitchen."

"That'll do. Show me the way."

Jacko picked up the balance of his money roll which he had deliberately left on the small table and followed her into the kitchen.

He took the back streets to Shaftesbury Avenue and looked for a cab. Kwang's man had not been there when he arrived so it left the question of whether Sharon was being watched for whatever reason. If Jason was a jealous man he might have an eye kept on her, but would he use Kwang's man, which meant Dine's? Or was Dine watching everyone in the hope that Jacko would show up to target himself?

10

James Atkins enjoyed staying in Jacko's house, because it was bigger and better furnished than his own and made a change. The area was not so good in snob terms, and that was something of a drawback for someone like Atkins who was a tax avoidance accountant. But the temporary move also meant he was not so readily available to an ex-wife who had a habit of occasionally dropping in on him at home, something he had forgotten to tell Jacko.

Atkins was in his early forties, apparently permanently tanned, with a ready smile and a sharp mind. Some people found him too sleek but he and Jacko had always got on. They came from similar backgrounds, one tried to hide it, the other never did; it was something they understood about each other.

Atkins came home about seven each evening. Sam, from across the street, had introduced himself and Atkins already knew about him from Jacko or would probably have ignored him. On the third night of residence, he arrived home, threw Jacko's spare keys on to the hall table and went whistling into the cloakroom, washed, and then went into the lounge to pour himself a drink. As he opened the door he knew at once someone was in the room.

Atkins had none of Jacko's highly developed instincts, nor had lived anything like so dangerous a life, but he knew something was wrong. He was certain when the door was closed behind him without him touching it. He spun round and a tough-looking character with a friendly smile leaned against the door with his arms folded across his chest. When Atkins turned back to face the room, another man was sitting in Jacko's favourite chair.

"Where is he?" asked the seated man.

"Where's who?" Atkins was not being deliberately obtuse but was frightened and confused.

The seated man shrugged. "We'll let you have that one. So I'll ask again. Where is Willie Jackson?"

Atkins had not encountered this kind of situation before. He tried to be brave; without conviction he replied, "I don't know. He simply asked me to look after his place for a few days."

"So you don't know where he went?"

"Absolutely not. I've no idea."

"Did you hear that, Ted?"

The man behind Atkins, said, "Yep. You believe him, Joe?"

Joe, still seated, grinned. "Nope. I reckon he knows. Buck up his memory a bit."

Atkins felt a crunching blow on the back of his neck and fell to his knees, and then to the floor face down, unconscious.

Joe angrily shot out of his chair. "That wasn't Jacko you belted, he's a softie. I reckon you've killed him."

Ted came forward. "I only tapped him. I'll get some water." He went into the kitchen and came back with a bowl of water and tipped it over Atkins' head, a deep stain spreading out across the expensive carpet. Neither man thought to test the pulse but as it happened Atkins stirred, groaned and then lay still again. They got him to his feet and helped him on to a chair and Ted helpfully slapped his face in an effort to bring him round.

Atkins was out for several minutes and they began to get worried. When he finally came round he was a wet, trembling wreck. He felt as if his head had been half severed, the pain excruciating. He heard them asking him questions again and himself pleading to be spared more pain. He had never known pain like this before.

He must have blacked out again for there was a blissful darkness that overrode all sensation until light began to penetrate his lids and this time he was much more aware of being conscious. He did not want to wake up, he could hide behind darkness but they were not going to let him. He had a much clearer picture now of what had happened. And yet a strong loyalty made him still reluctant to tell them that Jacko and he had exchanged homes.

He heard himself give his own name and it seemed to echo several times round the room. And then he felt the pain of them beating him again, but the original pain, still intense, seemed to cover everything else. He was slipping away again and the room was swimming and the voices fading yet hanging in the air as if for ever.

When Atkins finally passed out he was not sure whether he had betrayed Jacko or not. He had tried not to but his last recollection apart from incessant blows was that he was babbling and had no idea what he was babbling about.

As Atkins' resistance had held up, Joe, in spite of his criticism of Ted's initial violence, had joined in. What they had considered to be an easy routine job had proved to be anything but. Atkins had held out like a hero and they suddenly realised that they had gone over the top.

They belatedly went through his pockets then left him lying on the floor and hastily left the house.

Sam's live-in girlfriend, Bessie, saw the men arrive across the street and kept watch behind the curtains. She knew that Sam and Jacko had some sort of bond. She believed that Jacko had helped Sam once when he really needed it and Sam had never forgotten. That apart the two men had always been close friends. She knew a friend of Jacko's was staying in his house at the moment and there was no reason why he should not have visitors. But she did not like the look of them.

She did not know Jacko's friend was out but when she saw him arrive she realised that the men had let themselves in to wait for him. This worried her and she was further worried when she saw the two men leave hastily. She grabbed the phone pad and pen and went out on to the steps to watch the men disappear further down the street and get into a car. When they went past her she took the car number.

She did not know what to do then. She did not want to walk into something she could not handle so waited for Sam to get back from work. He arrived about an hour later. She poured it all out to him and he dashed across the street with a set of keys Jacko always left with him.

He found Atkins lying on the dampened lounge carpet, credit cards and driving licence strewn across the floor. He kneeled down and examined Atkins without touching him at first. He had been badly battered but was alive. He crossed to the phone and rang for an ambulance, leaving the police for the hospital authorities to contact.

While he waited he examined the credit cards and driving licence. Jacko had not told him who was staying beyond mentioning that it was a friend; to Sam that meant Jacko had dived for a while. As Atkins was using an old Jaguar belonging to Jacko he could not be traced through the number. He searched for a James R.T. Atkins in the telephone directory, and rang in the hope that Jacko was staying in Atkins' house.

When there was no reply he got agitated but could not rush off before the ambulance arrived. He went to the window; Bessie was standing on the steps and he waved and gave her a thumbs up he felt was entirely misleading. But Bessie had done a good, sensible job and he was proud of her.

By the time Atkins was taken away half the street had turned out to see what was going on. Sam crossed to his own house and gave Bessie a watered-down version of how badly Atkins was injured and told her she had done a good job. She gave him the car number and description of the two men and he said he would have to find Jacko in case he received the same attention as had Atkins.

He went by underground to the address he had raised from the telephone directory and, by the time he got there, wished he had put on a collar and tie. This was what he called a posh area. He wondered what panic he might cause if he suddenly shouted out he was moving in. It was a fleeting thought while he waited for someone to answer the door but nobody did. He rang again and was surprised when this time a woman opened the door as far as the chain allowed and almost closed it again when she saw him.

Sam stabbed his foot in the gap, and said quickly, "I'm looking for Willie Jackson. I think he's staying here."

91

Hazel eyes in a pretty but hard face stared back at him through the gap. "You've got the wrong address. There's no-one of that name around here. Take your foot away or I'll call the police."

"Are you Mrs Atkins?"

The hostile flare faltered. "It's none of your business. Now push off." But she was puzzled and did not press the door against Sam's foot quite so hard.

Sam did not know why he said it, perhaps because he felt there was something not quite right about her, but he asked, "Are you still married to him?"

"How dare you?" But the threat of the police had suddenly been dropped and he realised he was probably right. He did not know whether to tell her about Atkins or not. She had not even admitted to being his wife which he found strange. He felt it was not his duty to impart bad news to someone he did not know and who clearly resented his very presence. Let the police do it.

"So Willie Jackson isn't staying here?" he finished lamely.

"I already told you. Now please go." She was almost polite.

"Sorry I troubled you."

He walked to the end of the street and wondered what he should do. Was Jacko staying there? The only thing left to do was to ring from time to time and hope Jacko would answer, although he could not see Jacko staying with a woman like that; Georgie knocked spots off her. He found a call-box and rang Bessie to ask if there were any developments that end and to tell her he was on his way back. She told him that the police had called and from the way she spoke he guessed they were still there waiting for him.

The only people who could tell him if Jacko was staying at the house he had just visited were Jacko himself and Atkins. But he doubted that he would be allowed anywhere near Atkins even if he was yet in a fit condition to talk. He went back to face the police.

Jacko had worked a long day with only limited success. He paid off the cab a few streets from Atkins' house and

92

walked the rest of the distance. He turned the corner and froze. An ambulance was outside the house with two police cars, flashers on. The inevitable crowd had gathered, which took attention from himself, now a lone figure at one end of the street.

The ambulance moved off. There was no siren and no flasher and he found that ominous unless it was all a false alarm. The police were multiplying, however, as a plain car drove up and men who were obviously CID climbed out. Two uniformed officers were pushing back the crowd.

Jacko decided to take a chance. He joined the fringe of the crowd. "What the hell's happened?" he asked a man standing in front of him.

"A woman fell down the stairs. Broke her neck. One of the coppers reckons she was pushed. The door was wide open."

"A woman?" What woman? Jacko had been living there alone. And that thought sent him edging away from the crowd and easing back to the corner of the street from where he had come. He found the same pay phone Sam had, and rang his own number. A strange voice answered and he hung up quickly. What the hell was going on? He rang Sam. Bessie answered. As soon as she recognised his voice she said, "You've got the wrong number." She said it in such a way that she was sure he would know it was her.

"Is somebody with you, Bessie?"

"Try looking it up," she said. "I'm busy with a house full or I'd help you better." Bessie hung up and Jacko was totally confused. Were his house and Sam's also crawling with police? He suddenly saw himself as prime suspect for whatever had happened.

Jacko went back to his own home but only as far as the corner of the street. The police presence was less obvious but there was a car outside his house and a policeman standing on the steps of Sam's house. Perhaps the police had all come in the same car.

It then seemed that the police were leaving Sam's place and Sam came out on to the steps to see them on their way. So nothing had happened to Sam and Bessie. It was too risky

93

to call openly so he found another pay phone and at last got Sam on the line.

Jacko listened in dismay. Poor old Jimmy Atkins. And he could not visit him; the police would have someone by the bed. But Sam could visit and Jacko made an arrangement to see Sam at the Hot Pot that evening.

Both men took extra precautions and they met late, at half past ten. Jacko arranged for them to use the small room at the back; it was rather airless but at least they were alone. Sam told him in more detail what had happened and passed across the car number Bessie had jotted down.

Sam was worried because he did not think the police believed his story. The two men arriving and entering routine rang hollow with them. Why should Sam investigate anyway? And what was Atkins doing in Jacko's house in the first place? The police found it difficult to accept simple values like acting out of friendship, and Bessie too was apparently unhappy about the outcome with the police. The one irrefutable fact in Sam's favour was that it was he who had called the ambulance.

"So who was the woman at Atkins' place?" Jacko asked.

"I think it must have been Atkins' wife."

"He doesn't have a wife."

"An ex-wife then? Girlfriend?"

"He was divorced. She was a bit of a slag, always with this man or that." Jacko suddenly snapped his fingers. "I seem to remember that Jimmy once moaned about the way his ex kept prancing in every time a boyfriend kicked her out. She had kept her set of keys and he never got round to changing the lock. If she was killed, why?"

"For the same reason they beat up your friend. They want to find you."

"I can't believe this. I tucked Georgie away because she is close to me. But I never dreamed they would start on innocent people who have no connection with any of this, if only because of the risk. Just to get at me? I've slipped up badly, my God. This isn't Dine."

"You must know more than you think."

"Or they have something much bigger to hide than I

94

realised." Jacko gazed across the small table in exasperation. "They won't be happy until they've stopped me once and for all. And they won't accept a declaration of peace; I've already tried that. I can't go back. Are you and Bessie all right?"

"Oh, sure. Don't worry about us. They must have thought the woman was staying with you and she wouldn't have known what the hell they were talking about."

"I'll find a way of making it up to Jimmy Atkins." Jacko suddenly pushed his chair back. "I don't know where I'm going now. When Jimmy comes round and the police find out I was staying at his place they'll come searching for me. I can do without that complication." He realised he was isolating himself almost completely now.

Before they left the Hot Pot, Jacko put a call through to Georgie and this time raised her as she was about to turn in. He told her everything was working out well. Another few days should do it. When she replied that she must get back to the office or the partnership would fold up, he shouted at her that she must not. He hung up before she could argue.

He supported himself against the end of the bar. All the reassurances he had given her had been destroyed in one act of panic. But she must not go back where they could easily pick her up.

"You sure you can't duck out?" asked Sam after seeing Jacko's agonised expression.

Jacko shook his head. "Even if they agreed we wouldn't trust one another. I'd no idea they had so much to hide and I'm nowhere near knowing what." Before leaving the club he made one more call.

"Sharon? I can't help it if you're in the middle of a job. If you don't listen there might not be any jobs. If you have a friend or relative nobody else knows about, go and stay with them. Now. I'm dead serious. Give the bloke his money back." He hung up to see Sam grinning. He smiled back; it felt like the first time he had smiled in years.

He slapped Sam on the shoulder. "Thanks, Sam. I'd better push off and find somewhere to sleep." But before he did he made one more phone call, this time from a pay phone after Sam had left him, and woke Ewing up to demand one more car trace and read out the number Bessie had taken down. He gave Ewing the number he was ringing from, explained it was a call-box and that he would wait until Ewing rang him back as he was on the run and the police were after him as well as Dine. He hung up before Ewing could answer.

Ewing might now find himself in a very awkward position. Jacko leaned against the box and thought that Ewing had nothing to complain about; he should not have started it.

Jacko finally fell on to a bed at 2.00 in the morning. It was a seedy boarding house near Highbury and he doubted that he would stay there long. Other than what he had on him he had no clothes. It had been quite a day! He fell asleep before he could undress.

Jacko woke as soon as it was light. He could cope with very little sleep and he caught a bus to Piccadilly and to the underground toilets where he had a wash and shave. He found an all-night chemist, bought a shaving kit, and asked for small coins for telephone calls. It was too soon to ring his warehouse, it was impossible for him to return there, so he took a chance on returning to Len Tiler, conscious of how near Sharon's apartment was.

Len had worked long into the night. Like most good professionals, once the job was under way he could not stop until it was finished. Jacko viewed the card: Detective Sergeant Michael Stedman; a work of art.

"What about the Renoir?" asked Len as Jacko was about to leave.

"Keep it for me until I can come back. Charge me storage. Thanks, Len. Great job."

He left Soho as fast as he could. The address Ewing had given him when he had rung back at the call-box was in Kennington and he hailed a cab to take him there. The street was behind an ugly block of modern flats and was run-down like most of the immediate area. The street was short, comprising terraced houses from beginning to end. He found No. 16 and noticed an old Ford Capri standing almost outside. The registration number checked with the one Bessie had taken down. He rang the bell, heard nothing from inside then knocked loudly on the door. Lace curtains twitched in the front room but nobody came. Jacko hammered on the door, intending that the whole street should hear if it was not opened. "What the hell are you playing at you crazy bastard? You'll break the door down." At last the door was open and a man stood there in open-neck shirt and braces, with bare feet. He was a big man, well muscled, in his early forties. "I was just taking a kip. What do you want?"

"Are you Bob Allen?"

"Who wants to know?"

"I do." Jacko made a point of fiddling in his pocket to produce the new warrant card and briefly held it up. "Is that your Capri out there?"

"What is it you want? Don't bugger around, just say it."

"Can I come in?"

"No, you bloody well can't."

"Okay. I'll ask you once more; are you Bob Allen?"

"No. I don't know a Bob Allen. He doesn't live here."

"Our records say he does. So who are you? And one more crack and I'll arrest you for wasting police time and for carrying drugs."

"Don't come that with me, copper. You'll find no drugs here."

"Want a bet?" Jacko let it hang as he fiddled in one of his pockets.

"You bent bastard. What's the problem with the Capri?"

"It was seen last night near a place where someone was murdered."

The hard eyes went blank. "Someone nicked it last night. I found it round the corner this morning and parked it outside. Probably joyriders. No damage. Young buggers."

Unimpressed, Jacko said, "Do you ask me in or do I get a squad down? Your neighbours would like that." He went up the short path to the front gate and looked up and down the street. "Quite a few are interested now."

"You can have five minutes. I need some sleep."

Jacko went into a small sitting-room. Some trophies lined

97

the mantelpiece, one of a boxer on a plinth. It was quite a pleasant room. Jacko stood by the mantelpiece. "Is your wife in?"

"I haven't got a wife; not now. My girlfriend's at work."

"Good arrangement," said Jacko. "She does all the work and you put your feet up."

"You're asking to be done, copper or no copper."

"So we're alone," said Jacko.

"That's right. No witnesses. So watch yourself."

Jacko took his time gazing round the room, letting the silence build up; there is nothing more unnerving if someone has something to hide. He walked round the room, peering into corners.

"Have you got a search warrant, because you need one the way you're carrying on."

"Let's have a look at your hands," said Jacko suddenly, taking the man who had been called Joe the previous night, by surprise.

"Get stuffed. Look, are you going to get on with it? I still don't know why you're here."

"Yes you do. You beat somebody up last night. You were seen with another man entering and leaving a house where a man was later found dead," Jacko lied. "Who was the misguided fool who hired brainless trash like you?"

Allen just managed to stop himself from striking Jacko. He had sufficient sense to grasp that he was being deliberately goaded, and then one or two questions entered his mind. "Where's your oppo? You wouldn't be coming here on your own with an accusation like that. You'd have back-up."

Jacko shrugged. "I wanted to get you alone. If you want to go down for it yourself, that's up to you. But you're a mug if you do. Don't take the rap for someone else's orders. Was it Sonny Rollins?"

"Don't be stupid. Sonny Rollins wouldn't give me the time of day."

For Jacko that was tantamount to an admission. "One of his men then?"

Allen came nearer. "You're not very smart, copper. I didn't beat anybody up. And if you go round talking of

Sonny Rollins like that you'll be taking early retirement. Now sod off."

"Okay. But I'll spread it around that you told me Sonny set you up. That should make him happy."

Jacko had been waiting for it from the moment he entered the house. Allen swung a blow at his head and Jacko responded in the way he had been taught over many years. Allen struck air and something hard hit him in the stomach with tremendous force to leave him curled up, face down and barely able to get his breath. He was also in a great deal of pain. Jacko flipped him on to his side with his foot.

"Was it one of Rollins' crowd?"

But Allen was not yet fit to talk; he was still curled up and groaning with pain.

Jacko stood clear of him, watching carefully for animal cunning. When Allen's breathing became more regular he asked again, "Was it any of Rollins' crowd?"

When there was still no answer Jacko squatted on his haunches and pulled out the Browning. He tapped Allen's broken nose with it, hard enough to draw blood. "The bloke you did was a mate of mine, and you're in the frame for murder. If I don't get an answer I'm going to blow your bloody brains out, because I don't trust the courts and nobody is going to be bothered by your death." He started to attach the silencer.

Allen's eyes flickered with fear. He tried to speak but gagged and Jacko waited, moving away again.

Allen was trying to think clearly as he came out of pain. Before he could say anything Jacko added, "Before I put a bullet in your head I'm going to smash you bit by bit. You'll beg for the bullet before it comes; it will be merciful, an end you never offered my friend."

"If I tell you, I'm gonna get a bullet anyway so what does it matter?"

"Why should he know? Go away for a spell. Or would you rather we tucked you up inside?"

Allen tried to sit up. The movement brought the pain back. "What the hell did you hit me with?"

"My foot. They didn't train us to fight clean. No referees. Was it Rollins' crowd?"

Allen nodded his head slowly. He struggled to his feet, held on to the table to steady himself. He put an enormous effort into a back-handed swing that would have almost have decapitated Jacko had it struck him. It threw Allen off balance and when he looked round Jacko was not there. Belatedly, it occurred to him that a Browning was not police issue; so who the hell was Sergeant Stedman? The first deep pangs of fear then gripped him and he went upstairs to cram some clothes into a suitcase. He dared not leave a note.

11

Jacko was already outside the house when Allen made the back-handed swipe at him. He was satisfied there was a positive connection between Dine and Rollins and reckoned that Charles Jason and Simon Wherewell, MP were also involved. Sharon had mentioned a big wheel in politics; Wherewell was anything but that; it was extremely unlikely that the general public had ever heard of him except those in his own constituency who, according to Ewing, had been trying to get rid of him for some time. Wherewell was in the political wilderness and was unlikely to be returned at the next election.

It was a strange mixture. A top gangster, a minor politician, a man involved in leisure and clubs, and Dine whom it was difficult to place in any particular group, but who might just be the most dangerous of them all.

Everything stemmed from Dine. And yet Jacko had difficulty in believing that Dine had sanctioned the beat-ups and the murders. Rollins had provided the machinery of small-time hoods like Pete Selby and Bob Allen to process the violence. The pattern was familiar but with such a strange liaison what were they protecting? Rollins would not be involved in petty crime; it would have to pay in a big way to attract his interest.

Dine and Rollins might have been engaged in the same rackets and their paths had simply crossed and they had done a deal together. Wherewell and Jason were the odd men out. He must find out what the central racket was.

Jacko at last rang his warehouse and gave certain instructions. He then hired a BMW from a dealer friend in Notting Hill and felt the relief of being mobile again. He had settled up

101

with the boarding house and so had nowhere definite to stay. He could not compromise any more of his friends and was sure that the word would be put around the lesser-known hotels by leg-men of Sonny Rollins; they would not stop now.

A delivery service was used from the warehouse to Waterloo Station and he collected the grip from a motor cyclist, under the entry arch.

He rang Georgie again; just a few bright words, and then rang Sam to hear that Jimmy Atkins' condition was not as serious as it had first appeared, which was a huge relief. He had not yet been told about the death of his ex-wife.

He drove to the underground car park at Marble Arch and went on a shopping spree for a change of shirts and underwear, spare socks, and extra shoes, considering it too risky to make even a brief visit to his home. He then drove to the Army and Navy Club and managed to book a room and underground car space. He had belonged to the club for some time under the name of Lieutenant-Colonel W. Baxter, with the help of Ewing who had supplied proposal and seconding letters. He used it only in a crisis and as a relatively safe haven. He made no friends during his few visits, being stand-offish to discourage approaches.

He looked Wherewell up in the telephone directory, and found him off the Bayswater Road. He thought it slightly strange that none of the four men he was now investigating was ex-directory when they had so much to hide. Perhaps their openness was itself a disguise.

Jacko telephoned Ewing again at his office, could not raise him, left no message and tried twice more over a period of an hour before making contact. By this time Ewing was worried about the whole affair. What had started out as an effort to help a Frenchman regain some national property had got hopelessly out of hand. Now there were pressures from above, on Ewing himself to come up with answers regarding Reginald Dine.

Ewing wanted to meet Jacko to bring himself up to date but Jacko did not trust Ewing's ability to avoid being followed. He explained quickly, "Three dead, one injured, I've taken a dive, and Georgie is staying with a friend; I won't tell you where she is and I've told her not to go near her office. I've already given the names of those I think are involved one way or another, but I want more detail on Simon Wherewell."

Ewing knew he was getting out of his depth but could do nothing other than help. "I can tell you most of it off the top of my head. He's not a young man. Probably of similar age to Dine. He's been in politics since the middle 1960s and for most of the time has barely uttered a parliamentary word since his maiden speech. He was used on various committees which gave him a sense of purpose according to those who know him best. A frustrated man, I would say, one who would never hold a ministerial position."

"You told me earlier that he isn't liked," said Jacko. "Was there a point of change? Has he always been disliked?"

"This is ridiculous, Jacko. Why can't we meet and discuss this properly?"

"Because they're out looking for me and you wouldn't stand up to torture well. Answer, Thomas."

"He used to be a quiet sort of chap. Harmless, some would say, with a certain homely appeal which clearly won him votes. But he's changed over the last few years. He's become cocky, almost arrogant, and at times insufferable."

"Any obvious reason?"

"Something must have happened to make him more sure of himself. Maybe a rich aunt left him some money. He does not seem perturbed by the almost certain probability that he will lose his seat."

"What about those committees he sat on?"

"For God's sake, Jacko, I've no idea. There could be dozens, hundreds, over the years. They're the usual thing; parliamentary committees are commonplace, they're happening all the time."

"Can you rake them up from the time you think a change came over him?"

"It could take ages; a full-time job. If I got someone to do it then it would be a risky thing to do; they would want to know why I was ferreting. He would get to hear of it."

"Okay, but do what you can. Does he act as though he has money? And is he married?"

"I already answered that; it goes along with being cocky and suddenly self-assured and generally obnoxious. His wife left him some years ago. I don't know whether they ever got divorced." Ewing sounded exasperated. "When the devil are you coming in from the cold, Jacko? We are all worried sick."

"So am I. That's why I'm staying put. Thanks, Thomas. I'll be in touch. And give my love to Liz." Jacko decided to call on Simon Wherewell early the next morning.

It turned out to be one of those Edwardian houses converted into expensive apartments, just four in the one terraced building, with names and numbers in smart brass plates alongside intercom boxes. Jacko peered back down the street to the Bayswater Road. With imagination, if he could have seen through the mass of constant traffic to the far side of the street he would have seen Hyde Park. On a fine Sunday, rows of paintings with their artists would be on show. It was not the most salubrious of districts but expensive enough.

As there were five floors including the basement, Jacko assumed that one of the apartments must be a maisonette. He rang the bell of No. 4 which he assumed was at the top of the building, and waited. Nothing happened. He rang once more without result and crossed the road to get a better view of the whole building. He could see no burglar alarms; such quarters were difficult to wire up separately and provide each one with an outside bell or siren; it could be confusing. So occupants usually relied on the security of a well-locked door which could only be opened by a mortice key or a lock release from inside the apartments. Each apartment then had its own choice of locks and bolts and chains.

As he gazed across the street, Jacko thought of Walter Daley, better known as Wally the Creep. Jacko knew his own limitations when it came to breaking and entering and he had used Wally before for this sort of job.

Somewhere along the line he would have to break in to find what he could. Nobody was going to tell him what he needed to know. Sonny Rollins was the last man to enter his mind as a possible source of information; he would need an army to help him and then one to protect him. Dine was wired up to the hilt. Charles Jason was a possibility. But Wherewell seemed to be the weakest unit: cocky men thought they knew it all and could seldom be advised. But he needed to know something of Wherewell's habits and he did not have the time to have him followed for a few days. Ewing would curse him for this next request but somehow he had to ensure that Wherewell was in the House of Commons, preferably during an important debate.

He rang again. A resigned Ewing said, "Yes, Jacko?"

"Can you let me know when Wherewell will be in the House? I need him to be away from his apartment for a while."

"I never heard that, Jacko. Just what the hell are you up to?"

"Can you?"

"Of course I bloody well can't. I'm never in the actual chamber. I'm a personal administrator to the PM, not an elected MP."

Jacko could almost see Ewing shaking his head in despair. "I want to be sure he's away from home for a few hours."

"I'm not his keeper, Jacko. I rarely see the man. Anyway, you're barking up the wrong tree. As I understand it he's one of those who give the party a bad image. He's seldom in the House."

"What about a three-line whip? Wouldn't he have to be there?"

"Oh, you'd like me to lay one on, would you? That's no problem, I'll have a personal word with the PM and the Leader of the Opposition, and the Leader of the House and rearrange the whole damned schedule for you. How would that be?"

"That would be fine." Jacko could not fail to hear Ewing's desperation. Jacko had never before called on him to this degree. Ewing wanted to help, felt that he must, but could not. He was well aware of how his original request had placed Jacko in danger.

Jacko laughed. "I'm pulling your leg, Thomas. I just

thought it was worth a try. Don't worry. I'll find another way."

There was a long silence and Ewing finally said more quietly, "I'd forgotten. There's a three-line whip this afternoon. Unemployment. A vote of confidence issue. I was looking beyond today. I suppose the notice is too short?"

Jacko's heart sank. He'd never get Wally in that time; Wally liked to case his targets very carefully before operating. "What time does it start?"

"Immediately after lunch."

"I'll do my best. But thanks for the help, Thomas. I don't like harassing you but I'm being harassed myself. Cheers."

"No," said Wally, bluntly. "No way." He had smartened up since Jacko had last seen him: good suit, thinning hair brushed back, eyes bright, spindly figure filled out. He appeared to be prosperous.

"You look as if you've done some useful blagging. Glad to see you doing well, Wally."

They were in the Hot Pot and Jacko was paying for the lunch. He had been lucky to get hold of Wally so quickly but it now looked as if it would not help.

Wally swigged his beer and wiped his lips. "I don't blag, and you know it. I'm a peterman, one of the best."

"The best, some say," said Jacko mildly.

"Flattery won't help, Jacko. I need time for preparation."

"I've done the casing for you and the guy won't be around all afternoon. What could be easier?"

"Nobody does my casing for me. Anyway, working for you is non-profit-making. The last time I cracked a safe for you, you made me put the 'tom' back. Never seen jewellery like it. I can't work for a fee."

"Would you do it for the flag?"

Wally choked on his beer and it was some time before he could get his breath sufficiently to say, "The flag? You? You got drummed out."

Jacko gazed round the room. "It was a fix, Wally. It had to look like that." He leaned across the table and lowered his voice. "Why the hell do you think I made you put the 'tom' back? Believe me; if anything goes wrong I've got cover; it will all be hushed up. I'll pay you well enough. Plus a Government bonus."

"No, you crafty sod." Wally was shaking his head, smiling. "You should have been a con man, Jacko. I'm not sure you're not."

"Okay, Wally. No hard feelings. I can see you don't need the extra cash right now. So, I'll have to do it myself. You can do me one favour, though. Will you come with me to look at the place and tell me if you see any snags. Give me a tip or two? I'll pay for your time, of course."

Simon Wherewell carried himself like the soldier he had never been. He had good posture, had always dressed well, although these last few years he had been fitted exclusively by a well-known Savile Row tailor, and his accessories were of the best.

Age rode well on him, silver hair well cut and brushed back at the sides. His good looks were spoiled by a slightly supercilious air and a condescending nature. To speak to him made it easy to discover why he was not liked by most of his fellow MPs.

He strode along to St Stephen's Square swinging his umbrella like a guardsman lacking in height, and attracting a fair amount of attention. He was a nobody who looked like a somebody.

He received a salute from the policeman at the gate and swung his umbrella up in return. It was small things like that that he liked about Parliament: a sense of importance. And to be recognised after only infrequent appearances made him feel better still.

Wherewell resented having to attend at all but he had failed to get a 'pair', little realising that nobody wanted to do any sort of deal with him and that he was disliked by the Opposition almost as much as he was in his own party. The feelings others had for him passed him by. Well, another year at most should see him free of political shackles, although he would miss some of it, like sailing out of the House of Commons car park in his Daimler Sovereign and having a policeman hold up the oncoming traffic for him so he could get away. Just one of the small perks.

As he entered the House he hoped he might get away or even find a 'pair' at this late stage. He was going to find it difficult to listen to acrimony about unemployment far into the night. He would surely find some way to leave early. He was good at manipulating.

They gazed across the street at the house in which Wherewell had his top-floor apartment. Jacko was edgy, for the Commons debate had probably already started. "I thought I'd con one of the other tenants into letting me in the main door, you know, flowers or a parcel stuff."

"That old trick." Wally was disgusted. "So what happens once you're in and don't pitch up at that flat you're supposed to be delivering to? No, it's easy enough to slip the lock. If you have the right gear."

Jacko glanced at Wally. "I don't suppose you could lend me some of yours?"

Wally did not answer. He was still studying the house, and then scanned up and down the street. "I must be mad even to think of working in daylight. It's asking for trouble. You'll have to act as look-out. It might take a little time to release the catch."

"You mean you'll do it?" Jacko sounded overjoyed.

"You crafty bugger, you knew bloody well I would once I'd seen the place. You knew I couldn't resist a challenge. But it will cost you. I'll have to go back for my kit."

That was worrying but there was nothing Jacko could do but hope the Commons debate went on long into the night. Wally lived in Fulham and Jacko took him in the BMW using the back streets to avoid the bulk of the after-lunch build-up. But delays were inevitable and by the time they got back to Bayswater it was after half past three, and that was good going. Fortunately Wally always kept a bag packed ready.

Jacko kept watch at the foot of the shallow steps while Wally went to work on the front door. Mid-afternoon somehow attracted fewer people on to the streets; most would be working, and the lunch period was long over.

Jacko shifted position as necessary to block off from view what Wally was doing.

At last Wally called out, "We're in," and opened the front door.

The two men closed the door after them and mounted the stairs although there was a tiny lift at the end of the narrow hall. The lift hummed when they were halfway up the first flight of stairs and they waited until it had descended. The gates opened and closed and high heels clacked across the stone-flagged hall to the front door.

They continued up to the top floor, and Wherewell's solid door with the spyhole peering at them like a mini TV camera faced them almost opposite the head of the stairs. No.4 must be the maisonette, for there had been an apartment on each of the other floors.

Unless Wherewell returned they were safer up here. Jacko stood guard while Wally went to work on the door. The lift was not operated again but from time to time he heard the faint sound of the front door being released and realised how lucky they had been when working on the street door.

Time was passing and it was well past four but Jacko knew he dare not break Wally's concentration while he dealt with the locks. When they did get in they pushed the door to behind them and felt the quiet aura of the apartment. As they went from room to room both men were impressed by the dignified décor which somehow did not match up with Jacko's understanding of Wherewell who, Jacko concluded, must have used professional interior decorators.

A semi-circular wrought-iron staircase led to the upper floor and the bedrooms, one of which was being used as a study. The layout memorised, the time passing all too fast, Jacko said, "You find the safe and I'll look around." They separated, Wally searching for a place he would expect a safe to be.

Jacko went up to the study to find everything locked; desk and cabinets. He had to get Wally to use some of his precious time in opening the locks but Jacko wanted to leave no obvious trace of a break-in. He carefully went through all documents and papers in the drawers to find

109

most of them political, including unanswered letters from constituents who needed his help. The cabinets were also of no help and housed old Hansards, political newspaper clips and magazine articles. It was Wally who found the interesting stuff.

Wally had found the safe in the drawing-room, hidden inside a window seat. The seat itself could be raised on a hinge, and then the front panel could be lowered by releasing two catches at each end. After that, to Wally, it was relatively easy. The safe was a small modern design and he had lain flat to work at the combination.

By the time Jacko reached the bottom of the wrought-iron stairs Wally had the contents laid out for Jacko to examine. There was no money or jewellery, much to Wally's relief for their absence removed temptation. There was a leather-bound address book with some loose sheets inside the cover, and various insurance documents. There were also share certificates and bank statements. Jacko collected them up from the floor and took them to a long polished stone table in the middle of the room. He put the nearest side lamp on one end of the table, the flex just stretching far enough, and switched it on. When he produced a miniature camera, Wally said, "I never knew you had one of those."

"Part of normal gear, Wally," said Jacko seriously. "Like invisible ink."

He opened the book to the first page and lined up the camera. This part could not really be rushed but he was very conscious of the time and had yet to restore everything in the study to how they had found it. The time was 5.35.

Simon Wherewell was totally bored with the time-wasting and futile in-fighting taking place around him. It was like a kindergarten. He could better use his time than listen to the political jockeying about an issue which had once interested him but now left him stone cold. It was obvious the debate would last long into the night. Politically he did not give a damn either way; whoever was in would use the same tactics if it suited them.

He decided to slip away from the House and come back

later. He knew he was taking a grave risk, and that if caught, could be suspended or even kicked out of the Party if he missed the vote. It did not matter to him any more except in terms of adverse newspaper and television coverage which would do his general reputation no good at all. And certain of his acquaintances outside politics might take a very dim view if he offered too high a profile.

He was so sure he had time in hand that he decided the risk was worth it. It was not that he had anything urgent to do but that he must find relief from what was happening around him. It had once been different but that was before he found the source of complete freedom and no longer needed the supportive ladder of politics. He would go over a few things at his London apartment, go out and eat decently, then return to the chamber. He left the House at 5.30.

They tidied up, made sure everything was as they had found it and that all drawers were locked. To do this and not leave a trace took time but both men were professionals and did the job properly. Satisfied, they took a last look round and left the apartment, Wally using more valuable time in locking the door. They used the stairs again, skipping down them as fast as they could. They reached the hall and Jacko opened the front door.

A well-dressed man looked up as they almost knocked him over in their haste to leave. He had a key in his hand and it was clear he had been about to unlock the door.

Jacko said, "I'm so sorry. Are you all right?" He knew at once that he was looking at Simon Wherewell. He had never seen him or a photograph, but it was he, no doubt about it.

Wherewell gave a cursory smile but eyed them with suspicion; he could not place them and his expression suggested they did not belong there. For some reason alarm bells sounded but not because of his absence from the House. He took a good look at Jacko and Wally who had hurried up the street without turning round. He would remember their faces.

111

12

Jacko dropped Wally off in Fulham and drove back to the Army and Navy to park the car. He took a cab to Len Tiler's place and asked him to develop and enlarge the shots he had taken of Wherewell's documents; photography was all part of Len's talent for forgery.

While he waited, Len having disappeared behind a paint stripped door hung with forged miniatures, he reflected on seeing Wherewell. Wally, who like himself had never seen the politician, or even knew who lived in the maisonette, felt as Jacko did; it had been a very near thing and the repercussions would not have stopped with Wherewell. As it was, the politician had taken a good look at them and would not forget.

Jacko was aware of restricting himself with every move he made, almost like applying his own restraining harness. He looked at some of the paintings while he waited and noticed that the Renoir he had bought had been put out of sight. There were times when Len could be so honest that it made Jacko wonder how he had ever got behind bars.

Some time later Len came in, rattling the miniatures on the door, and passed Jacko an envelope containing the prints. Jacko settled the bill, still declined to take the Renoir, and went searching for a cab. It was the back-end of the rush hour and he finally decided to take the long walk back.

In his room at the club he examined the shots. The lists were confusing because they covered virtually all parts of Europe, headed by Italy with Britain finishing last, several pages on. There were lists of names against each country, Italy had several pages of them. Almost all had names crossed out and others added, and against each was a location but only a few had an actual address. The remainder were starred perhaps suggesting that there were addresses elsewhere.

Jacko went through all he had but could find no supplementary pages with addresses. He gathered up all the copies and propped himself up against the bed-head to go through them more carefully; there had to be more meaning to them than just a list of names and locations. He started on the tedious task of counting the names.

Italy had the highest number, 139, but most had been crossed off, leaving twenty-five. All were in Northern Italy. Britain had forty-five original names: they had been whittled down to four which had addresses as well. They were in Hampshire, Sussex, Dorset and Essex. The original locations had been roughly spread all round Britain, excluding Scotland but with one in Northern Ireland. There were four in Holland, ten in Germany and others in Scandinavia, France, Belgium, Luxembourg, Switzerland, Portugal and Spain, and just two names in Greece.

By the time he put down the photo-enlargements he was tired and very confused. When he checked the time it was after ten and he had not yet eaten. He put the prints away in his grip and went out to find a snack bar. Even if it had not been too late for the club he would not have eaten there; the less he saw of the members the better.

He had a sandwich and some coffee and decided he had to contact Ewing again, perhaps risk a meeting with him. He sought the nearest call-box to receive no answer. He supposed Ewing was entitled to go out some time but why tonight? He rang Ewing's office number but did not really expect anyone to be there and he was right. Ewing did not use an answering machine believing that if it was important enough people would ring back, and that all they really achieved was to inform burglars that the occupier was out.

Jacko was tired, increasingly irritable and frustrated. He needed Georgie then and wondered for how long she would stay away from her office without him giving her more informative reasons for doing so. But he had none to give.

Jacko trudged back towards the Army and Navy barely aware of those around him. It was a pleasant October night and the swishing of traffic became a lullaby against the gentle accompaniment of passing footsteps. Was loneliness at last getting to him? He shook himself from reverie and realised he should be looking about him from time to time. It could be fatal to assume he was safe where he was. By the time he reached the club he was pondering his next move.

When Harry Bates refused to meet him at the Hot Pot, Jacko realised there was something wrong. In fact it took a good deal of persuasion for Harry to agree to a meeting at all. They met mid-morning on the Embankment and Harry even refused to shake Jacko's hand, in case he was seen doing it.

"Nothing personal," said Harry, coat collar turned up partially to hide his lean features, and partly to ward off a crisp wind cutting across the Thames. They leaned on the parapet and faced the river so that passers-by could not identify them, but even then it was obvious to Jacko that Harry was uncomfortable.

"What's the matter with you?" asked Jacko. "I only want a small favour for which I'm willing to pay your exorbitant fees."

"Can't do it, old son." Harry kept his gaze on the grey turgid water. "I've stuck my neck out coming down here. I reckoned I owed you an explanation."

"Look, all I want is a couple of blokes to watch someone for me. You're the best fixer in the business, this is a dolly, Harry. No risk."

"I'm taking one right now, old son." Harry still had his gaze on the river as if hypnotised by it. "There's an open contract out on you."

Jacko gazed hard at what he could see of Harry's face. "A contract? Have you gone American or something? What are you talking about?"

Harry almost turned then but stopped in time, now fascinated by the Festival Hall on the opposite bank. "What else do you call it? A contract is a contract. Ten grand. A lot of the boys could do with that sort of money."

"Ten grand? The mean bastard. Who's put the word out?"

Harry did not answer the direct question. "It's no joke, Jacko. If I help you I put myself on the list. I can do without that. As an old mate I thought it best to warn you personally; I don't trust telephones."

Jacko looked down at the heaving water for a while. He was disturbed but not only because of himself. "I never thought I'd see you like this, Harry. You're suddenly jelly. What the hell has happened to you?"

The eyes above the upturned coat collar were reflective and sad. "I can deal with most things, Jacko. I've done my share. But this is more than I can cope with. Leave the country, old son."

"Sonny Rollins?" Jacko tried to penetrate beyond the eyes above the coat collar.

"I got married," said Harry.

For a moment Jacko found this more surprising than the threat against him. "I'm sorry about that," he said without thinking, meaning that he understood Harry's extra caution. "Anyway, you didn't answer; is it Sonny who's put out a contract?"

"Could be," Harry said. "His is one name I don't like mentioning. He got to know my part against Dickie Ashton. He let me know that he knew."

"That's history, Harry. He couldn't have done a thing without showing he was involved. Forget it. Lend me a hand, just for a few days."

At last Harry turned. Talking had steadied him down a little but he was still a very worried man.

"Jacko, you are not taking this seriously. The word is out and Rollins controls all the outlets, so that everybody knows. You are fingered, old son. I like you, mate. Everyone likes you. But that has to be weighed against how much they fear Rollins."

Jacko thought of Len Tiler and Wally, both of whom had only recently helped him. "When did you hear of this?"

"About two hours before you phoned. It's fresh and if you're quick you can be in time to take a deep dive where they won't find you."

"Thank God you're not short of ten grand. I told you it was mean."

"It won't be to most of them, Jacko. But I couldn't do that to you for any price."

"Thanks, Harry." Jacko knew that Harry meant it and that he had taken a risk meeting so openly. He thought that if Rollins had made a tactical error in spreading the contract so far and wide that even the police might get to hear of it, it would still not help Jacko if someone completed the contract.

"I'll have to watch my back," said Jacko lamely.

"All 360 degrees, old son, but your back is a good place to start. I'm sorry, Jacko. Have you any instructions for anyone?"

Jacko smiled because Harry was so serious. "You mean when I've gone?"

"Sure. That gorgeous bird, Georgie, for instance. Any messages? I'll see that they're passed on."

"I'll give you a tinkle from the other side," said Jacko. "I might be around for a while yet."

Harry shook his head sadly. "It hasn't sunk in, has it? Bit of a shock." To confirm how seriously Harry himself took the threat against Jacko he now held out his hand and took Jacko's warmly. Realising what he was doing he suddenly let go and gazed around self-consciously. "Good luck, old son. We'll miss you, mate."

"Cheers, Harry, and give my best to all the boys I know."

"I can't do that; they're the ones who'll come gunning for you. I can't let anyone know I've seen you. Make sure your magazine is always loaded, mate, and keep your back to the wall. Be lucky." Harry turned and wandered down the Embankment and was soon lost amongst the other walkers.

The threat had almost been comic in its delivery but Harry had been torn between warning and not wanting to upset or lose a friend; and Jacko had verged on the flippant for Harry's sake. But trying to spare each other's feelings would not make the problem go away. If Rollins had put out a contract then it was as serious as anything he could recall happening since he had left the forces.

He decided to check Harry's warning. He crossed to the

116

Underground station and telephoned Wally. Wally hung up as soon as he heard his voice. He tried again and Wally would not answer. To go into Soho was to ask to be seen with a contract out. Surprisingly, he found that Len Tiler had a telephone and he rang. Len was more lenient; when Jacko spoke he said straight away, "Who shall I send the Renoir to, Jacko?"

"Don't worry, I'll collect it myself in due course." To save Len further embarrassment he hung up. So Harry had not been exaggerating; Sonny Rollins had picked up where Reginald Dine had left off, but it must have been by mutual consent.

Rollins' empire was spread through the Greater London area, but concentrated in the West End and East End. He had contacts right round the country whom he could call upon in an emergency. And there were many sycophants who would only too willingly do him a favour.

Jacko rang Molly again at the warehouse to find that already that morning there had been callers looking for him. She described them as hoods dressed up to look like crooked business men. But they had scared her and that sickened him. Since the Ferrari had been blown up the second girl had not come back and that left Molly alone.

Molly was a resilient girl with an immense hang-up for Jacko she well knew could not be realised. For her, to work for him was enough. She also guessed that from time to time he got involved in matters she chose to see as in the interest of the State, right or wrong. When he rang up like this it gave her a sense of involvement which was the last thing he wanted. He did not want her to be in any form of danger. But the warehouse costume business was legitimate and parcels, sometimes several at a time, were despatched by van or motorbike, or with film people the costume department might collect themselves.

He gave her an order for immediate delivery and told her he would wait outside Embankment Underground station on the embankment side until it arrived. He sank into the shadow of the bridge where the steps came down towards the station, which was always busy. He knew it would not take Molly long

117

to pack what he had ordered, she could be incredibly quick, but a delivery man might take time despatching.

It was a long fifty minutes to wait and during that time Harry's warning lost all the banter and the real threat came through. The motorcycle drifted in just when the wait was really getting to him. Jacko stepped forward in relief.

It was the same delivery man as before so there was no problem in handing over and he took the cardboard container with the plastic handle and decided to walk back to the club rather than wait for a cab; certain taxi drivers might be on Rollins' pay-roll for it was mooted that he owned a cab company.

He rang Ewing from the club and caught him in his office. He had decided against meeting Ewing anywhere now, and briefly told him what he had found and asked if Ewing could throw any light on it. It was a strange list, much revised, which suggested its origins were rooted some time ago. Ewing said he would find out what he could and would Jacko send photocopies of the prints.

"I'm not too keen on that," said Jacko. "You don't understand security as I do. You sensibly didn't ask where I got them from for you wouldn't be too happy if I told you; if someone your end found them you could be in all sorts of trouble. One more favour and I'll ring back in an hour for an answer: Dine's son is at Oxford; can you find out which college?"

"I can't possibly do that in an hour. Give me a number where I can reach you." Ewing shook the phone in frustration; Jacko had hung up.

Oxford was not a city Jacko knew well, and he suffered the pangs of frustration everybody does with the one-way traffic system. To make it worse the car park for St Peter's College was in a difficult-to-find position round the back. He managed to find a slot and walked back to the main entrance of the old college.

He used his Detective Sergeant Willis identity card, feeling that he did not want Dine to discover he had another one so soon. So far as he knew the Stedman card was still a secret unless Rollins knew he had been to see Len Tiler.

He had timed his visit for late afternoon and had no difficulty in getting a message to Lonnie Dine who met him outside half an hour later. Jacko could not miss the oriental in the pleasant features of Dine's son who was surprisingly tall. Jacko liked him on sight and Lonnie greeted him warmly.

"The police?" enquired Lonnie. "What have I done?"

"That's your conscience," replied Jacko with a grin. He knew he was taking a dangerously calculated risk in seeing Dine's son. "It's nothing to worry about. Is there somewhere we can sit down and talk?"

It was too early for the pubs and Lonnie led the way to a café where they found a table up some creaking stairs and across an uneven floor.

"Mid-eighteenth century," explained Lonnie. "Mind your head on the beams." He laughed as he pulled out a chair. "I don't think they've done anything to it since it was built. Now, what is the problem?"

Jacko ordered tea then said with a smile, "An excuse for a day out really. It's about the Sèvres vase that caused the rumpus; you must know a little about what happened?"

"Oh, yes. Could I ever forget! My girlfriend's father knew something of its history. Apparently it was stolen from Paris; Government property. What a turn-up."

"We're trying to trace its route, because a lot was stolen at the same time." Jacko waved a hand dismissively. "Of course, we are well aware that your father did not take it but he genuinely can't remember where he did get it from. He has so much wonderful stuff. He showed me round, you know. We're trying to help the Sûreté over this. Is it possible that he told you something that he himself, with the best will in the world, has forgotten?"

"About that particular piece?" Lonnie seemed surprised. "I think it's common knowledge that after his death a good deal of Ceauşescu's stuff was put in a warehouse near the palace. Anything could have happened to it from then." He leaned back while a waitress arranged a pot of tea and cakes. When she had gone he added, "Father does not often tell me from where he obtains this piece or that. Sometimes he does but I usually forget within minutes. I know he often uses agents. He couldn't help you then?"

"No. He has better samples than that and I suppose, in the scheme of things, there was no reason why he should particularly remember the source of the Sèvres."

"A long way to come for a negative answer," Lonnie murmured over his raised cup.

"We're used to it. We won't get anywhere with this enquiry but it has to be done if only to satisfy the French. Do you miss Hong Kong?"

"When I'm not studying, yes. But it will soon be lost forever, so perhaps it's a good time to get used to not being there."

"I've never been there," Jacko lied. "Always wanted to. All that cheap jade and stuff."

"It's not so cheap now. But there's much more to it than that."

"Is your mother still there?" And then quickly, "I'm sorry. I had no right to ask that and I don't know why I did."

"It's all right. I never knew my mother and Dad won't talk about her so something grim must have happened. I would like to have known her very much."

"She produced a hell of a nice son," Jacko said sincerely. "Was your father actually born there?"

"Oh, yes. In Kowloon. Of British parents, of course. They both died out there long before I was born so I never got to know them."

"He'll speak Chinese then."

"Cantonese and Mandarin," Lonnie corrected gently. "Like a native." He grinned. "Like me."

"Did you live anywhere else before you came here?"

"No. We travelled a lot, though. Spent a long time going round Europe but we lived in London at that time."

"Europe I know a bit. Italy. Now there's a place. Rome, Sorrento, all that. Smashing. Lovely people, too."

"We were mainly in Northern Italy. Venice, Milan, the lakes. But we spent a lot of time in the lesser-known villages

120

around Verona and the southern Dolomites. Smashing, as you say."

"They can play football a bit, too," Jacko felt that if he probed further he might give himself away. He had pushed it as far as he could. He did not think that he had raised Lonnie's suspicions but it was likely that this meeting would get back to Dine in any event. It was time to go back. He was satisfied that Lonnie was not involved in his father's activities.

Reg Dine did not like the way the matter of Jacko had been taken from his hands. He had always handled his own problems but had made the mistake of underestimating Willie Jackson and, instead of warning him, should have killed him at the outset. The truth was that the idea of killing his own kind, the British, upset him and he had difficulty in understanding why. He had to admit, though, that Rollins had the contacts in this country for this kind of work, which he did not have. It was difficult to resist.

His nightmares had increased ever since he had set eyes on Jacko, yet there were moments when he knew that this was only partially true. What had thrown him off balance more than anything else was sight of the poor, elderly woman in South London. That, more than anything, had brought back the terrors and the early tortures and bad food, and the increasing hopelessness as life slipped by with agonising slowness. Life had not been worth living and there came a time when he had considered ending it, yet somehow that tiny spark of resistance would flare up and another day would drag past and then another and he would still be alive, wondering why he held on.

He had a fine son who would never know his mother was a boat woman, living on one of the junks in Aberdeen harbour on Hong Kong Island. Lonnie must never learn that. He would never understand without suffering in the same way and he would never allow that to happen. Whatever happened to himself, Dine had made sure that Lonnie would be well provided for and his son's well-being was now his main priority, although there was another. He vetted Lonnie's girlfriends from a distance and without him knowing. There was nothing wrong with the French girl who came from a good family, but it was a pity about her father.

The information Jacko had given him meant nothing to Thomas Ewing. At first he did not know what to do with it. He had jotted down what Jacko had given him but it was merely a bare skeleton of what Jacko had. Jacko had given some of the locations mentioned in Britain, and some of the Italian. He was annoyed that Jacko would not send him photocopies but accepted the need for at least some secrecy; Jacko was not inclined towards over-dramatisation. He also accepted that Jacko was in considerable danger although it had not been mentioned, and this worried him.

He sought out a friend in MI5 who had helped him in the past. They met after lunch in Ewing's club and found a corner seat in the near-empty lounge. Ewing faced the tall Georgian windows with his back to the room and Ian Brooks sat opposite him.

Ewing had memorised most of what Jacko had told him and as he trotted it out it sounded rather ridiculous. He was asking information about certain people in Britain against certain locations. When he had finished Brooks asked, "Is that it?"

"There is more but that is all I have."

"And you think there is some significance in these names and places?" Brooks was in his mid-forties, dark-haired, with a good-looking firm face and clear dark blue eyes. He wore an MCC tie.

"I don't know. I'm just bouncing them off you."

Brooks gave a twisted smile. "Well, let's have a go," he said. He frowned with concentration. "Hare coursing? Pit bull-terrier fighting? Bare-knuckle fighting? How's that for beginners?"

"I was hoping you would take this seriously."

"I am, Thomas. Come on, be fair. Where did you get this stuff?"

"I can't tell you. You know all about secrecy."

"You're making it sound bloody mysterious." The blue eyes were slightly mocking. "What else do you expect me to say? Why don't you get the Met to sus them out?"

"Because I stupidly thought that I could come to an old friend and get some help."

"Okay. Look, have you a written list?"

"Yes, but I don't want to part with it. I don't mind you copying it, though." Ewing went to the writing-room and returned with some notepaper. He passed his notes and the paper to Brooks who jotted them down as if performing a chore.

"Right. I'll let you know what there is to know, but I think you'll find they are local gigs of some sort." He sat back smiling. "I bet Glasshouse Willie gave you these. When will you learn to use us, Thomas? You use an amateur and then come to us when you're flummoxed. It's not on, old boy."

"Jacko is hardly an amateur but I do not acknowledge that it was he who gave me this information. The reason I did not come to you in the first place was because it started out as something rather small and not up to your exalted standards."

"Bullshit," said Brooks with a grin. "I'll give you a ring in a day or two."

"Can't you make it sooner?"

"Only if you can persuade the PM to grant us more money so that we can expand." Brooks winked as he rose. "Cheers, old boy."

In fact Brooks rang Ewing at his home that same evening.

"Thomas. Came up with it sooner than I thought. Forget about the whole thing. Nothing to do with us and nothing important. You're wasting your time."

"Well, what does it mean? You've told me damn all."

"Nothing to tell. A dead issue. Burn the list like a good Government officer."

"Not until you tell me what I'm burning."

"I can't. It's dead but still classified under the present time restriction. I know that's daft, but the law's the law and we poor Security mortals have to heed it above all others. But believe me, it's nothing to worry about. Those names have been dug up out of the ark. Dead as the dodo. Sorry I can't say more. By the way, can you tell me where I can find Willie Jackson? We might have a small job for him."

Ewing went cold. He had always protected Jacko and now felt a need as never before. If MI5 wanted to get hold of Jacko it was certainly not for a job. "I don't know where he is," he said warily. "I rarely see him these days."

"It would help us if you could get hold of him. After all I've just helped you. Be fair, Thomas. We just want his help."

"You find him yourself, Ian. And you've done nothing to help me." Ewing hung up aware that Liz was standing in the doorway; he would not want her to know that Jacko was getting in deeper than ever. But his main worry was that he had no way of contacting Jacko to warn him. If MI5 went looking for him then he would be at the centre of a pincer movement.

13

Jacko rang Ewing an hour later, much to Ewing's relief. Before Jacko could say anything Ewing blurted out, "Thank God you rang. This lack of communication is really intolerable. MI5 are after you."

"Keep those bastards off my back whatever you do."

"I'm doing my best. It's not easy. I wouldn't put it past them to tap my phone. We must be careful from now on."

Ewing had stumbled over his words and before he could say anything more Jacko burst out, "What the hell is happening, Thomas?"

"I saw a friend of mine in the Security Service about the names and locations you gave me. You thought they might be political. He took them down and rang me back in less than three hours telling me to lay off. Not in those words, of course, but that is what he meant. The information is classified. And he wants to find you."

"We've struck a vein. Oh, boy. For God's sake don't let them know where I am, Thomas. I've got trouble enough."

"I don't bloody well know where you are. That's the problem. I cannot keep in touch. We've got to think of something. Don't ring here again."

"You've no idea what it's all about? No hint?"

"None. He said it was a dead duck and the impression I got was whatever it is began some time ago. I'll have a word with the PM. After all, the original enquiry emanated from that office, but no-one wants to buck the Security Service."

"I can't drop it. I told you that. They won't believe me, or more likely can't take the risk of believing me. The best thing to say is that they'll lose the next election if any of this comes out. It's an enormous cover-up."

"Are you sure of that, Jacko?"

"Of course I'm not bloody sure. But nor will the PM be. If Five are involved it begins to stink, bearing in mind what they're up against – Dine, Rollins and that crowd."

There was silence between them for a while and then Jacko added, "Maybe they're all in it together."

There was a time when Ewing would have hotly refuted that possibility but now he had no reply except to say, "How do we make contact?"

"It might be better if we don't. I think you've gone as far as you can. If I need you again I'll think something up. Cheers, Thomas, love to Liz."

When Ewing saw the Prime Minister the following day he gave his assessment of what had happened and asked for help in safeguarding Jacko against MI5. Later in the day he received the reply he expected. Willie Jackson was in no danger from the Security Service; rather, they wanted to protect *him* from other sources. Ewing knew that if he accused the MI5 informant to the PM of lying, which he was very inclined to do, he would get no further and possibly be reprimanded. Prime Ministers had to rely on their Security chiefs.

The chalet-bungalow was in the New Forest, fairly isolated, and off the main Lymington Road leading down to the coast. The approach road was reasonably good and Jacko could see where the New Forest ponies wandered in to graze; there were bare patches in the pasture-land which largely surrounded the house and a thin tree-line formed a semi-circle which thickened out further away from the house.

With so many trees around, it would be a simple matter to maintain a vigilance, and with so much open ground close to the house it was impossible to approach without being seen. Jacko saw no easy way to tackle it except by night and at the moment he could see no advantage in that.

He parked the BMW well out of sight of the dwelling and started the long walk back. He had his Browning in his waistband at his hip and under his jacket. He carried a spare clip in his pocket. This was the first time he had really

126

felt need of the gun. The nape of his neck was prickling when he rounded the sparse tree-line as he neared the house.

There was no-one about. This made him more edgy for there was an upstairs window open, suggesting that someone was at home. As he came round the curve of the long, open driveway he could see a railed paddock with two donkeys in it who came to the fence as he approached.

He was feeling uneasy mainly because of what Ewing had told him. It had produced a new dimension and he did not trust an organisation which had once tried to terminate a friend of his in order to cover their own shortcomings. At least with Dine and Rollins he knew where he stood. It was particularly galling because nobody flew the flag higher than Jacko, and Ewing at least knew him to be the most patriotic and faithful of friends.

The unease increased as he drew nearer to the door which he could now see was ajar. Jacko stood on the earth drive and did a 360-degree slow turn, taking in everything he could. It was so still, even allowing for the fact that the place was so well protected from the wind. Most of the leaves were down and the ground was a mass of autumn colour. Then a dog started to bark somewhere behind the house. It was a friendly sound, but no dog came in sight.

When he neared the front door, instead of ringing the bell, an old-fashioned monster on a chain, presumably so it could be heard well beyond the house to what appeared to be a huge vegetable garden at the rear, he went to the side of the house, past a large wooden garage, and could see the space beyond, the dog on a running lead, and two small hot-houses. But there was nobody in sight.

He ventured round the back and found a rough patio with some upturned plastic chairs, stacked for the winter. No water was coming from the drain. He went back and rang the bell.

A man appeared as if he had been standing behind the door waiting. He gazed at Jacko quizzically and said, "Was that you I saw wandering around the back?"

"The door was ajar and I couldn't see anyone around." Jacko found himself staring into the watery eyes of a medium-built man of fifty-odd years, who was wearing braces over his shirt and baggy trousers that needed pressing. He was almost bald and strands of loose hair had been trained across the scalp.

"So you've sized me up, now what do you want?" The tone was more aggressive than the look.

"I'm sorry." Jacko produced his newly forged warrant card. "Detective-Sergeant Stedman. Can I come in and have a word?"

"Sure. Mind the ruck in the rug." As he went past the foot of the stairs the man called up, "I've got a visitor. I'll be up later."

The feeling of danger would not go away. He thought the man let him in too readily; most people would want to know what it was about. As they entered a dark, heavily furnished room he said, "I hope I'm not interrupting anything." It was gloomier in the house than he expected.

"No. We're going out this evening." The man raised his brows in resignation. "My wife has started to get ready. Takes her hours. Sit there, that one's safe. Have you come about the chickens?"

"The chickens?" Jacko sat down and could feel the springs.

"I reported them last week. Poachers cleared out the whole hen house and the dog let them do it; too bloody friendly that dog."

Jacko smiled; he had been offered a chair with its back to the door and was looking for some kind of reflection from the facing windows. "No, it's not about poachers, sir. I'm not local. I'm from Scotland Yard. Special Branch. Is your name Frederick Miles?"

"Frederick Miles? I'm Sam Walters. You've got the wrong man and the wrong house. Special Branch eh? You're not so special if you come all the way from London and make that kind of mistake."

Jacko produced a single sheet of his lists and appeared to study it. "I've got Frederick Miles. It's the same address. How long have you lived here?"

"About twelve years. I'll give Lill a shout, see if she knows of a Miles."

Walters went to the door behind Jacko and shouted up the

128

stairs again. Jacko could not hear the reply but he caught the tones of a woman's voice and heard someone move in the room above his head. Some sort of explanation seemed to be floating down the stairs for Walters stood there for some time while the woman kept shouting. Walters came back and sat down. He gazed up at the ceiling as if his wife had not yet finished and then said, "Apparently there was a Miles who lived here. But it must have been years ago. We didn't buy this house from anyone of that name. Lill must have picked it up from village gossip."

"Do you think I could speak to her?"

"Lill? She wouldn't thank you for that; she's half-dressed with her make-up off. I don't think she can add anything; gossip is gossip, it might not be right. Oh, there was one thing Lill mentioned: someone told her that Miles had died some time ago. She was only interested because he once lived here. But how can it matter now, after so long?"

Jacko realised he had to give some sort of explanation. "His name cropped up in what we thought was a dead file. Something that was not satisfactorily wound up and which he could probably explain. These things happen. People move away; police officers retire and, they too, move away. And then something crops up and all those who might have remembered have pushed off somewhere and nobody knows the answers."

"I'm sorry I can't help you," said Walters in the friendliest tone he had so far used. "Want a cup of tea?"

"No thanks," said Jacko, rising. "Sorry to take up your time."

"It's your time that worries me. I mean it's us who have to pay for it."

"I pay taxes, too," said Jacko and headed towards the front door. He could still hear faint movement from upstairs, but now, he was sure, from two positions. He offered his thanks at the door and had the feeling he was being watched all the way up the drive and even when he rounded the curve at the top. He felt more comfortable when he reached the BMW. He sat behind the wheel for a while doing nothing but look in his rear-view mirror. Some ponies appeared behind him and wandered off into the woods. By the time he started the engine he was reasonably satisfied that he was not under observation. He drove off slowly, thinking that Walters knew far more about Frederick Miles than he had admitted. He got back on to the main Lymington Road where, even at this time of year, the road was packed with traffic and constant bottlenecks.

He reached Lymington, found a parking space near an art shop by the harbour, and watched the yachts and the sea from a bench near the front. He climbed slowly up the steep incline of the main road and found a restaurant where he had an early dinner and then returned to the car. By now it was well past lighting-up time. He drove slowly back to the house, using only sidelights as he approached it. He pulled up and reversed over uneven ground and tucked the car away from sight as far as he could. He covered the windscreen and the lights with bracken so that passing vehicles would not raise a reflection from the glass. He put on a pair of surgical gloves, took a powerful flashlight from the dashboard and locked the car. He started to walk back towards the house.

When he reached the corner of the drive he positioned himself so that he had a good sighting of the house but was not visible from the road. It was a secondary road, deep in the forest, which still attracted the odd passing car in either direction, but the advancing headlights were ample warning for him to draw back.

Most of the house lights appeared to be on; a couple of rooms upstairs, the main room where he had talked to Walters, and a very capable porch light. It was eight o'clock.

It was another half-hour before anyone appeared. The front door opened and Jacko heard Walters' voice and, much fainter, a woman's. Walters gesticulated angrily, ran indoors, and the lights began to disappear one after the other until even the porch light was out. The resulting darkness in such a remote position was total. Jacko could not see a thing until a flashlight came on and he could hear the woman complain about the unevenness of the ground as they crossed towards the garage.

The wooden doors swung back but no lights came on,

suggesting the garage had none. The flashlight picked out the car and focused on the nearside so the woman could see to get in. Then the light went out and the engine started and the full beams came on and seemed to be directed straight at Jacko. The car moved forward and stopped and the man got out, closed the garage doors, climbed back in the car and drove forward.

Jacko did not move. He had not been foolish enough to venture too far from his cover but the glare was increasingly uncomfortable as the car came up the drive. It swept past him and he had the vaguest impression of Walters at the wheel with a woman beside him. Walters looked neither left nor right and the car took the Lymington direction.

Jacko waited. It was something of a strange time for them to go; rather late for dinner or a show. And the woman had been getting ready so early?

The house was now completely out of sight. Even the trees around him were difficult for Jacko to see. And yet, as he began to tread carefully down the edge of the drive, he refrained from using his flashlight. After the glare of the lights his sight gradually improved and as he advanced he could make out the outline of the house. He now had the same feeling as when he first arrived. It was not just the eeriness of darkness in an isolated location in a forest, with the sounds of the night creatures around him, it was much deeper than that.

Something was missing and he suddenly realised it was the barking of the dog. A dog's acute hearing would pick up the most silent approach, even indoors, and as the slight breeze was blowing towards the house it would also have picked up his scent. He had not seen a dog in the car but could have missed it. He continued on, stepping off the drive completely and keeping to the grass.

He reached the house and stood in the porch. There were no burglar alarms; he had satisfied himself on that when he had called earlier. At first it struck him as lax but who would hear it even if there was one? How far away was the nearest house and how far the police station? Just the same he would expect some form of security but had failed to see any.

131

He pressed against the door, and, as expected, found it solid and locked. He started to go round the house without using his torch and felt round the frames of each window as he passed. The house had probably been built in the 1920s and had sash windows. There was still no sign of the dog and he accepted that it was no longer near or around the house, which, as he saw it, was another breach of security. It was almost as if he was being invited to go in. Perhaps they were as harmless as they portrayed.

Jacko squatted at the rear of the house, outside the kitchen by the outlet pipes. He lifted the kitchen window, surprised to find it unlocked and now he was really worried. Sash windows were easy to make secure even with loose catches, but this catch had not even been applied. It was not easy to climb into a kitchen, there was always a sink or something in the way. He remained squatting for about ten minutes without anything happening or a sound from within the house. He drew out his Browning and attached the silencer.

He crawled back to the front of the house, leaving the kitchen window open, and tried the window to the left of the front door. It opened just as easily as the kitchen one. Again he squatted, waiting for something to happen. After ten minutes he crawled off again and tried other windows. Some were locked and some were not.

Jacko waited again and smiled to himself. He was being tempted in by certain routes. Time was passing but he was not concerned. He did not believe that Walters and his wife would return until told. His impression was that they had been taken out of circulation until the job was done. There were hours of darkness ahead of him and he was well used to waiting.

After a while he decided to open all windows that were off the catch. There were four, one each side of the house. If anyone was waiting inside for him, they must by now have felt the cold air coming through and they must also be puzzled as to what he was actually doing. Let them sweat.

He sat against one of the walls, pistol held loosely between both hands, and he reflected on why there was virtually no security about the house yet Walters had made a point of closing the garage doors before leaving. He crawled over to the garage.

It was wooden, as he had noticed on his first visit, but was very solid. Surprisingly, it had only one frosted glass window at the rear so nobody could peer in. It was difficult in the dark but he judged that the garage was more recent than the house. It was a good size, would easily take two large cars and there was an enormous padlock on the double doors. There was also an alarm high on the apex of the sloping roof at the rear, which accounted for why he had not noticed it before.

A secure garage but a house any vandal could break into. He examined the building by touch, running his fingers round the frame of the doors and the window at the rear. As he searched for wiring he realised that the alarm was simply to warn those in the house if the garage was being broken into and he was willing to gamble that it was not connected to the nearest police station. He started to look for a way in.

By climbing on a water butt he managed to get on to the low roof but the planks were too well set for him to prise off. He straddled the roof and decided that it would be better to immobilise whoever was in the house, after which he could take his time and noise would not matter.

He gazed towards the dark shape of the house. Whoever was in there were professionals. Anyone else would have been tempted into some sort of action with four downstairs windows open and nobody coming in. It was a game of nerves and Jacko had played it many times. His problem was he did not know how many he was up against and where in the house they were positioned. There was one certain way of drawing them out. He slid to the ground, went to the back of the garage and smashed the frosted window with the base of his torch. The alarm went off immediately, a siren wailing into the night. He sprinted away from the garage and the house, not quite making the tree-line before throwing himself flat.

Even then those in the house did not panic, as if they knew they had the situation well under control. They made use of the opened windows and came from three different directions. It was difficult to see them in the darkness and at first he had to rely on his hearing. They ran quietly, the nearest just a silhouette moving fast at an angle towards the garage, and Jacko was sure he was hooded.

Jacko aimed low at the moving shadowy legs and fired twice in quick succession. The man went tumbling down and Jacko did a series of rolls away from the garage and the flash point. He came to a halt against a sapling and lay still. The man he had hit was moaning but drew no attention from the other two Jacko had barely glimpsed.

Jacko would have felt happier had he been further into the trees but the men had reacted quickly as good pros should, and he had got as far away from the garage as their response had allowed. He could only wait.

The siren was still wailing and he hoped they would turn it off but when they did not he guessed they had left it on to cover their own movements. It indicated that they were satisfied that the sound was out of earshot of any neighbours. But if the continuing sound helped his enemies it also helped him, and bit by bit he edged back into deeper cover.

It became a cat-and-mouse game. They were not sure where he was and might even have missed the point of his shots as the silencer kept down the gunflash to a minimum. But he had no idea where they were. He could no longer hear the moans of the man he had shot. He edged back even further for it would be better for them to get to the tree-line and work their way back to the garage area.

There was a movement close to him. Like him they were not using flashlights, the more so since they now had hard evidence of his skill with a gun.

Jacko rolled slowly over on to his back to get a better view. It took him a fraction of time to realise that a man was standing almost over him but did not really see him until he moved; the continuing wailing from the siren had covered both their movements. He rolled again as the gun above him went off at point-blank range and he felt a shot tear through the fabric of his sleeve. He rolled again and again and again knowing the visibility on the edge of the woods was extremely poor. The shots followed him, hollow plops, unearthly as the bullets sprayed up little puffs of dead leaves near to him. And

134

in the middle of this life-or-death crisis the alarm suddenly cut out and the silence was painful and uncanny.

Jacko was too busy to take notice but in one of his frenetic rolls he glimpsed just the slightest hesitation in the dark form closing up on him again when the wailing stopped. Jacko fired from a difficult position, saw the man swerve, and fired again. The man fell in the direction of his movement, crashing sideways.

Jacko was on his feet in an instant and tore the gun away from the man's hand. There was no real resistance and when he bent down to feel the carotid artery he knew the man was dead. He tore off the hood but the light was too poor for any kind of identification and he realised then that he must have dropped his flashlight.

The third man must have heard his colleague crash down. Jacko faded into the trees and waited. And while he waited he fervently hoped that the man he had killed did not belong to MI5. But there was still one more man to deal with and his nerves would be as taut as Jacko's.

14

Jacko crouched with his back to a tree and waited so long he began to think that the third man had gone. Both the house and the garage were out of sight and it was so dark that he had to hang on to his senses to know which way he was facing; he could barely make out the next tree.

He peered at his watch. 10.30. He had been there for almost two and a half hours. From the time he had smashed the garage window to the present must have taken up about forty-five minutes. The temptation was to move but he resisted and continued to squat, slowly straightening up against the tree just once in a while without moving his feet, in order to ward off cramp.

It was a stand-off. If he was to discover anything at all he had no option but to stay. The night stretched ahead; there was plenty of time but the unrelenting concentration of listening played on the nerves.

After a while the normal night noises like the hooting of owls, and the nearby grunting of hedgehogs in the bracken became intrusive. He continued to stay at the same spot, knowing that any movement would carry through the night to ears as attuned as his.

He heard a faint movement about an hour later at a time when his legs were losing feeling. Sound at night is almost impossible to place accurately. He remained still. It was quiet again. And then he heard the sound a few minutes later; rustling in the leaves so faint that it could have been caused by the intermittent breeze, except that it appeared to come from only one direction, somewhere to his right between him and the house.

The next time he heard it it was more prolonged and now

he was certain that the movement was towards the house. Again it stopped. The next time it carried he moved just a fraction after he heard it, made long strides and stopped after a few paces. His judgement was good and the sound stopped just after he did.

It was a long-drawn-out, dangerous game. As it continued Jacko detected a degree of panic as the movements became longer and slightly louder. Once beyond the tree-line the stakes were higher as the visibility increased.

Once Jacko was reasonably sure of the actual direction he speeded up his own movements while still trying to synchronise with the other's, but always keeping his quick dashes short. After a while he lay prone. He could just see the outline of the house now, and nearer to him, the garage. And then he both saw and heard a figure running in a crouch towards the house.

It was too far away for any kind of accurate shot and the man was travelling fast. Jacko waited until the figure disappeared round the corner of the house and then sprinted as fast as he could. He went to the nearest open window at the front and swung over the sill. It was the riskiest thing he had yet done for he had no idea where the man was, but he guessed what he might be doing.

Jacko crossed the carpeted room, carefully opened the door and rolled round it into the hall just as he heard the telephone tinkle. "Put the thing down or I'll blow your bloody head off."

The figure stood with his back to Jacko, the telephone at his ear, finger ready to tap out the number. It was impression rather than actual vision, for it was almost as dark inside the house as amongst the trees, but the telephone was on a hall table which faced a window near the door and there was just sufficient light to see what was happening.

The man went rigid and Jacko silently approached in an arc so that he came in the direction of the hand that held the phone. He could now see that the hood had been removed.

The man spun, gun in his left hand and fired at where he expected Jacko to be. There was a sound of breaking glass but Jacko was near enough now to be able to hit the man at the nape of the neck with his gun. As the figure folded, Jacko followed up with another blow.

He tore the wire from the phone and used it to tie the man's wrists behind his back. He picked up the spare gun and slipped it into his pocket. He crossed to the wall beside the door and stood there for some time until satisfied that there was nobody else in the house. He realised that somewhere outside might still be an armed, wounded man; he had to take the risk. He closed his eyes almost shut and groped for the hall light switch.

The hundred-watt bulb was blinding after the long hours of darkness and he stayed where he was until he could tolerate the glare. The man was still motionless. Jacko moved the body to get a better view of the face but could make no recognition. He supposed the man was in mid or late thirties with rather coarse and brutal features. Jacko searched around and found a tea-towel which he cut with a kitchen knife and bound the feet together. When he straightened he saw the shot had smashed a framed print hanging at the side of the door he had come through.

He did not feel reasonably safe until he had dragged him into a small utility room off the kitchen. He made a thorough search but was not surprised to find the pockets empty of identification. He locked the utility-room door, collected the flashlight the man had placed on the hall table, and left the house after switching off the hall light.

He did not use the flashlight until he reached the approximate position where he had first thrown himself flat. He aimed the beam at where he thought the wounded man had dropped but there was now nobody in sight. He switched off at once and moved quickly away. He ran away from the spot and circled round to the rear of the garage. Someone called out softly, "Dan! Is that you?"

Jacko grunted a reply and went round the garage to find someone propped up against the side. "Where's your gun?" he demanded.

"Oh, Christ, are you the bastard who plugged me? Come to finish the job?" There was weariness and pain in the voice.

"Where's your gun?" repeated Jacko.

"God knows. I dropped it when I fell. It's out there somewhere. I'm losing blood. I need a doctor."

"You need a hospital, mate. When I've sorted a few things out I'll send for an ambulance. I see you've bandaged the leg? Use your shirt did you?" Jacko noticed both hands were visible, one holding the crude bandage in place over the track suit trousers.

"I want a doctor, not an ambulance. I can give you a number to ring."

"Why are you afraid of going to hospital? You need a transfusion."

"You know bloody why. I don't want the police around. The doc can fix me up."

Jacko had to judge the situation and the actual plight of the man whose voice was weak and whose pain was obvious. "You think I'm suddenly on your side, you silly bugger? You were trying to kill me. You can stay there and bleed to death. It won't worry me. I've already killed one of your men and the other is trussed like a turkey. Is there any reason why I shouldn't finish you off?"

"For God's sake, you said you'd get an ambulance."

"Did Sonny Rollins send you?"

"Look, we just get a phone call. We get together and are told what to do. The bloke who lives here knew all about it when we arrived. He was to piss off and we were to wait and deal with anyone who tried to break in. When we'd done that we were to ring him, he comes back from wherever he's been and we've disappeared with the body to bury it deep in the forest. A straight job."

"Three of you?"

"We were warned you were tricky."

"So who actually briefed you?"

"Never seen him before. He gave us half up-front and you don't ask questions of that."

"Who do you normally work for?"

"Anyone who will pay us. We work as a team."

"Not any longer. Hit men? How the hell have you got away with it? What's your name?"

"Horatio Nelson. Look, I'm bloody well dying here."

139

"Tear some more off your shirt. Be quick about it."

'Horatio' fumbled in the beam but finally managed to rip the rest of his shirt right off and threw it to Jacko who tore some strips off.

"Turn over," said Jacko who had been unable to identify Horatio. Three new faces; he was losing touch, but then he had never mixed with the hit-man fraternity. When Horatio complained and made it difficult, Jacko lost his patience and swung the man on to his face, pulled back his arms and bound his wrists and ankles. He then heaved him on to his back again while Horatio repeatedly cried out in pain.

Jacko stared down without remorse; at least he had fired to protect himself; these men were paid killers. "Do you know who I am?" he asked.

"It doesn't matter to us who you are. We'd rather not know. We know you're not a bloody copper from Special Branch. Impersonating a copper is a serious crime, mate."

"Don't get too brave, Horatio. Now let's go through your pockets." Like the others there was no identity but there was a wad of money and presumably Horatio was acting banker to the rest until the job was over. He left him there, ignoring the calls for help, and searched the spot where he believed Horatio had first fallen. He found the gun a little distance away and picked it up, emptied the magazine and threw the rounds towards the tree-line, and then tossed the gun near to Horatio.

Jacko went to the garage. The doors were still locked and he supposed Dan had climbed through the window to switch off the alarm. Jacko needed more space than that; he might have to make a sudden run for it. He shot loose the haft holding the big padlock and wrenched it away from the wood. He slipped out the used magazine and replaced it with the one in his pocket and then cocked the gun. He pulled back the heavy doors and swung the flashlight beam round the interior. Surprisingly, he found a light switch just inside the door and wondered why Walters had not used it; perhaps to confuse the issue.

Shelves right round the walls were neatly stacked with cans of oil and paint and numerous tools. A rotary mower and a leaf sweeper were positioned along one wall. There was an old-fashioned inspection pit covered by easily movable planks with faint oil traces where the car had stood but otherwise the garage was far cleaner, much tidier, than some parts of the house he had seen. It was a model garage, space for two cars, and contained a sophisticated alarm system for whatever reason. To protect one not very modern car, and equipment, the most expensive of which was the mower?

The floor was concrete and well brushed. He moved the planks off the inspection pit and placed them to one side. He went down the steps to find it deeper than he at first supposed and his head just poked out above the top. There was really nothing to see but oil stains. The pit was as any pit should be though probably far cleaner than most. There was nothing here. So why the alarm?

He stood there, flashlight in one hand, gun in the other, and wondered about what he was supposed to find; unless it was a deliberate dummy to hold the attention. His gut feeling told him differently, yet he was puzzled. He went round, gently tapping the walls with the base of his flashlight. The concrete sides went up to a level six inches below the garage floor level suggesting the garage foundation was six inches deep. Where the floor and the walls met there was a ridge right round which had not been concreted over, presumably because it would have been only cosmetic and would have been meaningless down here.

He followed the walls round, still tapping, until he reached the far end. At the bottom of each corner was a tiny pile of concrete dust. He ran his fingers down the sides then stood back and kicked hard with the flat of his foot at one end. The force had not been necessary; the end wall swung on a well-oiled central pivot and opened like a crypt to reveal a dark cavity.

Jacko stood back smiling. It was so simple and had been beautifully engineered. He crouched down and poked the flashlight through. The cavity was not all that big, there was no standing room and he would have to crawl through. He got down on hands and knees and entered. The interior was nowhere near as finished as the inspection pit. The walls were rough earth supported by timbers. Occupying some three-quarters of the space were rows of ammunition boxes, and stacked plastic bags. He undid the nearest, tied at the neck by a plastic strip so that it would not rot. A faint smell of grease reached him as he shone his flashlight inside. Automatic rifles of slightly old design but seemingly untouched and well greased. He counted five rifles in the pack.

By painstakingly sorting out the packs he eventually estimated that there were fifty rifles, a similar amount of Smith and Wesson .38 pistols, a large number of ammunition boxes for both weapons with their batch numbers painted over. On one he could just make out the faded number of 52, or 82, but they were the tail-end digits of a longer number. There were ten sub-machine-guns, several boxes of grenades, carefully packed detonators and plastic explosive, and more than ample fuse wire. There were also three two-way radio transmitters.

It was impossible to go through everything and the boxes were solidly locked but when he tried to lift one he was in no doubt that it contained ammunition. It would take more time than he could risk to open every container, but what he did open merely bore out the rest.

He crawled back into the inspection pit for air and considered what he had found. It did not make sense. He swung the concrete door back in place and was surprised at how easily it moved considering its weight. The door looked like a wall again. He climbed from the pit dissatisfied and puzzled, and replaced the boards.

He switched the light out before leaving the garage and pushed the doors to; there was nothing he could do about the haft. As he crossed towards the house he heard Horatio calling out.

Inside the house he switched on the lights as he went from room to room so that finally the house was a blaze of lights. He started upstairs, searching for anything that might fill in a massive gap in his thinking. He simply tipped drawers out on to beds or floors and rummaged through the contents but found nothing significant.

There were no arms in the house but he could not believe that Sam Walters did not know what was in the garage; he would be in on it, probably as caretaker. Jacko considered it pointless to tidy up. He found a small study downstairs and ransacked the place, crudely breaking open anything that was locked. He found nothing that would explain the arms and the extraordinary protection they received. He did not even find a list similar to the one stolen from Simon Wherewell.

The one thing they could not be certain about was whether or not he had found the arms cache in the garage for he had re-tagged the bags he had opened and carefully packed them as found.

The house had provided nothing, which explained why there was no alarm installed; it was apparently unimportant that the video and television and anything else which might bring ready money might be stolen, which told a small story in itself.

But there was no explaining why an arms cache, which would equip about sixty men, should rank such a high level in security. The profit from it would have to be weighed against the cost of security and the lives already lost. It didn't match up.

Jacko checked the time. It was 2.30 on a cold October morning. He had been there for well over six hours. He pulled out the gun he had taken from Dan, who was still locked in the utility room, emptied the magazine and the chamber and threw the rounds out of one of the open windows. He unlocked the utility room to find Dan staring up at him balefully; he had obviously been unsuccessfully trying to free himself.

"You've cracked my skull, you bastard," Dan snarled.

"It won't make any difference, Dan, there's sod all to come out." Then he said, "You've got one man dead in the woods. Another is propped up at the side of the garage; he's got a leg wound and probably needs a transfusion. The phone won't work because you are wearing its wire so you've no way of warning Walters, or whatever his name is, and I've no immediate way of calling for an ambulance. Are you listening to this?"

"Piss off."

143

Jacko smiled. "I'm going to. But when I reach the nearest phone I'm going to call for the police and an ambulance. I don't know how much time that gives you to get free, find your dead and wounded partners, and get away before the police arrive. You haven't done very well so far and I'm not going to loosen anything."

"You don't want the Bill here any more than we do, so untie this wire."

"That's true. But I don't want the complication of setting you free either. You don't know who I am and as sure as hell you won't be giving the police an accurate description because that might lead back to your boss and he wouldn't like that; old Sonny has ways of dealing with people who draw attention to him. So it depends on how good an escapologist you are. See you, cocker. And if you see me don't forget to duck."

Jacko went outside. The house was still ablaze with lights and he almost felt sorry for Sam Walters when he finally came home to the wreck he would find and the police waiting for him. He trudged wearily back to his car, throwing Dan's empty gun away as he went, and thinking that he still had the long trip back to London. He cleared the bracken from the car, climbed in, stripped off his gloves and enjoyed a minute or two of peace.

It had been quite a night but at the end of it he was not really satisfied. Survival was only part of the game; he had managed that all right, but he had left himself with more unanswered questions than before. His discovery was still disproportionate to the events and the loss of life. Somehow, he had to get at Dine, because he was sure that all the answers lay with him, in spite of Sonny Rollins' deadly involvement.

As he drove back he kept a look-out for a pay phone.

15

Reginald Dine received the news after breakfast the same morning. He took the call openly because he had long since installed a sophisticated and very modern telephone coder which made telephone calls safe from tapping anywhere, but by the use of only one highly developed machine. He kept it permanently plugged into the socket. He listened to Rollins' curt tones without expression. Things were serious, yet he was not surprised.

The hit-men had managed to escape the police, who had not arrived until 3.30, due to the timing of an anonymous call about a break-in. The men had not been able to reach their car, parked some distance away, but the one fit man had managed to carry the dead body deep into the woods and then help the wounded man to the same spot until it was reasonably safe to head for the car near dawn, before the police returned with dogs.

The dead man would be dumped or buried at sea when safe to do so. The wounded man was being attended to. It was all a bloody big cock-up and left many elements of risk, and much unanswered. Nobody knew if Jacko had found the cache; he had certainly ransacked the house but that did not matter. Walters had had the sense to act out an innocent victim of somebody else's outrage; both he and his wife were under sedation.

Dine listened to all this from Rollins, who was clearly very angry, and replied quietly, "I know you have the manpower but you should have left it to me. I think I know something of the man."

"He's an ex-SAS thug who served time in the glasshouse. He's well trained and that is all there is to know."

"I disagree. There is much more to him than that. So what happens now?"

"We've still got to winkle him out. I can't understand why we haven't."

Dine smiled to himself. "As I said, there is much more to him." He hung the phone up because there was nothing more to say and because he was almost pleased that the overpowering Rollins had failed. But he accepted that that was merely a personal feeling. Of course Jacko must be found, he was stirring too much up and attracting far too much attention.

Jacko sat in the BMW at the far end of the street with his eyes barely above the dashboard. He had driven back to the Army and Navy, breaking the journey to make the phone call, shaved, snatched two hours' sleep, taken a wig and a moustache from the box that Molly had sent, stuffed them inside his jacket and gone down to the underground garage. He used the rear-view mirror to don his disguise; it was simple but effective with long fair hair and a straggling moustache.

He was desperately tired as he drove off, not only from lack of sleep, but because events had taken it out of him. It would be easy to brush them off in the light-hearted way he had with Dan, but they had taken their toll.

By the time Jacko reached the Chelsea Embankment he reasoned that Dine would already have learned of what had happened and it might force some sort of move. Dine would not expect Jacko to be so active so soon after last night's events.

Jacko had been waiting well over an hour when Dine left the house and walked down the street. Some half-hour later he was carefully following Dine's Mercedes across Chelsea Bridge heading south of the river. He had not known what to expect. The journey might be meaningless and probably would be, but he was convinced that by following up so quickly on the New Forest fracas, Dine would be at his most vulnerable.

The traffic was not so thick going out of London but was bad enough. Dine was driving quite well and was heading generally south, possibly towards Croydon. Jacko did not allow himself to get too near; while he was part of a stream he was reasonably safe and he could think of no point on this route where it would ease up unless Dine intended to head for the country or the sea.

At this kind of speed it was easy to nod off and Jacko switched on the radio with the volume up to help keep him awake. Shortly after reaching Streatham, Dine drifted to his right and put his right blinker on. Jacko drifted with him; two other cars ahead of him were turning. Jacko closed up as much as he could.

Dine continued on at right angles to the London Road and then turned left. By now there was nothing between Jacko and Dine and Jacko drove on, eventually found a slot, and ran back to the corner. At first he could not see the Mercedes and then he saw Dine climb out and check that the doors were locked. In his haste, Jacko had not locked the BMW and on the London streets that was an open invitation but he had to take the risk and hang on to Dine. He followed him on foot, conscious that the street was not all that busy, forcing him to hang back.

They walked for some distance and Jacko decided that Dine was following a familiar route. Dine turned a corner, and Jacko jogged to it and peered carefully round. He could not see Dine anywhere.

There was a mixture of shops and terraced houses and the street was busy. He walked along slowly, scanning both sides. He quickened his pace and suddenly stopped dead, forcing a woman to bump into him and complain. Had it not been for the woman he would have bumped into Dine instead. Jacko apologised profusely, turning his head away from Dine as he passed him. But he managed to glimpse Dine staring with a fixation that saw nothing other than what held his attention across the street.

Jacko strode on until he felt it was safe to stop. He turned into a shop doorway to look back briefly. He could not see Dine again and was forced to step from his cover in order to find him.

Dine was still standing up against a grocer's shop window

147

and staring across the street, with people going round him as if he was not there. Jacko realised that Dine was so preoccupied that he doubted if he would see him even if he approached close to.

Jacko resisted the temptation to get closer, to get a better view of Dine's set expression, and it was a good half-hour later that Dine showed any kind of life. As an elderly couple stepped from a doorway opposite him, Dine stiffened, and took his hands from his raincoat pockets. As the couple moved up the street Dine followed on the opposite side, a pace or two behind.

Jacko was fascinated. He watched Dine keep the almost shabby couple in sight and decided not to follow. Instead he crossed to the doorway from which the couple had emerged. There was nothing to indicate who might live there. There was not even a street number on the door although there were numbers on the doors on either side.

He looked up the street and was just in time to see the couple cross the road as Dine hung back until they had gone round the corner. Then all three were out of sight. He rang the bell. He did not expect a reply but rang again to be sure. He then rang next door's bell and again nobody answered. He gazed across the street to the grocer's shop and crossed over. Choosing a quieter moment he entered the shop, ignored the pretty young girl serving and approached a middle-aged woman who was refilling some of the shelves.

"Excuse me," said Jacko with an apologetic smile. "But do you know the name of the couple across the street?"

The woman continued stacking but turned her head in not too friendly a way. "Everybody knows them. The Parsons. Doesn't shop here unless she runs out of something. What do you want to know for?"

"I'm sure I know him from way back. I just caught a glimpse of them as they went up the street. Is his name Fred?"

"Eric. You've got the wrong man. His wife is Annette, they have a daughter almost my age." The information came with a vague vindictiveness as if she did not want to talk about them but was quite happy to have the opportunity to knock

148

them. She finished packing and Jacko thanked her and agreed that he did have the wrong man. He left the shop, crossed the street again and made a note of the house number by getting the ones on either side.

He walked slowly back to the BMW, relieved to find it still there, locked the doors and went to the corner of the street where Dine had parked his car. He was surprised to see the Mercedes just pulling out; Dine had really spent little time here so why had he made the trip?

Dine was asking himself the same question as he drove back. He had decided to give up making the weekly call yet here he was again, making a fool of himself. And then he was angry with himself for thinking that way; the visits had nothing to do with being foolish but they had become obsessive. He had noticed that, whenever he was emotionally disturbed, a condition which until recently he believed he had banished for ever, he found a need to visit the South London address. It was a crazy thing to do, and pointless. Yet it seemed he had no control over it.

This time he had not gone as far as the bus stop but had tailed off and meandered aimlessly for a few minutes. As he walked he considered the previous night's events and had reluctantly developed a certain admiration for Jacko; there were qualities in the man he not only recognised but understood only too well. He would have much preferred to be his friend rather than his enemy. Dine felt badly about what he saw as the inevitable; men like Willie Jackson were difficult to find, one-offs, it was a gross injustice that he had to be removed, yet, however regretfully, it had to be done.

Jacko rang Georgie from Streatham praying that she would be in. She was, but just about to go out to have coffee with a friend.

"Georgie, I've got a job for you, love. An easy one."

But before he could go on Georgie exploded down the telephone and told him what he could do with his job. She went on, "I'm going back to the office tomorrow, Willie. It's intolerable that I'm cooped up here not knowing what's going on. It's well over a week now and I've had enough."

"They're trying to kill me, Georgie." He had not wanted to say it but it was necessary to keep Georgie away from her office.

"That's unfair, Willie. Terribly unfair to say that to me when I know you won't explain." She did not want to believe him, at the same time she knew it must be true; normally he would protect her from this kind of thing.

"You know I wouldn't say it if it wasn't true. I know what your partnership means to you. But your life must mean more. This thing is busting wide open. I'm making real progress but it makes things tougher. They haven't managed to get me so more than ever they will try to get at me through you if they can find you. I'm sorry, Georgie. Do you honestly think I want this?"

There was a long pause before Georgie said tearfully, "What is it you want?"

"Will you take this down. There's an Eric and Annette Parsons living at No. 45, Willmode Street, SW16. Married with one daughter. Woman late fifties to early sixties, man could be about seventy. See what you can dig up for me. Where they originally came from, her maiden name, when they got married, all that guff. The marriage certificate will be a good starter. But don't go anywhere near the place or send anyone else. What I want should all be on paper." Jacko gave her time to take it down then added, "I love you, Georgie. Nothing has changed."

"No, it hasn't changed, Willie. I still hang around day by day without knowing what is happening to you. I have no way of contacting you and simply have to hope for the odd call from you. In future we'll have nothing to do with Thomas Ewing; he can find someone else to do his dirty work."

"It's not his fault, Georgie. He had no idea this thing would go this deep. He can't ring me either and don't try ringing him or Liz whatever you do; his calls might be bugged. I'm well on the way to wrapping things up, so just hang on for a few more days."

"Thomas's phone tapped? I thought only the police or the

150

Security Service could do things like that. Is that what you're saying?"

"It's not as bad as it sounds. It's a long story and will have to wait. Will tomorrow be too soon to ring for the detail about the Parsons?"

"I might have the answer to the marriage details later today. The rest depends. I'll be as quick as I can because I want you back, Willie."

Jacko went back to the BMW and wished it was his Ferrari, which had always felt part of him. He drove back to Central London thinking he had better get some sleep. He did not realise how lucky he had been in choosing a day to follow Dine who visited South London once a week. It would have made no difference in the long run for he had decided to keep an eye on Dine for several successive days; but he now felt it might be better to wait for news from Georgie first, and then decide the next step. By the time he reached the Army and Navy he was almost asleep over the wheel. When he reached his room he slept for several hours and it was dark when he awoke.

Jacko immediately reached for the phone and got through to Georgie who said, "Do you realise how many Parsons there are? How many Eric Parsons? I hope I never see the name again. Eric John Parsons married Annette Mary Barr at St Jude's Church, Thornton Heath on 15 June 1959. She was twenty-seven and Parsons, whose address was in Dulwich, was thirty-five."

"Where did she live?"

"She lived at 24, Ronaldi Street, West Croydon."

"What about the daughter?"

"Nothing on her so far. It would help if I had her full name and date of birth."

"If I had that you would not need to bother. Perhaps that won't help. Just dig up what you can about the Parsons, Georgie, and thanks for being so quick. What would I do without you?"

"You just come back safe, Willie."

Jacko drove down to Croydon early the next morning. Ronaldi Street was one of those short roads tucked away between Purley Way, where the old Croydon Aerodrome used to be, and the main London Road. There was a small chapel at the T-junction one end, directly facing down the street.

The type of cars parked usually gave some indication of the neighbourhood and he was surprised to find two Jaguars, and several of the more expensive foreign cars; the rest were standard models. All the houses were terraced and had been built around the turn of the century. The originals would have had tin baths, but Ronaldi Street had risen in status, most of the insides of the houses having been gutted and modernised. But there was no room for garages.

He only managed to park after someone obligingly drove off. He slipped into the slot aware that the message was passing along the grapevine that a stranger had arrived. Whatever changes had taken place this was still a closed community. He walked back to number 24 and rang the bell. The original knocker was still on the door.

Jacko was still wearing his wig and moustache as a precaution. A well-dressed woman answered the door; she was a redhead and suspicious of strangers. "If you're selling anything we don't want it, if you're debt collecting we've paid all the bills, and if you're religious we're all bush heathens."

"You've rehearsed that," said Jacko. "You forgot to ask for my identity. Does Annette Barr live here?"

The pleasant features changed. "Annette Barr? I don't know of anyone of that name and I've lived here for over fifteen years."

"And your name is?"

"Why would that help you? What is it you want?"

"I'm sorry." Jacko produced one of his many visiting cards. "I'm a solicitor. Annette Barr, if she is still alive, has been left a small legacy. The only address we have come up with is this one. I suppose it was too much to expect her to be still living here."

"I wouldn't want anyone to lose an inheritance but I really have not heard of such a person. How long ago was it she was supposed to have lived here?" She saw Jacko hesitate then glance behind him, and added, "You're probably right, you'd better come in."

They went down the narrow passage and into a cosy room

152

that had probably been half the size when Annette Barr lived here; Jacko could see where the wall had been and the room extended. Jacko stood in the middle of the room and answered the question. "The last time she was definitely known to live here was June 1959. Does that help, Mrs . . .?"

"Judith Williams. You've got a bloody cheek. I wasn't born then. No wonder I've never heard of her. I don't think I can help."

Jacko said hurriedly, "I didn't think for a moment you were born then but you might still have known something about her. Is there anyone in the street who might know?"

Mollified, Judith considered the possibility. "Old Mrs Potter might know. She's been here for yonks." She went to the telephone in the hall, spoke for a while then re-entered the room to say, "She's on her way over. She says she knew her."

"Good. Thank you." Jacko would have preferred to see Mrs Potter alone but it was clear that Judith wanted to share the act.

Mrs Potter turned out to be an elegant, well-preserved woman in her sixties. Her hair was pretty and she was still an attractive lady. Judith introduced Jacko as a Mr Thomas after glancing at the card she was still holding, and then took over in briefing Mrs Potter about Jacko's quest.

They were all sitting down when Mrs Potter began her reminiscing. "They lived here for years. The Barrs were here before Jack and I came. Annette was married from here. A lovely girl. They were childhood sweethearts. Knew each other from junior school. It was such a tragedy. Terrible thing to happen."

Jacko was trying to equate Eric Parsons to a childhood sweetheart of Annette; the age disparity surely precluded them from going to junior school at the same time. He said, "They got married in June 1959; does that tie in with what you remember?"

Mrs Potter gave it some thought and shook her head slowly. "Oh, no. I can't remember the precise date or even the actual year but it was years before that. Years before." She concentrated hard. "Memory has never been my strong point but it can't be that bad. Besides he was just going off to war. I think Annette was still in her teens. I remember they made a big fling of it, all the street took part. He was in the army and I seem to remember that they wanted to get married before he went away." Her eyes glazed from recollection. "He never came back. He was killed in action. The poor girl tried to commit suicide."

"Can you remember the name of the man she married?"

"That's difficult." Mrs Potter's brows furrowed. "I never really knew him, and I didn't know the Barrs all that well. He did not live in the street and although I must have seen him once or twice I only actually met him at the street party. It was so long ago and memory plays tricks."

"Yes it does," agreed Jacko. "Did she move away from here soon after?"

"I can't recall how long she stayed. Her mother was still alive, of course, and looked after her. I think she must have stayed on for some time. Then the whole family moved out and I never saw them again."

"How many were there in the family?"

"Oh, Lord. She had a brother. He left home long before she did. He went travelling, I believe; one of those restless young men who couldn't stay still. I recall that because he sometimes told me of some of his travels before his sister married. I suppose he was two or three years older than her but still young to get around the amount he did. I seem to remember a sister but she might have been a cousin; there were a lot of relatives at the reception. I remember that because they kept cropping up. Her father had died years before."

"I don't suppose you know where she moved to?"

"Oh, no. As I said, we weren't very close. Once they had gone they more or less left my mind." She smiled. "Until you came asking questions. It's quite an exercise for an old lady."

"You're not old, Mrs Potter, and you've been most helpful. And it has been kind of Mrs Williams to let us use her house like this. I'm grateful to you both." He hesitated at the door; "I don't suppose you know the name of the husband's regiment?"

"Oh, no. I don't think I ever knew. I would not remember something like that. He was in uniform when they married, though. Perhaps you can find some of the original wedding photographs."

"Do you know who did them?"

"He used to live in the next street but he died about ten years ago. But I believe his business closed long before that."

"Thank you both again."

As Jacko drove back he wondered why he was concentrating on the woman and not the man. He assumed that what he had discovered, Dine must surely already know. It was clear that Annette Barr had remarried after the death of her husband, but that it had been some time later, June 1959. Why would Dine have such an obsessive interest? What had happened down the years to make this happen now?

As Jacko grappled with the traffic he at first thought that Dine must be the travelling brother suddenly awakening with a conscience but it was difficult to swallow and anyway he had been born in Hong Kong. And what was any of this to do with what he was trying to find out? And, yet, Jacko felt there was a connection; not an obvious one, but it was there and it was peculiarly strong, as if some spiritual dimension had entered the scene, leaving him with an odd feeling of unease because this enemy was in the air and unseen.

16

Jacko, still disguised, found a help-yourself café in Brixton. The place was virtually full but he found a seat at a table for four, fumbled around for space to put his plates and coffee and squeezed himself on to the chair, keeping his elbows in. He was aware of the noise and the clatter but the people around him did not register while his mind was so anchored on the history of Annette Barr. He knew the beginning and the end but nothing of the middle. Why was she so important?

The only person who could fill in the gaps was probably Annette herself. Or Dine. But what was this to do with an arms cache in the New Forest, several killings, the loss of the Ferrari, the going to ground of Georgie and, to a lesser degree, of Ewing who now had to be careful of his telephone calls, which raised questions about any part M15 might be playing in all this. The Sèvres figure had long since lost importance.

Jacko considered going through the marriage records at the church in Thornton Heath, where Annette Barr presumably got married, but it could take ages without the year of the marriage and Mrs Potter could not remember that far.

He did not know why but instinct warned him not to approach Annette Barr at this stage. He had the feeling he might be stirring up something that was best left alone. It was a difficult decision but Annette's early expectations had taken such a knock as to make her suicidal and he would not want to remind her of that. Whatever her lot now, from what little he had seen, she seemed to be content.

Jacko decided to pass on what he knew to Georgie and hope she could dig something up from records that he might miss; going through old documents was not his strongest point.

He removed the wig and moustache and drove to the club

from where he rang her, but could only get her friend Susan, whom he annoyed because he would not leave a message. He finally raised Georgie after eight that evening. He gave her what he had and could tell that she was becoming intrigued herself. She was happy to do the paper detective work if it helped keep him from trouble. After a thoughtful pause he said, "Do you think you can hire someone to go through the records at St Jude's church at Thornton Heath? There is something that doesn't tally and the answer might be there. I think Annette Barr got married there. It's only a guess. Could someone check through the years 1943 to 1945 and from 1952 to 1953?"

"That's a tall order, Willie. I can certainly get someone to check. You'll have to underwrite the cost; I'm afraid to go near my bank; I'm doing everything on credit at the moment."

"I'll send you some cash. I know it's a lot to ask but I can't spend the time on it myself right now. Thanks, Georgie. It could make all the difference."

When he had hung up he went through Wherewell's list of names and countries again and something began to stir.

Jacko had not paid too much attention to the make of the arms he had found beyond recognising them as old but in pristine condition. They were probably World War Two stock. He would have to go back to the New Forest or try one of the other addresses.

Simon Wherewell, MP, was not feeling quite so confident during a meeting with Sonny Rollins. The nature of these meetings was never pleasant but there was too much at stake to ignore them or to show disapproval. And the venue would be so clandestine as at times to be ridiculous. Rollins took enormous precautions to ensure that he was not seen with this person or that. Wherewell accepted that it was an immensely sensible thing to do but as an extrovert found it tedious.

They had met at an out-of-town motel which neither of them would normally dream of using and Wherewell hired a room in which the two discussed the current problems. They sat in the only two chairs in some discomfort.

Rollins was never a pleasant person to spend time with. Apart from counting his money nobody knew what other interests he had. He was burly, hard-featured, yet, at times when it was necessary, could produce a surprising charm. It was not clear whether or not he was married and nobody was willing to ask. He was not noticeably seen with women and certainly not with men. His aim in life seemed to be, to those who knew him best, to make other lives a misery and to profit by so doing. He had always ruled by fear but just once in a while, along the line, he would meet someone who was not intimidated by it. Such a person was Reginald Dine who had declined to come to the meeting on the grounds that he would learn nothing from it; he knew the problems and it was up to Rollins to deal with them as he had already chosen that role.

No-one else would dare speak to Rollins in this way, and like all bullies, and Rollins was supreme amongst them, he backed off. There had always been something about Dine he could not place, but he was as sure of his honesty in his dealings as any man he had met. He did not have to look over his shoulder when dealing with Dine and there were extremely few men he could say that about. Just the same he did not like losing any form of control and it rankled that Dine had been so contemptuous of his idea that a meeting was important.

There was little harmony at the meeting; it was a straight forward appraisal of what had gone wrong and was there a need for redistribution? Had Willie Jackson been successful in finding the arms cache? Nobody knew. They all knew the real answer: find Jacko. This was a subject that Wherewell veered from; he was a politician not an assassin.

And then Rollins raised the issue Wherewell hoped would not come up. "How the hell did Jacko find the address in the New Forest?"

The question was an accusation that hung in the air with Rollins' gazing at Wherewell as if accusing him.

"Don't look at me," said Wherewell. "Those lists are firmly locked in a well-hidden safe. And they are still there."

"You've checked?" asked Rollins while pulling out a pipe he believed gave him an image.

"Of course I checked. They are all there."

"So the thought must have occurred to you that it was possible that someone had got at them?"

"Not really. It was just a precaution. I check from time to time."

"Someone's seen them. Mine are safe in a safe deposit and there are no others. Someone has seen yours or one of the caretakers has talked."

"Well it can't have been Walters. He sounded the alarm as soon as Jackson appeared. He did everything he should. It wasn't his fault that it went wrong from there."

"You can never be sure. Are you certain that you've found nothing disturbed at your place?"

"Of course. I'm a creature of habit and I'm tidy. I would have noticed." The truth was that, once he had checked that nothing was missing from the safe, he had taken the rest for granted.

"Yet Jacko got hold of at least one address and we don't know how far he got."

"The police did not find the cache; they came back the next day."

"They wouldn't have been looking for anything like that. And the stuff is solidly hidden. It means I'll have to do a check on all the petermen and wring the truth out. There aren't many up to doing a safe like yours."

"Petermen?"

"Safe crackers. A dying breed. Kind of sad; it always is to lose a good pro. When I find him it will leave a little more space for the rest."

Wherewell did not think Rollins realised the contradiction and he did not like the assumption that his safe was broken into in spite of his denial. He could not see the point of any of this. "Do you want the stuff redistributed?"

Rollins smiled for the first time. "Now you're talking. But that is up to Jason. Let's be sure first. My boys have checked everywhere for Jacko. But nobody can hide for ever. He's around; we'll find him and his bloody girlfriend who's

159

dived down a foxhole. I'll make him suffer for the aggro he's caused."

Jacko packed the army uniform in the grip and left the club at 9.30. He went on foot to the nearest public toilet and changed his clothes. He would not wear the uniform at the club, members never did, and anyway, it would be difficult if he was greeted by someone who had served in REME who wanted to exchange gossip. He caught a cab to Ewing's house, arriving well after 10 p.m.

Liz answered the door; gorgeous Liz who had killed a man in order to protect Ewing, a secret guarded by the only person who knew other than herself: Jacko, who would always see it as the execution of a sub-human multi-murderer. The passing of time had not changed his opinion.

He gave a salute on the doorstep and at first she did not recognise him. He gave her a sharp warning look and said, "Mrs Ewing? I'm Lieutenant-Colonel Baxter. I'm so sorry to disturb you at this time of night but may I see your husband? There's some information he needs for his meeting tomorrow."

"I'm sure he'll understand. Do come in."

Once inside he dropped the grip and they embraced like the good friends they were.

"Oh, Jacko. You really had me fooled for a moment. It's so nice to see you again. Thomas," she called down the hall. "Come and see who's called."

Jacko took his cap off and put it on the marble hall stand as Ewing appeared. The two men shook hands and moved towards Ewing's study as Liz hived off to make some coffee.

They sat in the elegant room, a reminder to Jacko that Liz was a very wealthy woman; Ewing would never have managed this on his salary but the couple had long since come to terms with the monetary aspects. Jacko accepted a Cognac and told Ewing what he had discovered, explaining Georgie's present part.

"Did you find out what committees Wherewell sat on?" asked Jacko at last.

"Some. It's a very tedious and long job and I don't know

160

how far back I'm supposed to go. I do have my own work, Jacko and I dare not let that slip. And I can't delegate the other without questions being asked. The quickest way is to ask Wherewell himself but that's a non-starter."

"You haven't come across anything to do with arms?"

"Defence meetings, you mean? He wouldn't be on them." Ewing swirled his Cognac round his brandy balloon. He gazed across the room thinking that Jacko looked tired. "You are not connecting a small-arms find with any meeting Wherewell has sat on? From what you say there is enough to arm about sixty men. That's small stuff to discuss on committee, Jacko."

"Not if there are a lot of dumps. I'm thinking that Wherewell has been in Parliament for a long time; he goes back much further than you, Thomas."

"I keep telling you I'm not in Parliament. I'm an adviser, not a Member. A political errand boy."

"Who the PM puts great store by. A political trouble-shooter might be a better designation. You carry a lot of knowledge and do a lot of confidential jobs best not done in Parliament as such. Come on, Thomas, who are you kidding? You even have access to the Security Service, which a good many MPs must resent."

"I wish you would stop using that army jargon. Designation. I ask you. What contacts I have I've largely built up myself. I've taken the oath of loyalty like everyone else."

"But it's not everyone else who heeds it, is it? Wherewell for instance. He couldn't give a monkey's about allegiance to the Crown." Jacko leaned forward. "I think he's used his position and has come up with something to make a lot of money. I think it dates back a good way which is why this is all so difficult."

"But even if there were a fair number of these caches it would still be small fry in money terms. Arms are profitable but you need an awful lot of them and some bigger stuff than small arms and explosive. You're not suggesting he and Rollins are building up a private army for some reason?"

"No." Jacko was thoughtful for a while and then Liz

161

brought in the coffee and after she had gone the subject seemed to lose impetus for a while.

"No," Jacko said again some time later. "Apart from the explosive, and that's not modern-day Semtex, and the few SMGs and pistols, they are the wrong type of arms for crime. Villains don't use rifles, which comprise most of the haul, but sawn-off shotguns. Wherewell has picked up something inside the House. I'm sure of it. Otherwise I can't see his usefulness."

"I can only keep plodding. There are committees going on practically all the time. Just how far back do you want me to go?"

"From, say, 1946."

"Good Lord, stuff like that will be in the archives, somewhere under the streets of London. Anywhere. Nowhere. Probably destroyed long since. Anyway, Wherewell does not go back that far politically; he's not old enough."

"I suppose it's too risky to ask one or two who have been in Parliament as long as he?"

"There are some much longer, but, yes, it would be far too risky unless you wanted it to get back to Wherewell."

"Okay. I'll have to find out my way."

Ewing looked startled. "You are no longer in the Regiment. We can't have you pushing a gun in his ear."

Jacko drained his coffee and stood up. "Thanks for the drink and the coffee. I'll slip out quietly. Give Liz my love."

Ewing rose, too. "She'll expect you to say goodnight."

"Do it for me. I don't want to lie to her about what I'm doing and I don't want her to think you are in any kind of danger."

"Am I?" asked Ewing as they walked to the door.

"You have too many powerful political and Security friends for you to be in real danger. But if Rollins' crowd thought we were still in touch about this they might try to wring you out and leave you crippled. I don't think they would kill you. It would invite too much attention."

"That's such a comfort, Jacko. It will make me sleep much better."

"Best you should know. You're not too hot on security."

Jacko held his hand out. "Don't come out on to the step; just show me out. I'll be in touch." He picked up the grip.

Ewing opened the door for Jacko to leave and said with a slightly raised voice, "Thank you, Colonel. Give my regards to the Brigadier."

The door closed behind Jacko who stood on the steps pulling on his gloves. He went down the few steps slowly, paused to decide which way to go, then set off. The streets were discreetly quiet at this time of night in St John's Wood. He did not hurry and already knew that someone was behind him. He pulled the peak of his cap well down over his eyes and kept going, taking corners as they came.

Suddenly he turned round and went back the way he had come. The man following him had no option but to continue walking on and as they passed each other Jacko hit him hard in the stomach, dragged the retching figure into the nearest doorway, and went through his pockets to find a police warrant card. Special Branch doing MI5 a favour no doubt.

Jacko said in his most cultured voice, "I say, I am sorry, old chap. I thought you were going to mug me; official secrets and all that. But it does pose the question of why you were following me."

"I thought you were someone else. Sorry. Mix up." The words were strangled with pain.

"Be more careful next time, eh? Or I'll report you. You really should know better." Jacko strode off before the policeman could recover enough to continue.

As he changed again in the nearest toilet, he pondered on why only one man had followed him and decided that the uniform had thrown them; it had worked. They must be watching Ewing and had despatched only one man to follow a colonel on the you-never-know basis.

Reginald Dine was beginning to worry about himself. For the first time he was finding the house too large and too empty. Mrs Morris was in her quarters, where she sometimes entertained a friend, but he could hardly turn to her for company without some repercussion.

The house had the space he had always craved. Nobody

163

crowded him and that was terribly important. He could change bedrooms as he felt fit; in fact he had only ever used the one, but the option was there. Freedom. What a magic word. But he was beginning to believe he was creating his own prison, physically and emotionally.

As he sat in the lounge about the time Jacko was visiting Ewing, he had a mad craving to have a chat with Jacko, whom he believed he was beginning to know in spite of the fact that they hardly knew each other. Jacko, he was sure, would understand. The Rollinses of this world were rubbish and he despised people like Wherewell who took the Queen's money and betrayed her behind her back. So much had changed; values had plummeted. To fight for survival he could understand, to make money for money's sake was beyond his comprehension even though he had enough to live luxuriously for life. But was that safeguard enough? That was the eternal question.

He became confused when he tried to struggle with fine points of morality. His thinking processes seemed to collapse. He knew part of the reason for this and those reasons were sound, nor did he have to excuse them. There were other reasons too, over which he had had no control and which he had been forced to fight for survival. But he had come through. Yet it now seemed to be starting all over again, on a different playing field, with different people, and he wondered if he had the strength left to fight it. He had wondered that for most of his life.

The next morning Jacko reverted to the wig and moustache and went to the Imperial War Museum. He told Reception what he wanted and went upstairs to study the material in the gallery. He spent the whole day there because he was searching for the nebulous without a real starting point. During the lunch break he telephoned a journalist on the *Daily Telegraph* who had helped him previously, and asked if he could go through back numbers the next day.

Meanwhile, Georgie had appointed an agent to go to Thornton Heath to search through the marriage records in the forlorn hope of finding something useful. She had lunch with her friend Susan and then returned to the apartment. While she was actually working for Jacko she was quite happy and could accept the restrictions on her life because she knew her man; she just prayed that they would not go on for ever.

She entered the apartment and someone closed the door behind her and someone else placed a hand over her mouth. She almost fainted from shock but they held her upright and dragged her into the small, bright living-room and the man behind her whispered in her ear, "My friend will take his hand away if you promise not to scream. Nod your head if you agree. If you do scream it will be your last. Do you understand?"

Georgie, terrorised, nodded slowly.

"Okay. Now sit over there and put your hands on your lap and keep quiet and still."

They helped her into an armchair and then stood back. Georgie put her hands on her lap as she was told. She was trembling.

They gave her a little time to recover from the shock and then one of them said, "This should be quite painless; we just want to know where Willie Jackson is. Tell us and we'll go."

Georgie was trying to find her courage. These men were rough but did not speak as she would expect a hardened villain to do. She had been so afraid that she had hardly noticed them but she now took stock. She put her hands to her mouth as if she was about to be sick.

One was slightly taller than the other and wore glasses, but there was a basic similarity. Their clothes could have come from the same high-street tailor and were fairly well cut. The accents were semi-cultured and possibly disguised. It was obvious that they were fairly fit and there was no way she could deal with them physically. She estimated they were in their early forties. During this quick appraisal she realised that even if she did scream she doubted if anyone would hear. The house had three apartments and she was usually the only one left in them after 9.30 each morning.

"You are taking too long to answer," said the one with glasses.

She gazed from one to the other, thought they were

unarmed and then saw the butt of a pistol protruding from one of the jackets. Her heart leapt. "What do you expect?" Her voice was shaking. "You nearly gave me a heart attack." It would be stupid to deny knowing Willie so she said, "I've no idea where he is."

"Now don't be difficult. You two are lovers. Of course you know."

"If I did I'd be with him."

They glanced at each other. The shorter one said, "Miss Roberts, we're trying to help him, he's in grave danger."

"I can see that. If you are so bloody do-gooding why did you break in and scare the daylights out of me? Couldn't you ring the bell? Never heard of a telephone?"

"We did not think you would respond to a normal request."

"I'm certainly not responding to this except to tell you to get out quick. I don't know where Willie is and if I did I would not tell you. You must be mad to think I would."

"We don't want to hurt you. We really don't."

"But you'll do it just the same. It must be terrible for you, you sadistic louts." Georgie had recovered fully now, her spirit had returned and she was glad that she did not know where Willie was; he had anticipated something like this might happen and she understood without rancour. Willie was Willie and she knew what she had entered into and would marry him at this moment if she could.

"You'll have to come with us."

"Over my dead body."

"That can be arranged." The shorter man had pulled out a pistol and attached a silencer to it. "Walk quietly to our car or we'll drug you."

"My God, I don't believe this. It really is too melodramatic. I'm not going with you, anyway."

"These situations are always larger than life. We don't like them either. They are rather ridiculous. But they work, Miss Roberts. Old-fashioned methods have stood the test of time. Now what is it to be? The needle or common sense?"

Georgie took a shoe off and flung it at them but it hit neither and was a futile gesture.

"It would seem to be the needle," said the man with glasses.

166

17

Jacko left the Imperial War Museum only when it closed. He was weary from going through records and dropped into a pub for a drink and a meal on his way back to the Army and Navy. He took his time because there was little more he could do until the next morning. He wanted more information than he had before taking the risk of returning to the New Forest.

He eventually arrived at the club about 8.30 and rang Georgie straight away. He accepted the hit-and-miss affair of finding her in but it was at least some form of security. Susan answered the phone and told him Georgie was not in. Had she gone to a theatre or cinema? Not so far as Susan knew. Susan had expected to find her home when she herself came in; they had lunched together. Jacko apologised for the hour but told her he was on his way round. He put the disguise back on in the BMW.

Susan was a willowy blonde with a wicked sense of humour which she suspended when Jacko arrived. She knew something was going on between Jacko and Georgie and that Jacko sometimes moved in strange ways, but she asked no questions. She was as worried as Jacko.

Jacko thanked her profusely for letting him in. They had met before but she made no comment about Jacko's change of hair colour or the moustache which did not suit him. But she was puzzled.

"You don't know if she came back here after lunch?" asked Jacko.

"That's what she said she would do. I don't know whether she did."

"Was everything as you'd expect it to be? Was anything disturbed?"

Susan looked worried. "Am I understanding you right? You think someone came and took her away?"

"There are reasons I can't tell you for believing that could have happened."

"Only one thing was obviously different. She left one shoe by that chair and I found the other under the TV stand. She might have changed her shoes, of course, but Georgie is a tidy person. It was unusual."

"Have you a flashlight?"

When Susan produced one he went to the front door and examined the lock to find scratches around it, some of them deep. "They must have broken in and waited for her," he said half to himself.

Susan clutched her arms round herself. "I don't like the idea of that. They could do it again."

Jacko tried to give her a reassuring smile. "If they did that it was Georgie they were after. Can I use your phone?"

Jacko rang Ewing uncaring of whether the phone was tapped or that Susan was listening. "I think they've got Georgie," he said at once. "If it's Five then the bastards are listening and they'd better give her back quick or I'm going to stir the can until they pop out screaming from the heat. Thomas, for God's sake do something your end."

"And if it's not Five?"

Jacko had thought it through. "Five have better tabs on me and my friends and their friends than Dine and Rollins can have. They have had a dossier on me for years; they'll know my bank balance and the number of costumes I have at the warehouse and the number of times I clean my teeth. The bastards want me for whatever reason. They don't like playing second best mainly because that's what they are."

"The others want you too, Jacko," Ewing said quietly. He fully understood how Jacko must be feeling.

"I know they do, Thomas. Maybe there's a way I can find out. Do your best." He turned to Susan. "Sounds like gangland doesn't it? Would you mind if I ring you periodically just in case Georgie comes back?"

"Can't you give me a number?"

168

"I'm afraid not. It would not be fair for you to be lumbered with it."

Shrewdly, Susan said, "It didn't do Georgie any good not having your number did it?"

Jacko hurried to the door. "That was a low blow, Susan, but I take your point. If I hear of anything myself I'll let you know at once. Thanks for your help."

He found a pay phone and rang Dine who answered quite quickly; he had long since accepted that as Dine used his telephone so freely he must consider it safe. "It's me," said Jacko. "You might be able to help me."

"I was thinking of you," said Dine pleasantly. "It's such a pity we are enemies."

"It was you who made us enemies. I wanted out and you wouldn't believe me. It's too late now. They've taken Georgie. I want her back."

"Georgie?"

"She's been snatched. Probably to get at me. Do you know anything about it?"

"Would you expect me to tell you if I did?"

"Yes. I think you would. In exchange for me."

"I don't recall ever using a woman as hostage. I didn't know she was in the firing line. I can't help you, Jacko."

"Would you know if Rollins had snatched her?"

"I suppose I could deny knowing anyone of that name but that would be insulting you, wouldn't it? I have no knowledge of this at all. I think you're wrong."

"You wouldn't lie to me about it, would you, Reginald?"

There was a long pause and when Dine came back his voice was strangely subdued. "No, Jacko. I would not lie to you about it. It changes nothing between us, of course."

"Would Rollins do it without your knowledge?"

"You are very persistent and I really don't know why I am answering you. He might do it without my knowledge but I would have expected to hear almost immediately afterwards. If it was done to root you out I would certainly be told. I repeat, I know nothing of this."

"Okay, I accept what you say about Georgie. My thanks."

Jacko was about to hang up when Dine said quickly, "We

169

will still get you, Jacko. Don't mistake a liking for a weakness. I can't afford to be weak. I think you know that. We can't mark time for ever, you'll find there is really too much stacked against you."

"That's the story of my life. Nothing is ever bloody simple. Would you like me to give myself up?"

"I could have said we had the girl; would you have given yourself up then?"

"Oh, yes. A life for a life. Hers is worth saving far more than mine. You missed an opportunity."

Dine sighed slowly. "I don't want you that way. But it is not wholly in my hands. We make strange enemies, Jacko."

"Yes, we do. Thanks for your candour, Reginald." Jacko hung up satisfied that Dine had told the truth.

He suffered a long restless night. He could not go to the police; there was already too much he should have told them and he knew the answer did not lie with them. For reasons he did not understand he knew the Security Service would block all police efforts even if they tried to help him. But he was no more popular with them than the others. He was on his own. He had always been on his own.

The next morning he rang Ewing who at once told him that MI5 had absolutely no knowledge of Georgie's disappearance. But they were eager to meet him and believed they could help find her.

"They want to lay their hands on me," said Jacko bitterly, convinced that they were listening. "What the hell for? And whose bloody side are they on? They've never been on mine."

"I can't force them into a confession particularly if they are right. They contact me as a favour; I have no real pull with them. But who has? Even the PM doesn't know the half of it."

"What do they want me to do apart from walking through their doors in Curzon Street?"

"There's a man called Peter Jennings. I have a private number for you to ring. You can take it from there."

Jacko took the number down. "It might be easier if I just talked to the guy with earphones and a tape recorder who's listening to all this. I don't like it but if that's all you have to offer I'll give him a bell."

Jacko rang the number Ewing had given him, well aware that the call would be taped and a trace put on where he was ringing from, which was another pay phone well away from the Army and Navy.

"Peter Jennings?" Jacko was suspicious before he started, gaze roaming beyond the box.

"Willie Jackson? I'm so glad you called. Can we meet somewhere?"

"What for?"

"I understand your fiancée has been kidnapped. I thought we might be able to help with our considerable resources."

"And why would you want to do that? Kidnapping is a police business."

"Then why haven't you gone to them, old boy? Oh, come on, Jacko, don't piss about. We look for the girl in exchange for information you might have to help us on another issue."

"Thomas Ewing knows everything I know about whatever it is you want to know. Why don't you ask him?"

"Well, Jacko, in the first place we strongly doubt that Mr Ewing knows everything you know. He may have the bare bones but you'll be keeping quite a lot back because that's the way you work. You like to be sure about everything and that is commendable. Secondly, Mr Ewing is far too close to the Prime Minister for us to apply crude pressure. If he chose not to tell us there is little we can do."

"You could snatch his wife like you have Georgie. Or you could rig something against him like you tried to do with Sam Towler, a good friend of mine, and which you would do to me at the drop of a hat. Peter, old son, I don't trust any of you. So what's the deal for you to release Georgie?"

"We don't go round snatching innocent people, Jacko. You should know better. All we want to do is to compare notes. You name the meeting place and we'll be there."

"I bet you will. An army of you. Let me think it over. I'll give you a ring later." Jacko hung up not sure that he had done the right thing. If Five had Georgie then he was sure she would come to no harm. They must be satisfied by now that she really did not know where he was. Thereafter, although a prisoner, she would be fairly well looked after. Georgie's biggest worry would be in not knowing who her captors were, although she might by now have guessed.

In spite of his concern for her he decided to take a chance. If Five had her she was safe from Rollins. If Rollins had her he could not afford the time to spend talking to Five so that they could pick his brains; they clearly thought he had information they needed. He realised that he was placing great store on his belief in Dine and that it was risky. It was all risky.

He went to the *Daily Telegraph* offices and looked through their back numbers. It was a mammoth task because he did not know precisely what he was looking for or even that it would be there. If he knew that, the staff could probably have pin-pointed the issues for him.

He broke off for lunch and returned to continue and found something of interest dated 17 November 1990. He made some notes, realising that what he had found might be totally misleading and should be handled with caution. It was tea-time before he left and he considered himself lucky to have taken such little time and that the issue was so comparatively recent.

He rang Ewing again at his office because he thought that the telephone there was the least likely to be tapped, particularly now that MI5 had come on the scene more openly. The chances were that they would have removed any tap from that source in case of repercussions, if there had ever been one; a tap on a home phone was a different matter and could be blamed on almost anyone. He explained that the deal Five had to offer was no more than he had expected and that he had refused it for the moment. Ewing was slightly irritated, not going so far as Jacko in his appraisal of Five's devilry. Jacko asked Ewing to keep pressure on Five because he was convinced they had Georgie Roberts.

He hoped he was right about the phone tapping but it was becoming difficult to use pay phones all the time and expect the people he was calling to run out to find one. He knew he was getting reckless but he doubted that he had said anything that Five did not already know. As Ewing's home was obviously under surveillance it would be difficult for him to call there in person again, whatever the disguise.

He thought the arms he had found and told Ewing about were the type used towards the end of the Second World War and shortly after, well before his time. With the batch numbers painted over it was impossible to give precise dates and he had not been looking for particular detail; at that time it did not seem important. Even so, he had no intention of passing that information over the phone. So far as he knew Five had no idea he had found arms.

From the same box he rang Susan, hoping she would be home. "It's Willie Jackson. I've no news about Georgie but I have a hunch that she might be safe. I hope I'm right but hunches are all I've got to go on right now. Nobody's rung you, have they?"

"No. But a letter has come for her. Unstamped so presumably delivered by hand. Do you want to see it?"

Jacko took the BMW and arrived at Susan's about forty minutes later having tried to force his way through traffic jams. Susan poured him a drink after handing over the letter which he did not hesitate to open.

It was a copy of a marriage certificate and a bill for services. Michael David Deering had married Annette Barr in May 1951. It did not take Jacko any further but merely confirmed that Annette Barr had been married twice. If her husband had been killed in action soon after the marriage then it was almost certainly in Korea. To Mrs Potter one war might have seemed the same as another, and the Korean war had followed on close to the end of World War Two. It did not matter, except to get some form of chronological order.

As Jacko stood there holding the copy marriage certificate he suddenly thought he was going mad and was aware of Susan looking at him strangely. What had any of this to do with Georgie being missing and an arms cache in the New Forest? He was side-tracking. Whatever Dine's interest in Annette Barr it could make no difference to the real issues of the case; what were Dine and Rollins really up to?

Jacko pulled out his cheque book and wrote out a cheque for the amount of the bill. "I wonder if you'd be kind enough

173

to bung this in an envelope and post it when you go in tomorrow. It will save Georgie having to worry about it when she returns."

"Of course. Anything else I can do?"

Jacko put the certificate in his pocket. "You must wonder why Georgie hangs about with a nut like me."

"She loves you." Susan smiled wickedly. "There's no accounting for tastes. At least things happen around you."

"Yeah. The wrong things. I do intend to get her back, you know."

"I know. I wish someone would work that hard for me."

Jacko left wondering why someone wasn't. Back at the Army and Navy Jacko put a call through to Hereford to an old friend still serving in the SAS in admin.

"Jimmy, can you do a routine check for me on a Michael David Deering? I don't know the regiment but he was killed in action during the Korean War, somewhere between, say, May 1951 and the armistice July '53. Sooner rather than later I would say. I just want to tidy up something. I'll send you a case of Scotch. And you can ring me here at the Army and Navy, ask for Lieutenant-Colonel William Baxter." The Regiment at Hereford was the only exception Jacko would make to issuing this number. Jacko hung up to Jimmy's laughter; they had been sergeants together.

He had gone as far as he could for that day, and the frustration of inactivity set in as he had a meal near the club. All he could now do was to wait for information and, apart from being deeply worried about Georgie, on a purely practical level he missed her help.

Night-time, unless he could go exploring, was becoming difficult to bear. He felt that matters were on the move yet he had to exercise patience until the right moment. He really had nothing in terms of real knowledge, but there were all sorts of bits and pieces and from experience he knew that they would come together. Yet there was one big factor missing – he felt he had been near to it but had somehow missed it. He was as satisfied as he ever would be that Rollins did not have Georgie; if he had he would have found some way of letting Jacko know through the grapevine. That Five probably had

174

her only showed how seriously they were taking this affair to go to the extreme of kidnap, even if benign kidnap. But he could not be absolutely sure and Five would know how to play on it.

There were times when he felt he should co-operate with them, but he did not like the way they operated, as now, having taken Georgie as hostage to get him to help them. But there was a larger question hanging over them. Just what business was it of MI5's to search for a cache of arms unless they believed they were to be used against the State for some form of treason? The arms cache was surely a police affair, the Anti-Terrorist Squad; he wondered if C11, more recently designated SO11, knew anything about the matter. Unless Five really knew nothing about the arms at all and were just following up a suspicion. What sort of suspicion?

Jacko sometimes thought he was chasing moonbeams. There were so many imponderables, particularly about Dine himself, who was really difficult to place in context. His association with Rollins was strange and so was that of Wherewell. Jason was closer to Rollins than the others but money was a good blender.

The next morning Jacko viewed his options, pulled out a dog-collar attached to a black silk front from the stuff he had ordered from Molly, and with the wig and the moustache went down to the car park. He donned the disguise in the car as usual and now looked like a priest. He drove off to Wherewell's apartment block and rang the bell.

Wherewell's voice was tetchy through the box. "Who is it?"

"The Reverend Driscoll, Mr Wherewell. I wonder if you can spare me a few minutes to talk about the Child Care Foundation?" That Wherewell was on the committee of the Foundation as one of his earlier ploys to win popularity was one of the snippets of information Ewing had passed on to Jacko.

"You really want Sir John Perryman. He's the President and has all the information."

"I've already seen Sir John. I'm seeing all the committee members in turn. We have a new scheme for fund-raising that needs to be mooted by all involved. So I've agreed to do this rather than a full meeting be called which might inconvenience some members. Just a few minutes is all I need."

"It's a bit early in the day, Reverend, but you'd better come up. A few minutes no more."

The buzzer sounded and the catch was released and Jacko entered the familiar hall. The door closed behind him and it was a symbol of the risk he was taking in trapping himself in this way. Avoiding the elevator he went up the stairs slowly keeping his ears attuned, but it was uncannily quiet. Anyone who worked would be out by this time, but Jacko had banked on Wherewell going to the House late, if he went at all.

The front door to the penthouse was closed and Jacko rang the bell and faced the spyhole squarely. The door opened and Wherewell stood there in a dressing-gown, hands in pockets, in one of which Jacko was convinced he was holding a gun.

"I don't know a Reverend Driscoll," said Wherewell, the bulge in his pocket moving. "There has never been such a person on the committee."

18

Jacko gave no indication that he knew a gun was pointing at him. "I don't believe I said I was on the committee, Mr Wherewell. I have never been on the committee as you know, although I am with many other charities. No, no, I am acting solely for the charity's fund-raisers; I am involved with them in other ways and I must say I think they have come up with a particularly good idea."

"For goodness sake, Reverend, this is not a matter for door-stop chat. Let the publicity agents call a meeting; it cannot possibly be dealt with in this way. It's highly irregular."

Jacko stepped back a pace. "If you feel that way, sir, then I have no option but to report back. I'm sorry to have wasted your time. And mine."

Jacko saw an expression of exasperation cross Wherewell's face but he became more relaxed as he realised Jacko was leaving. Jacko knew he would not get a better chance. He stepped forward quickly and hit Wherewell hard on the jaw and caught him as he collapsed. He pulled the body inside the hall and closed the door before pulling Wherewell's gun from the dressing-gown pocket.

He dragged Wherewell into the drawing-room and pulled him on to a chair. He went to the kitchen and returned with a jug of water which he threw in the politician's face and then sat down opposite him to wait for him to come round.

Wherewell spluttered and he had paled, the jaw already swelling; the immaculate Wherewell suddenly looked more than his age, and his hair now partially hung over his face. His eyes were glazed as he tried to focus on Jacko who thought he was about to be sick. Wherewell had never been on the wrong side of violence and was finding it extremely painful and distressing. He tried to sit upright and one hand dived into a pocket.

"I have it here," said Jacko amiably, holding up the gun. "Fancy not trusting a clergyman, and I wonder if you have a licence for this thing? Or did Sonny Rollins supply it from his considerable stock?"

"You must be Jackson. God, you're sub-human." The words came out painfully.

"Everyone calls me Jacko, Wherewell. You can if you like. And if I'm sub-human, then you are a piece of slime who takes the taxpayers' money for a crooked return. You're bent, Wherewell. Everybody knows you're bent but I'm the one who can prove it."

"What is it you want? There was no need to punch me like that."

Jacko watched carefully as Wherewell pulled himself up to a more comfortable position. Jacko held up the gun again. "You were going to shoot me. You were lucky to be punched." Jacko pulled out his Browning. "I could have plugged you with this. My hand was in my pocket too. And I dare say I'm a better shot. I've been here before, you know."

Wherewell was startled. "That's ridiculous."

"Went through your safe hidden in that window seat over there. Some interesting documents. I wondered if you could give me more background to them."

"There is nothing missing from the safe." Wherewell sounded unconvincing, worried that Jacko knew where the safe was.

"I photographed the lot. Where did you think I got the New Forest address from? Has Rollins cottoned on yet? He wouldn't be pleased if he knew." Jacko was trying to compromise Wherewell, to put sufficient fear into him to make him talk. "I just want a little additional material." He took a chance, knowing it could backfire. "I know you got this stuff from parliamentary committees you sat on and that you've abused your position as an MP. I don't know where that stands in law, but as sure as hell the press will make mincemeat of you, whatever else happens. That wouldn't please Rollins either. You are in the shit, Wherewell, one way or another."

Wherewell was recovering, rubbing the painful swelling on his jaw, but his eyes were now alert and years of experience in evasion, lying, and bending facts were forming a formidable barrier in his mind. There was also another aspect to give him comfort but he would have to hold his corner first. "You're groping. And you are wildly wrong. You are also guilty of breaking and entering and of theft. Don't try to intimidate me, Jackson. You are the wrong side of the law to be able to do that. Now get out."

"I suppose you've conned so many people for so long that you think you can get away with it for ever. How would you like your teeth smashed in? I haven't your pseudo polish, Wherewell. But then you would only expect physical threats from someone who is sub-human. I want to know what those lists mean in full. I can guess but I want to be sure. Now what do they represent?" He produced his silencer and quietly fixed it to the Browning without looking at Wherewell at all as if he really did not matter.

"You are bluffing, playing around with that thing. It doesn't fool me."

Jacko looked him straight in the eye. "Did Rollins tell you that he's already killed three or four people to protect what is on those sheets? I'm losing count. Did he tell you that he sent three of his hit-men after me in the New Forest? Did he tell you that I killed one and wounded another? Or does he protect you from the gory details and just give you an outline? No, I'm not bluffing. But you are. Feel free to call the police. I won't stop you." Jacko levelled the gun.

Wherewell went white. He at last realised that he could not slip from this crisis by bluff or filibuster. He woke up late to envisage the nerve of a man who could call on him like this dressed as a priest and who incongruously pointed a gun at him. And he thought he had just heard the truth about the deaths.

"If I tell you I am dead anyhow." The voice wavered.

"Who will know? How can they know? I won't tell them."

Wherewell licked his lips, extremely nervous now. "Events

179

will show that only I could have told you." Where were Rollins' men? He had phoned for help before letting Jacko in. He realised he was beginning to panic but he did not like the bleak look of the man sitting opposite or the incredible steadiness of the gun. He added, "If I tell you, I am finished. My friends will be outside by now so I would be very careful if I were you."

Although the claim was very near to being a plea for mercy, Jacko picked out the truth of it. Wherewell was waiting for something to happen and had woken up to the fact that it would be on his own doorstep. Wherewell was not only scared of him but of what he might have started in order to protect himself.

Jacko rose slowly and backed behind the door. "What have you done?"

"I phoned for help once I realised you were a phoney. Had you not been I would have cancelled it. It's too late now. You are trapped."

"And you are near to dying. How would they get in? You haven't released the front door." When he saw Wherewell's hesitation he added, "You're not bullshitting some opposition MP now, Wherewell. This is for real: your life or mine."

"There are two ways: the fire escape or from the roof; there are maintenance stairs leading down to a short corridor at the rear."

"It looks as if you're going to have a shoot-out on your own patch. That should make you happy."

"Oh, God." Wherewell buried his head in his hands.

"Is there any way to call it off?" Jacko was straining his ears.

"It's no use my ringing. They will be here already. There would be no way to contact them. Why were you stupid enough to come? You'll never get past them."

"You just want the money without the aggro? Close your eyes when the rough stuff starts. But you're good on corruption. That's okay. Nobody gets physically hurt and what does it matter if a few morals are bent?" Jacko gazed contemptuously across the room. "You bloody fool; there's always the physical side where there's bent money; if not from you then from someone else like Sonny Rollins who you had to go to to get the operation off the ground. That man has only to raise an eyebrow and there's violence. You're a weak-kneed, conceited, self-seeking pratt, Wherewell. Sod everybody else. Well, the price has caught up on you, chummy. If they are out there, you are in the front of the firing line. You'd better tell me a way out."

Wherewell shook his head in despair. "There's only the fire escape and they are sure to have it covered. It leads down to a mews at the back."

"Let's try it. You go first."

"I'm not moving. I'm too scared. If they saw me they would take the worst possible view."

"And you are not scared of me?"

"Oh, yes. But I'm more scared of them. I can't stop you from going. I don't want your death on my hands. The gun you took from me is empty; I couldn't shoot anyone."

"I knew the gun was empty by its weight. You've spent a lifetime at bluffing. And you do it well. It seems we have plenty of time. Maybe they'll get fed up with waiting and go away. So you can fill in time and tell me what those names and locations are all about."

"I thought I explained. I have to face them after they've got you."

Jacko smiled ruefully. "Rollins isn't going to believe a word you say. He knows you're a con artist and he knows what every copper knows: con-men con themselves more than they con their victims. You've produced the goods and he's taken you on board but your real use has long since been over. He'll take no risks. At least you stand a chance with me. Come on, let's try."

"No. You might just as well shoot me now."

Jacko was surprised at the sudden show of courage. Wherewell had quickly surveyed his options and decided where the main risks were.

"Okay. Then I'll tell you what I think. It's quite simple and obvious really. Each name and location represents an arms dump, perhaps similar in size to the one in the New Forest. Some have been moved about and some minders have passed on for one reason or another and others have taken their place. The dumps have been built up over the years and some have been closed."

Jacko was watching Wherewell closely but the politician was showing no reaction other than distress at what was happening to him. He went on: "Now the question is, what are the arms for? They are spread far and wide throughout Europe with the main concentration in Northern Italy. Why?"

"You're so bloody clever, you give the answer."

"Come on, Wherewell, your manners are slipping. Are we now seeing the real Wherewell? The street brat? The delinquent who rose to greater things?"

"You crazy fool. Don't you realise that there are men out there who are going to blow your stupid head off." Wherewell tailed off almost to a sob. Then he slowly lifted his head, his jaw now so swollen that his face was distorted. "That's a crazy premise. There wouldn't be the kind of money in something like that which would interest us. Big, maybe, but nowhere big enough."

"That's what I thought," Jacko agreed. "So what's the catch?"

Wherewell intertwined his fingers. He seemed to have sunk into a permanent state of despair. "You are a bit of a fool really, aren't you? Up to now we weren't sure whether you had seen the arms or not. We were inclined to believe that you did not find them. It is now clear that you did." Suddenly he brightened and gave a wan smile. "That's something I've learned from you. I think I'll pass that on straight away."

Wherewell moved over to the telephone and as he lifted the receiver Jacko shot the cradle off the table and it shattered and crashed with an enormous clatter to the floor. Wherewell jumped back in fear and dropped the receiver.

"It's my favourite trick," said Jacko. "You're not going to exonerate yourself at my expense. And that's exactly what Rollins will think if I'm dead and unable to corroborate what I've told you. Think about it."

Wherewell's confidence went again. He had never been that close to a bullet before. It was made worse because he barely heard the shot.

182

"Come over here," Jacko ordered. "Come on. I've decided to make a run for it."

Wherewell was finding his legs had gone weak. He came round the settee, holding on to its back, and faced Jacko as he came forward from the door.

"Turn round. Come on." Jacko helped push Wherewell round and then cracked him on the back of the head with the Browning. Wherewell fell across the settee.

Jacko ran lightly to the hall door and peered through the spyhole. He could see nothing, nor could he hear a sound. He believed that Wherewell had told him the truth about ringing for help; his 'charity' act had not been as convincing as he had believed. It was broad daylight; there must be a limit to what they could do in full view. He ran upstairs to the bedrooms and entered the main one at the rear. He opened a window and looked down, and there, at the bottom, a lone figure in the narrow mews, was a man dressed in a cleaner's overalls who peered up to grin and wave. As Wherewell had said, that route was blocked off.

He went down to the drawing-room. Wherewell was still sprawled across the settee and now a bump on the back of his head protruded through his hair. Jacko went back to the front door and thought he heard a movement. He peered through the spyhole again but if anyone was there they were either side of the door or crouched below the spyhole level. As there was someone at the foot of the fire escape he knew there must be others.

He stood back, aimed low at the door and fired a couple of shots. He dived to one side as someone groaned with pain and the next moment he witnessed the uncanny spectacle of the door splintering, and a series of holes appearing and the thump, thump as shots tore into the furniture in line with the open drawing-room door.

As Jacko crouched he now knew they were using a silenced SMG and that the only sound from the other side of the door was the movement of the bolt action and the splintering of the wood. Jacko had declared himself but they already knew he was in there so it made little difference.

He ran up the stairs and stopped close to the top to crouch

low by the balustrade. He had almost a full view of the drawing-room. It took them another few minutes to open the door, they would want to avoid smashing it down because of the noise. Jacko slid down to a prone position.

He anticipated that they would approach carefully at first, and then suddenly there was a rush of bodies hurling themselves into the room spraying shots at random and he caught the first man as he came through. The man spun round, dropped his gun and collapsed across Wherewell. The others scattered behind the nearest furniture which was little protection but at least hid them from view.

"You've got to come up and get me," Jacko called softly through the wrought-iron banisters. He was firmly on the floor and well protected.

"We can wait all day, mate. You've got nowhere to go," a voice called back.

Jacko tried to locate the position of the voice, took careful aim and fired through one of the armchairs.

"Jesus Christ!" The alarm in the shout indicated a near miss and Jacko fired again. This time there was a loud gasp of pain and it sounded as if someone was writhing behind the chair.

"Now who's trapped?" Jacko called out. "Show a leg, anything, even nothing at all and I'll have you."

He knew what would happen next because they had no real options. They could burst from cover firing at him with everything they had while one of them rushed up the stairs. It would not be a situation he could escape from; the firepower against him would be overwhelming. But he was more worried about the man in the mews; if he came up the fire escape he would get Jacko from the rear.

Jacko slid back along the landing towards the main bedroom door which he had left open, as he had the window. He reached the window and slowly rose.

He had no idea of how much time he had. The men in the drawing-room might wait until they thought he had lost concentration; it could be their best tactic as none of them would relish the mad dash up the stairs, knowing how accurate he was. But he was sure that the man in the mews

184

would not stay there forever; he would start to get worried at the non-action and would come up the escape to investigate.

Jacko climbed over the sill and on to the fire escape platform and peered down below where the man was still waiting but not at that time looking up. And then he saw why. A group of hippies had noisily entered the mews and were playing around seemingly half drunk, or more likely drugged up.

Jacko chose the moment to climb the ladder but as he glanced down he saw he had been seen. He did not expect to be shot at even if the hippies were not there, the angle was all wrong for both of them and the range not ideal. The hippies were almost at the other end of the mews and shouting greetings at the symbol of the working class, who, unknown to them, had a hand clasped over a gun butt in his overalls pocket.

What disturbed the gunman was that Jacko was climbing up and not descending. Jacko was on to the flat roof just as the gunman jumped for the bottom platform as the hippies disappeared.

Jacko ran for the maintenance stairs; the door was still ajar where the others had entered. He ran down the stone steps and pulled up sharply when he reached the corridor which was on the same level as Wherewell's front door.

He had to hurry but he had to be quiet. He rounded the corner and could see Wherewell's door. It had been closed but the terrible rents were on full view. He tiptoed past and it was like a grave. He strode on afraid to call the elevator because of the delay and the noise it might make. He started to go down the stairs as fast as he could and heard a yell from above when he was about halfway down the first flight. He now took the stairs two at a time, realising that the mews man had moved fast and arrived in the apartment to tell the others what had happened.

He reached the hall and sprinted across with two sounds in his ears, the elevator whirring and the rush of footsteps above him. He reached the door, opened it, saw a man in overalls with a window cleaner's bucket and pushed him down the steps as he hurtled out. Jacko fled across the street to exclamations of incredulity from people who saw a priest racing away with a gun in his hand as if his life depended on it. Jacko ripped the dog-collar off as he rounded a corner and put his gun away at the same time. He turned another corner and another, found himself on a main road and raced for a passing bus which he just managed to catch. He leaned against the stairs while passengers barely took notice. His breathing was rasping and he felt in bad shape. He had no idea of how far behind Rollins' men were. But he hoped he had lost them for now.

19

Jacko was relieved to get back to the club. He threw himself on to the bed and clasped his hands behind his head to gaze at the ceiling. He had escaped but he was angry with himself for believing he could so easily fool a man who lived by deception. He had learned nothing except to satisfy himself on something he already accepted. He had placed himself in the gravest danger and had been lucky to escape; it was not enough to convince himself that he had outwitted Rollins' men; he should not have placed himself in the position of having to do it in the first place.

If he pulled a stunt like that again he could expect the worst. He could not go on for ever beating the odds. Rollins would not just be furious, he would be more determined than ever to get him; two more of his men were wounded, although how seriously it was impossible to say. They must have dragged the first injured man into the apartment hall for there had been no sign of him.

Jacko showered and changed and consoled himself with a strong whisky. He was satisfied he had been right about the arms dumps, but was no nearer to understanding their purpose. He went out to have a sandwich and a coffee and returned to the club, reluctant to keep placing himself on public view. Yet he had to continue the momentum.

He listened to various news programmes on a portable radio he had bought for his room and was shocked to hear, on the early evening news that Wherewell had been shot dead in his flat by unknown gunmen; the place had been ransacked and valuables stolen to the value of many thousands of pounds and the safe had been broken into and cleared out. Jacko could not believe it. Had Rollins decided that Wherewell had become a liability and had taken the opportunity to kill him? Or had he been killed by a stray bullet when the gunmen had rushed in? Either way, Rollins would not be disappointed; he had probably got rid of an increasing liability and his profits would now be higher.

No mention was made of injured men or even the front door being holed, so Rollins must have arranged a quick cleaning-up job at which he had always been good, before the police got anywhere near. Jacko felt the odds shortening against him. He wondered if there was any point in flying to Italy or one of the other countries mentioned on the list. If they had no more to reveal than what he had discovered in the New Forest there seemed to be little point.

He looked up Peter Jennings in the telephone directory to find he was not listed so that he could not check the address. He rang the number Ewing had given him hoping Jennings would not answer. A woman did.

"May I speak to John please? This is Colonel Baxter."

"There is no John here, I'm afraid you have the wrong number, Colonel."

"I'm so sorry." Jacko hung up, waited a few minutes then rang again. As soon as the woman answered he said, "It's seems that I've done it again. I'm dreadfully sorry. I've obviously been given the wrong number." He gave the Jennings number and added, "Major John Brooks, 3 Lorne Mews. That doesn't ring a bell?"

"Not this bell, Colonel. And, offhand I don't know a Lorne Mews. You'd better check with directory." She hung up before Jacko could ask his next question which was the street she lived in. The lady had been too shrewd for him and he smiled ruefully. He phoned Ewing at his office.

"I thought you might have gone home, Thomas. I'm trying to get Peter Jennings' address; the number you gave me is ex-directory. I'm surprised they gave it to you."

"I can't attempt to get his address without them knowing. I can hardly ring MI5 and ask for it."

"What about Telecom? You must have sufficient clout for them to help you."

"Jacko, I sometimes wonder what sort of contacts you think

188

I have. I'm not in security or the police or any of those things. I can't help you." He then added quickly, "Yes I can, or I might. I have a top police contact. Ring me in an hour at this number and we had better hope to God that this phone is not tapped, because I am sure the one at home is. And before you say it, Jacko, some of us do work long into the night."

Jacko sat in the BMW at the end of the street, the tail of the car protruding beyond the corner because it was the only space he could find. It had been dark for some time and he had been sitting there for about half an hour. He wore no disguise.

Jennings might have been home for some time, of course; it was now 7.45. Jacko decided to give it longer because he did not relish the prospect of actually calling at the house.

Gerrards Cross was a quiet, upper-bracket district, and few people passed by. The station was about a mile away and Jacko had to use his judgement on when to make his move. The street was almost clear of cars which were mainly parked on drives or in garages. Jacko decided to move nearer to the Jennings house, which lay well back behind tall hedges. He climbed out and stood by the car.

A tall man with a briefcase hurried round the corner and as he approached Jacko stepped out and asked, "You're not Peter Jennings, by any chance?"

"He lives over there." An umbrella rose like a baton and pointed the way. The man hurried on.

It was almost eight o'clock and Jacko was beginning to feel the chill when a car approached, slowed, and turned into the Jennings' drive. Jacko sprinted across the road to crunch his way over the gravel and called out as a man climbed out, "Are you Peter Jennings?"

The figure stiffened and slammed the car door. "I know that voice." He turned.

"Willie Jackson," said Jacko, holding out a hand. "Sorry to waylay you like this. Can we talk?"

"You want to come in?" In the dark, in spite of the outside house light, Jennings appeared rather like a short, dumpy silhouette with his glasses reflecting what little light there was.

189

"I'd rather we sat in one of the cars."

"Okay. I must pop in and tell my wife or she'll wonder what I'm up to."

"She'll have to wonder. Let's get it over with. Your car or mine?"

"You're an unreasonable sod, Jacko. It won't take me a minute."

"I know. That's what I'm afraid of. Your wife is very competent. She'll raise the alarm even as we speak."

"You've spoken to her?" Jennings stepped nearer, peering up at Jacko in an owlish way.

"She doesn't know it but, yes, I have. She's a security credit to you. I had to get your address from another source. Come on, Peter, don't make me threaten you, I'm getting tired of doing that. Just a short talk."

"All right. May I drop my case in the porch first?"

"I'll be right behind you."

"You're a suspicious bugger. It's just that I don't want to sit with it perched on my knee." Jennings crunched over to the porch with Jacko right behind him.

"There are no secret buzzers in the porch," said Jennings in derision as they walked back to the car.

Even climbing in was a performance, with Jacko insisting that they got in either side simultaneously. It was hot in the car and Jennings must have had his heater on full blast.

"Right," said Jennings. "You have a captive audience. Make it quick; my wife will have heard me arrive."

"I want to do a deal. I want you to hang on to Georgette Roberts but tell her she is perfectly safe and that you are holding her for her own protection. I will give you a note to confirm the arrangement. And she is to have the maximum comfort."

"We haven't got her, Jacko." Before Jacko could explode, Jennings hastily added, "But we probably know who has and will convey your wishes subject to a fair exchange from you."

"Have you the authority to promise this?"

"Not immediately, but I don't see any problem provided you co-operate. We'll have to know where to contact you."

190

"No. I'll ring you at Curzon Street."

"Can't you trust us that much? If not why the blazes are you here?"

With the fan and the heater off the car was steaming up but Jennings made no effort to clean the windscreen.

"I don't trust you. I'm having to compromise. Georgie must be worried sick at what has happened to her. I haven't forgotten how you lot tried to top Sam Towler when he was working for you."

"I heard about that. It was one man; one renegade who cocked something up and tried to find a scapegoat. We are not all like that, Jacko."

"It was not one man," retorted Jacko angrily. "Your Chief Cook was also protecting his rear end. Don't bullshit me. And you wonder why I don't trust you."

"Look, the fellow directly involved had a heart attack shortly after, and died; probably as a result of that caper. The Head Chef resigned a year later under pressure. We've been under new management for some time now. Are we going to do a deal or not? We really do want to help and we are very much interested in what you might know."

Jennings turned to gaze at Jacko. "Okay," he continued. I'll come absolutely clean. We have your girlfriend and she's living off the fat of the land. She may even know who we are but we would, of course, deny everything particularly when we know there are others who would like to get hold of her. We wanted to draw you out and we were right, weren't we? We snatched her and here you are ready to do a deal. We have a great respect for you, Jacko, even if you do sometimes tread on our corns. For goodness sake, trust us."

"That will always be difficult." Jacko then added, "I'll give you what I know but I might need some help in return. I have a list of names and locations around Europe one of which I broke into to find a cache of arms. I would guess it to be early NATO vintage but in pristine condition. I am sure that Sonny Rollins and his mob are behind it alongside an unlikely but charismatic character called Reginald Dine."

"That would have been the New Forest shindig. You were sticking your neck out there."

"I nearly lost it. Now I can't make out what the hell it is all about. The list has been changed many times, some entries completely crossed out. I would not have thought there is enough money in a cache like that, even a lot of them, to get Sonny Rollins to make such elaborate plans for protection and to send out torpedoes to top me."

"Did you get this list from Simon Wherewell; the MP just found shot dead? We've been interested in him for some time."

"Yes. Don't ask me how. That is really all I have. What's it all about?"

"It's more than you think. Wherewell used confidential information, saw the commercial value, contacted Rollins, who, presumably with Dine, saw far wider possibilities than Wherewell could ever have dreamed of and put them to a use we are still trying to uncover. In spite of what you say there is a lot of money in small arms, particularly spread far and wide as these are. It goes back to the early 1950s, Jacko. Operation Sword. Or in Italy Operation Gladio, from the Latin for a short lethal sword, and in Germany, Operation Schwert and so on. In Greece for some incredible reason it is known as Operation Red Sheepskin. You see, I'm telling you much more than you have told me because we need your particular skills."

"And I'm bloody expendable."

"Aren't we all? But then we chose to do what we are doing. The whole thing was a CIA brainchild and they financed most of it. Those were the Cold War days and nobody trusted Russia and Stalin's intentions. If he thought he could have got away with overrunning Europe he would have done it.

"To guard against the possibility secret arms dumps were buried all over Europe with the idea of arming guerrilla groups to operate in the event of occupation. The scale of the operation is still obscure but has perhaps been best revealed in Italy by a crusading judge named Felice Casson in 1990. To go into the detail of his campaign would take far too long. But it emerged that in Northern Italy alone there were 139 secret dumps. Some say there were at least 12 more.

"At the time, 1951, American and British Intelligence

192

trained 622 guerrillas in Sardinia but each of these was allowed to pick 15 men to serve him. We are now talking about 10,000 men, largely out of control, in one country alone. Spread it through the rest of Europe in varying degrees and you have a well-armed army."

Jacko was listening intently to every word and then the spell was broken as the front door opened and a woman came out with a flashlight to see what had happened to Jennings, who lowered the car window immediately. "It's all right, darling. I'm talking. Won't be long."

"Why don't you come in and talk? It's warmer."

"No, it's okay. We won't be much longer; really, I am all right. Don't fret. I'll be in soon."

"You have a good wife there," said Jacko as Mrs Jennings went reluctantly back into the house. "I hope she doesn't call anyone?"

"No. Don't worry. Where were we? Yes. Now President Andreotti admitted that Gladio was born in 1951 but that most of the arms caches were recalled in 1972." Jennings turned to Jacko. "How many do you think is most? There is quite a history of their usage up to recent years and there is little doubt that some of them have been used for various terrorist activities.

"The Dutch admit there are still some around. Boys playing in Rhedan found a cache. But it would take all night to give you an inkling of how they have been used and by whom. We, in Britain, don't even admit they existed here. But they did and still do. Some of the original gladiators still exist but are now old men, some have passed on, but who has the arms now? Why are they so difficult to find? How many of them have been moved around? The fact is, Jacko, that this problem is so serious that there are now Gladiator investigators operating all over the place and not getting too far. The European Parliament has agreed to set up a Commission of Inquiry. There are a lot of arms out there and a lot of wrong people trying to get hold of them. That should fill you in. Now, can you get a copy of your list to me? I want to compare the changes with the list we have. Some may have been crossed off simply because they don't exist any more, but others may have been changed by Rollins and Dine for their own reasons."

Jacko leaned forward and wiped his side of the windscreen but the temperature had dropped sharply since they had got into the car. He gazed through the misted glass and said, "I can do that. But just what the hell do you think I can add to that? My own research was leading in that direction but you have told me far more than I knew already. What's your point?"

"I've just given you a brief outline of the history of the dumps. There is little doubt that some have closed down and little doubt too that a good many have been nicked. And some dumps have been moved for all sorts of reasons, some of them disturbingly sinister, depending on the way one looks at things. On the lighter side, some dumps have been built over, one site has a multi-storey hotel over it. We think there is still a comprehensive network of dumps which has come under organised control and is being used, or will be used, for God knows what. It's scary because it is not just Rollins and his crowd but his equivalent around Europe and the bond we believe has been formed between them."

"But this is for SO11 to deal with. And where do I come in?"

"If it's political, then it's for us. At times it's a fine line between the Services and often quite a problem. We're hanging on because, so far as I know, we know more than the rest and have a good liaison with the other intelligence services; we are all working together and have limited success. There are two reasons why we need you. You can do things where we are restricted, like the other night. But you also seem to have built up some form of contact with Reginald Dine and he intrigues us very much. It's difficult to see where he fits in."

"Have you checked his background?"

"Far more than we've checked yours. It stands up."

"Which doesn't mean a bloody thing."

"Which doesn't mean a bloody thing," Jennings conceded. "It's not just the arms. The New Forest dump is not at its original burial place so far as our information goes. But most of the records are missing if ever there were any; at that time everybody thought everybody else was a red agent so nobody trusted anybody and probably little was committed to paper."

"I can't go back to the New Forest so soon. I can't expect to get away with it again."

"But you found the arms; why should you go back?"

"Because I'm not satisfied. There is another angle on Dine I am following up but it may come to nothing. There's something about him that simply doesn't fit in with Rollins and if it came to choosing who would come out top between those two I would plump for Dine. There's a lot of experience there. And that makes him a very formidable man."

"What kind of experience?"

"That's the question, isn't it? What about Georgie?"

"After this chat I think we have no option but to let her go. I don't see how we can hold her now, if you are co-operating. But we can arrange some protection. By the way, just how did you get involved in this in the first place?"

"I was asked to do a favour for the French. A simple thing really. But I trod on toes that I didn't know were there. When Dine blew up my Ferrari and sent me a dummy letter bomb I knew that the enquiry was far from simple. When I wanted to pull out I found that they would not let me simply because they had too much to hide and they didn't know how much I knew, which at that stage was damn all. I don't think they know I found the arms."

"Are you sure?"

"Pretty sure."

There was an uncomfortable silence. Jennings blew his nose loudly and then sat staring ahead. "Did you kill Wherewell?"

"Would I tell you if I had? No. He was either killed accidentally by bullets meant for me, or the opportunity was taken to get rid of him. I think he had served his usefulness to Rollins. Whether his death was accident or design Rollins won't be shedding any tears."

Jennings nodded his head in the dark. "You've proved my point. You can do things we dare not try."

"Balls. But with me it doesn't matter if I'm caught. I'd better get back."

They climbed from the car, slamming the doors, and walked to the porch. Jennings said, "So we still don't know how to contact you."

"Better not. Take the phone tap off Thomas Ewing. He's about to complain to the PM and as the original enquiry stemmed from that source you'd better be careful. You wouldn't want your funds suddenly cut."

"You assume too much, Jacko. Guilty conscience. Do let us know what you come up with. It's been a real pleasure to meet you."

The two men shook hands and Jacko was just about to walk back down the drive when he said, "Do you see Dine as any kind of security risk?"

Jennings stood thoughtfully for some seconds before replying, "That's a good question. Perhaps you'll be able to find the answer."

Jacko walked slowly down the drive and out into the street to return to the BMW. When he reached the car he looked back towards the Jennings house but could not see it behind the tall hedges. The road was quiet again. He climbed in wondering why it had all been so pleasant and how he had come away with far more knowledge than he had given. They had taken great pains to find him for so little, particularly when Ewing had told him they could not tell him anything because it was classified. What had suddenly unclassified what Jennings had told him?

Jacko drove off slowly, watching his mirror. He turned a corner and stopped, double parking. Nothing happened, no car went past behind him although one coming towards him gave him a couple of flashes for parking so awkwardly. He decided he was becoming paranoid, that his basic distrust of the Security Service was so great that he could believe nothing good about them. He saw nothing wrong with that but he did accept that he could not work alone. He needed the information just given to him, and he might need other help.

He drove all the way back to London at a speed so sober he did not believe it to be possible. He parked the car, went up

196

to his room and rang Susan. Georgie answered and he could not believe his luck. He almost broke down as he talked to her without letting her know that he had done a deal to see that she was looked after. He wondered if she knew that she had minders? But it was not the time to ask. She was none the worse for the experience and as Jennings had said, she had lived off the fat of the land, and her locked room had been extremely well furnished. She had been driven back by limousine. They talked as lovers will and when they finally hung up Jacko had to admit to himself that Jennings had not only kept his word but had been incredibly quick about it.

He went out to snatch a late meal and when he returned he found a message to ring a Mr Cole at a Hereford number. He rang back straight away.

"Michael David Deering: reported missing in Korea in January 1953," said Jimmy Cole. "Reported dead in March the same year. He ran out of luck, Jacko, the bloody armistice was in July 1953. He died of wounds to chest and legs. A mortar bomb. He was twenty-three. He was awarded a posthumous MM. Is that what you wanted?"

"Just the job. I'll send the case of whisky, Jimmy. You must have pulled out the stops to get that so quickly."

Jimmy laughed. "We have ways of influencing people. Come up and see us some time."

Did it help? Jacko decided to fly to Hong Kong the next day.

20

Jacko rang Peter Jennings at his home early next morning. "I didn't want to go through the red tape of ringing Curzon Street," he explained. "Thanks for releasing Georgie so soon. What I need now is a contact in Hong Kong. Not too upright a citizen, or at least someone with his ear to the underworld. And I want the return air fare and hotel expenses."

Jennings laughed. "I'm having my breakfast; that's always a bad time to spring that sort of problem on me. I can give you a contact but the expenses are another matter."

"The Security Service is the only outfit that does not declare its budget. You're swimming in the stuff. I've already spent a lot out of my own pocket. Do you want me to go or not?"

"Ring me back in ten minutes and I'll give you a contact; I need to check first."

Having someone like Jennings behind him had its uses, like getting on a heavily booked plane. He flew Cathay Pacific because he wanted to feel he was already there. It was the first real relaxation Jacko had experienced for some days and it was not until they were taking off that he realised just how tired he was. He slept for most of the way, often flying over territory he had operated in for one reason or another. By the time the plane was descending in the canyon formed by hills on one side and skyscrapers on the other to land at Kai Tak Airport he felt refreshed when most passengers were feeling weary.

He was using his own passport and it seemed that Jennings had smoothed the way for him because he was through immigration and customs while the others were still queuing. The usual Rolls-Royces were waiting outside to take clients to the Peninsular Hotel, but for him there was a battered Cadillac.

A tall, thin European approached, cream jacket open to show a white silk shirt. The face was narrow, lined and weathered but in it were two twinkling blue eyes which looked out with amused cynicism at all they saw. "Willie Jackson?"

"Jacko. Are you Sam Winterman?"

"It's been my name for too long. I'm thinking of changing it."

"To Fred Winterman?"

Winterman smiled. "The oldies are always the best. Get in. She's ancient but she can move." He spoke in a weary sort of way as if it was all too much effort.

They climbed into the car, the upholstery in surprisingly good condition showing that the cynicism did not extend to the vehicle. "I've booked you in at the Hong Kong Hotel. I thought you might lose yourself more easily into the depths of obscurity there, than say, the Peninsular or the Mandarin. And it is handily placed for reaching Hong Kong Island."

"I know it," said Jacko easily. "I've stayed there before."

Winterman gave a glance of surprise. "They didn't tell me you knew the place. I'm sorry."

Jacko grinned. "Along the mainland border, mostly. You'll know all about it. If you can supply me with what I want to know I might need to stay only the one night."

"You're full of surprises. Most people would give their ears to stay longer. It must have left a nasty taste in your mouth."

"Not really. Although I did get fed up seeing empty and hopeless expressions on disillusioned faces when they were sent back. But it's not that; I must get back, I've spent far too long on what I'm doing. I'm grateful for your help."

They drove through Kowloon to the hotel which was adjacent to the ferry and the Chinese shopping arcade. It was a slightly sprawling place with plenty of room and an enormous foyer where they selected a place to sit.

"You sure you don't want to freshen up first? You haven't checked in yet."

"That can wait. I wouldn't mind a coffee, though."

"They prefer us to go to the cafeteria over there but I think I can swing it." When the coffees had been ordered Jacko said, "I don't know how much London has told you, but I want to check up on a character called Reginald Dine. I believe he was born here."

Winterman leaned back on the padded circular seat. The foyer was loosely packed with people, active in a leisurely sort of way. Across the way a man was being interviewed by a woman who was obviously a press reporter, and a photographer was moving around taking flash shots. "I remember Dine. It must be ten years or so since he left here." He mused for a while, eyes screwed tight. "He had a son. It was rumoured that the mother was one of the boat people at Aberdeen. I don't think they were ever seen together. She's probably still alive although you'd have one hell of a job in finding her."

Jacko said, "I've got to know Dine just a little. My impression is that he may have deserted the mother for hard realistic reasons but he would not have left her destitute; he would have looked after her financially."

Winterman gave one of his slight cynical smiles. "So we'd be looking for a boat woman who had come into money and did not know to which section of the community she belonged. That makes it a lot easier."

At first Jacko was angry at the response but quickly saw that Winterman was right. The Chinese were a very close-knit society and even if someone knew her, it was unlikely they would tell. He dwelled a little on a woman who had had her child taken from her because she did not fit in, and he felt a little less respect for Dine. But then, that was the whole problem; he knew nothing of the circumstances that had led to such a sad situation. The fact that Dine had gone with a boat woman at all made no sense. And it was some twenty-odd years ago. To try to find Lonnie's mother would be hopeless. He said, "How far back can you remember Dine?"

Winterman waited while the coffees were put down and stared thoughtfully at them. He was sitting with his legs crossed, his wiry body turned slightly away from Jacko, his gaze shrewdly roaming the foyer. "That's a bit difficult. As I recall, Dine was always something of a loner, didn't mix a great deal. I seem to remember that he would attend those functions where it would look odd if he didn't but would never stay long. A wealthy man, but that's nothing new in this place; millionaires are common. That's why I never became one."

Jacko smiled. "How did he make his money?"

Winterman swivelled round. "Jacko, my boy, you should know that that is not the sort of question one asks in Hong Kong."

"You don't know, or you don't want to tell?"

"You're persistent; I think I'm warming to you, but that does not mean I know, or if I did, I would tell you."

"Then you're a dead loss to me. I need all the information I can get."

"You're asking about someone who left the colony over a decade ago, whom nobody knew very well because he kept himself to himself, and who was never my personal friend. I don't know how he made his money, only that he was never short of it."

"You mean he flashed it around?"

"Don't be obtuse, Jacko. He lived in a mansion up Victoria Peak. Apart from the Peak tram and a road that winds forever, it was not all that accessible. Which was probably why he bought it. It had splendid views towards Kowloon, and before you ask, yes, I was there once at one of his rare parties. And even then he did not put in too much of an appearance. I remember that because everyone was so surprised he held a party at all."

"Was this shortly before he left Hong Kong?"

Winterman raised a brow sensing a trap in the question. "I don't know what kind of memory you think I have but that's a fine detail."

"You have the type of memory," said Jacko picking up his cup, "that London rate or they would not be paying my expenses in order to meet you, nor would they recommend you. Was it?"

"I think it was. I believe he left a few weeks later. Sold up

201

completely. An Australian magnate has the house now. He's freer with his parties. What is in your mind?"

Jacko wished there was somewhere less public than a busy hotel foyer, no matter how large, but there appeared to be no-one near them. "You know how difficult it is to get UK citizenship these days unless you were born in the UK. I gather he was born here. That can't be too common with Europeans. Most of them are doing a tour of duty in one form or another; there are plenty of civil servants, airline personnel, and military here. Businessmen who live here come from all over the place, but did not start here. They can't all be celibate so some are born here. But does anyone know anything about Dine's parents?"

"I believe they were born here. It's difficult to dig it up at this stage but I think they were killed during the war. I'm pretty certain."

"So who brought Dine up?"

"You really do want to get to the bottom, don't you? At that stage he was old enough to look after himself. As far as I could make out at the time he was not short of money when they died. I think they were merchants; he probably carried on in the same way."

"Merchants! That's a good description for so much in Hong Kong; the colony grew on merchants." Jacko gave Winterman an old-fashioned look. "It can cover a multitude of sins, that name, and tells us nothing." He finished his coffee and put down the cup. "Is that all you know about him?"

"Just about. There is a man, a Chinese, who was Dine's chief accountant. He's over on the island. I can give you his name and address although I doubt that he'll help. He's probably on a fat retainer."

"Okay. Just before I check in, tell me this. How difficult would it be to get false papers?"

"No problem at all. Depends on how much you want to pay. There are more than a few around here with false papers. But if you are talking about the kind of false papers that stand up to close police and intelligence investigation, then I would say it is very difficult indeed. When those boys dig deep they dig all the way."

202

"You mean there's no such thing as bribery here?" Jacko was quietly laughing. "For a sceptic, and I could have said cynic, you have suddenly gone all naïve, matey."

"Well, I suppose if the money is big enough it will corrupt. I'd better give you that name and address."

By the time Jacko checked in and the porter carried his single case to his room, he was beginning to feel a little jet lag. He undid the case and put his clothes away in the wardrobe then ran a bath and washed off the sweat of travelling. He lay on the bed in his underwear and thought it had been a long way to come for what little he had learned from Winterman.

He sat up and opened the drawer of the bedside table to look at the piece of paper with the address Winterman had given him: Li Chai, Juniper, Wan Street. He returned it to the drawer; Winterman was probably right, he could expect little from someone who had worked for Dine unless he had reason to dislike him.

There was a discreet knock on the door, Jacko called, "Enter", and a porter came in with a trolley on which was a bottle in an ice bucket and a splendid arrangement of flowers in a cut-glass vase. "Shall I put the flowers over there, sir?"

The porter took them over to the dressing-table and placed them in front of the mirror so that it appeared to be a double arrangement.

"What's this? Compliments of the management?" Jacko was sure he did not rate the treatment.

"The card is on the tray, sir." The porter left without waiting for a tip and Jacko climbed off the bed and crossed to the trolley.

The bottle was Moët, the ice packed around it. Beside the bucket was a plain champagne flute. On a salver was an envelope which he opened with misgivings and drew out a short letter. He knew who it was from before he read the first word. "Enjoy the champagne, Jacko. I hope you can manage all of it. The flowers are because I know you have a good eye for things of beauty. Do enjoy Hong Kong while you can. It has always been a very special place to me. I still have many friends there, most of whom will do anything for me. Anything, Jacko. Take care. With affection, RD."

Jacko stood quite still for a moment then realised he should not be surprised; this was Dine's domain. His influence was still strong here. Jacko uncorked the champagne and poured a glassful, sad that he could not share it with Georgie who did not know he had left Britain. He raised the fizzing glass and said, "Thanks, Reg. Your warnings have toned down quite a lot." But he reflected that they were no less menacing. Even when he was absent it would be easier for Dine to operate here than in London. His scale of contacts was already clear by the fact that he knew Jacko was here. It was impressive and it was scary.

Jacko decided to spend what was left of the day in wandering around the arcades. He bought a superb pony carved from agate, and the total oriental flavour surrounded him and brought Dine even closer as if he was following every move. And when Jacko looked around him at the milling crowds he realised that could well be true. Dine knew what Jacko was up to and would protect himself to the limit. Jacko had brought no gun into the colony because of the airport checks. If he wanted a weapon he knew he could get one but it would take time to organise, and meanwhile he was unarmed.

He slept well enough that night, thinking that Dine would not be so crude as to take the risk of having someone break into his room. The next morning he caught the ferry to Hong Kong Island, preferring the old-fashioned way to the underpass. The slow pitching and tossing of the junks brought back many memories.

Except for the backcloth and the sudden view of Victoria Peak rising like a scarred monument, the approach to Hong Kong was like seeing a mini New York. He disembarked and lost himself in the myriad bustling streets of varying attraction. There would always be a fascination about this place and, not for the first time, he wondered why Dine had left it; there were still a few years left before annexation and Dine had left so long ago. Somehow he seemed to belong here.

Jacko found a cab to take him to Wan Street and was surprised when he arrived. It seemed to be a world apart and solely for the very wealthy. It was difficult to understand that a short distance away was the commercial bustle of a wealthy island. Yet in this unexpected backwater, a curved, rather narrow street, high walls protected expensive mansions.

The huge gates between the white pillars of Juniper were hand-forged wrought iron and must have cost a small fortune in themselves. There was a buzzer and a voice box. Jacko paid off the taxi and rang the buzzer. A man's voice enquired, "Yes?"

"I would like to speak to Mr Li Chai. I'm just in from London. My name is Willie Jackson."

"I've been expecting you, Mr Jackson. You should have retained the cab, it's rather a long walk up the drive."

Only one gate swung back and Jacko started walking over gravel. It was a circular drive and as he crunched on, the house came slowly into view section by section and it was not at all what he had expected. It was a white Corinthian-columned manor, superb in architecture and generous in its spaciousness. Two uniformed Chinese servants waited for him under the canopy at the main entrance.

As he approached they bowed and waved him forward and it was soon clear that they spoke no English. He entered the capacious hall and they led the way to a room on the right. They opened the door, ushered him in and left, closing the door behind them. He was in a room of oriental luxury, exquisite Chinese rugs were scattered around the marbled floor; silk tapestries portrayed early battles.

"I thought you might have called last night," said the slight figure at the end of the room. "I believe you are a man of action and I was rather disappointed that you didn't. You would have been perfectly safe." The English was clipped but otherwise perfect.

As Jacko walked towards the figure he saw that Li Chai was dressed in European clothes and was almost diminutive. The little man had cheerful features and was smiling as if at some private joke as he stepped towards Jacko to proffer his hand. Jacko took it feeling little flesh but a good deal of bone, yet he did not place Li Chai as being older than Dine.

"Do sit down. Anywhere."

Anywhere was right. There were so many substantial chairs, all of which looked comfortable, that Jacko had difficulty in choosing one and when he did it seemed to mould round him. This was a palace.

"I can see you are impressed. You should have seen Mr Dine's place at Victoria Peak. It made this one look like a lodge."

Jacko did not believe it. Li Chai would seem to have done very well for himself but it was perfectly clear that he still had strong links with Dine. "How did you arrive at the name?"

"Juniper? It was the name of Reginald's yacht. It still is; I bought it from him."

"It is kind of you to see me, Mr Chai, but I doubt now that you can help me."

Li Chai, now seated, seemed to have chosen the biggest chair and was almost lost in it. "That entirely depends on exactly what you want of me. Don't mistake hospitality for goodwill, Mr Jackson. What is it you want?"

"Please call me Jacko, everybody does."

"Not me. We Chinese set higher values on formality. Don't evade the issue. You are here, tell me what it is you want."

"You probably know already. And I can see that visiting you was a mistake. I was stupid enough to think that you might be a one-time disgruntled employee of Reginald Dine. It is obvious that you are not."

"You might also observe that it is unlikely that I was ever his employee. We were partners, Mr Jackson. We still are. We have always been close, as close as an oriental and an occidental can ever be. We are virtual brothers. We taught each other a good deal. You see, you have learned something for your trouble after all. Do put your question to me."

Jacko noticed one of the servants come in with a tray containing tall glasses filled with what looked like orange juice. One glass was placed beside him on a coaster on a small Chinese-Chippendale table.

"Fresh oranges," said Li Chai. "Just squeezed. Delightfully refreshing."

"What sort of business do you do, Mr Chai? I hope I'm not being rude but it must be extremely profitable, to provide such luxury." Jacko felt the question was too bold and that he

206

would get nowhere at all with this small, cheerful character who knew he was in total control.

"No one thing. There is a lot of money to be made here for those prepared to work and I have lived here all my life. We also have one of the most active stock exchanges in the world. The colony is massively wealthy and, like so many wealthy countries, full of deprivation. Does that answer your question?"

"Did you ever deal in arms?"

"We still do. We don't create their need but supply those who want them, if we are able to obtain the stock. But that is a relatively small part of our business. What you are dying to ask is what Mr Dine was up to when he was here. Why is that so important to you?"

Jacko felt that as he was in the lions'den he might just as well go all the way. "His background seems to be obscure and it intrigues me. I am sure he has already told you of the circumstances in which we met. But strange things have happened since then. There have been attempts on my life which I would like to get to the bottom of."

"But Reginald likes you, even admires you, why would he want to kill you?"

"Because he's a realist, no matter how reluctantly he might do it. He sees me as a threat."

"And are you a threat?"

Chai's orange juice remained untouched whereas Jacko felt a great need for his. But he left it where it was and said, "I'm trying to stay alive. Part of the threat to me is anchored in his past. It may be suicidal for me to say that to you but you must already know from him."

Chai spread his small hands in surprise. "There is nothing strange about his past. My parents knew his parents, and I remember them well. It was tragic that they died so young, but many did at that time. It was a distressing period. He was not left wanting and has been successful ever since. He left Hong Kong because he wanted to get back to his roots and be close to his son while he was at university. I miss him a good deal. A fine man."

Jacko was bursting to ask for more detail about the deaths

but to do that would cast aspersion on what Chai had just told him and it could be dangerous to question his word in that way. He was not going to learn anything he did not already know. He could check through old press reports but this man would know almost as soon as he turned the pages. But Li Chai was right, he had learned something but that only increased his fears. His questions had been answered yet he had effectively come up against a wall of silence. It would be difficult now to find anyone who did not like Dine sufficiently to talk about him. They had probably been eliminated long ago.

When Jacko gazed across at Chai, the little man was smiling as if to say, 'You'll never get past me'. But Jacko felt in a more dangerous position than before. If Dine wanted to get rid of him then this was the place to do it.

"You appear to be uncomfortable, Mr Jackson. And you have not touched your orange juice." Chai laughed in a softly chiding way. "It's not poisoned." He picked up his own glass and drank from it to prove the point.

Jacko was disturbed enough not to touch the drink although he believed Chai. "Well, that seems to be that," he exclaimed. "I'm sorry to have taken up your time."

"Don't apologise, I've enjoyed our chat. I don't get many interesting visitors." Chai eased himself off his chair. "I'll let Reginald know we met just in case you do not get the opportunity yourself."

Jacko was seeing a threat in every innuendo. He rose, took hold of his glass and raised it to his lips and drank. "Very nice indeed," he said. "I wonder if I can ring for a taxi from here?"

Chai approached with his hand held out. "It has already been done." Their hands met.

Jacko wondered how Chai had ordered a taxi; there had been no move he had noticed, no pressing of buttons.

"No doubt you will fly straight back?"

Why did that sound like an instruction? But really, it did not matter what Chai said; Jacko could put no credence to any of it. Chai struck him as a man who could tell smooth convincing lies in his sleep.

They walked over towards the massive door and it was opened by one of the servants just before they reached it. Jacko reflected that Chai must have some form of communication on him. What he noticed at once, which had not been on view when he arrived, was that the servant now wore white gloves. There was nothing new in that but why put them on for his departure? The pressure was subtly being applied without a wrong word being spoken. In criminal terms it reduced men like Rollins to the fourth division.

Chai escorted him on to the huge porch as the taxi arrived on cue. Jacko climbed in the back. "The Hong Kong Hotel," he instructed. He looked up at the porch as the taxi drew away but Li Chai and his servant had already gone indoors. He sat back thinking over the futility of the trip as the taxi slowed down at the gates. Why had he not noticed before that the driver was also wearing white gloves? Then he noticed the glass partition between himself and the driver like in a London taxi. But this was not London and the taxis here were virtually saloon cars.

With an empty feeling of resignation he tried to lower the window to find it would not move and when he tried the door catch the same thing happened. He had enacted the whole scene like an amateur and had been trapped like one. He accepted the situation without rancour but with a good deal of self-disgust. There was no point in yelling or struggling, he had to let matters take their course and try to keep his wits about him, something he had not done since arriving here.

As he sat back he reflected angrily that he had been sewn up in Hong Kong since stepping off the plane and he began to wonder at Winterman's part. He had no idea where he was being taken until they took the underpass to Kowloon. At least he was going that far. When the driver veered away from the direction of the hotel Jacko started to get worried.

It was then that he missed having a gun, but if he had learned anything at all about Li Chai it was that he would already know that he was not carrying one. It was not often that Jacko felt he had lost all control of a situation but it had happened now. He was helpless.

He began to brighten a little when he realised they were on

the airport road and when the driver finally turned into the concourse at Kai Tak he began to feel a sense of relief. When they pulled up the driver spoke through an old-fashioned tube. The speaker was somewhere behind Jacko's head. In bad English he said, "A man has your ticket inside. Your seat is booked. And the man has your case. You will only leave the airport on the aeroplane. We wait to kill you if you step outside. People will watch you inside. You understand?"

"I understand. But I haven't settled my hotel bill."

"It is paid. You lucky. You do what I say. You get out now."

Jacko tried the door again and it opened. He climbed out. The deep roar of aircraft engines seemed to be all about him but suddenly they were like a lullaby. He walked towards the departure bays knowing he was being watched all the way and wondering why they were letting him go. There must be a reason; he felt he was stepping from the dock after being pronounced guilty, to a place of execution where he would be buried without trace.

21

The moment Jacko was back at the Army and Navy he rang Georgie, and then Ewing, to let them know he was all right. Only then did he tell Georgie where he had been but without explanation, finishing by telling her that it would not be long now. He had been saying that to her all along but, after her kidnap, she no longer argued. He added, "If you see anyone hanging about who does not look too sinister, he's keeping an eye on you. Don't fret."

He rang Dine to get no reply. He did not call Jennings, who probably already knew that he was back. But he did wonder about him and whether there was something he was holding back; Winterman, Jennings' contact in Hong Kong, had not added much to what he already knew and seriously misinformed him about Li Chai.

What he saw as the most important call, he could not make until early evening because of the time difference, but he booked a person-to-person to Glenn Patton at the FBI building in New York. Glenn Patton had been in the Green Berets at the time when Jacko had been serving in the SAS. They had sometimes trained together in Wales, Germany and the USA, and had remained good friends.

Meanwhile Jacko had to curb his impatience and wait. He still could not get used to the idea of how easily he had been allowed to slip the leash in Hong Kong. It could only be by arrangement with Dine and he must have a motive.

Jennings was sitting at his desk when Pat Ramsey knocked on his door. Ramsey went in and waited a few minutes while Jennings illustrated his seniority by ignoring him as he studied some papers. After a while of restlessness

Ramsey said, "I can see you are busy, I'll call back. You probably know already what you need to know about Willie Jackson." He opened the door to leave as Jennings called out, "Sorry, Pat. Everything is piling up. Come back and close the door."

Ramsey came back and sat down without invitation; he was tired of Jennings' little foibles.

"What's this about Willie Jackson?" demanded Jennings.

"Did you know he was christened Willie? Most people think his name is William but it's not." Ramsey felt better when he saw Jennings was irritated.

Jennings leaned back and threw a ballpoint on the desk. "If you are going to play games, piss off, Pat. I'm too busy. Now what is it you know that I don't know?"

"I hear you are looking for him?"

"That's no secret. But we are in touch. So where is he?"

"It was secret enough not to reach me. I've only just heard about it. We are hiding him ourselves."

"Are you trying to be bloody funny?"

"We were using him about a year or so ago. Things got rough, I suppose much the same as they are now, from what I've heard. He needed somewhere safe to billet, somewhere nobody would think of looking. There was pressure on us at the time and the matter was important enough to try to keep him out of trouble. We were also still getting repercussions from the way we had treated his friend Sam Towler, so were under some obligation to help Jackson even if it stuck in our throats. And it almost did because we had a lot of resistance."

Ramsey looked smug knowing he was telling Jennings something he did not know but might have looked into. "Upstairs decided to get him membership in the Army and Navy. We knew that if we did it openly their committee would resist and almost certainly refuse point blank. After all Jackson was only a non-commissioned officer; they wouldn't wear that. But we have several members in the club and national security comes before club rules however much they did not like it. We had one man on the committee who, rather than agree, resigned from the committee. That left the way

212

for a proposer and a seconder who resisted until they saw their prospects here dwindling by the day. It was easy to fix his background; I think he became a Lieutenant-Colonel in REME. In fairness to the man I believe he used it for only a short time. He did not mix too well with officers."

Jennings gazed across the desk; he did not like Ramsey and the feeling was mutual. "Are you sure about this?"

"It's on record. Very few knew. Very few wanted to know. It was the perfect place when almost certainly his enemies would be looking at sleazy boarding houses and hotels and doss houses in general."

Jennings smiled slowly, then caught up with his own satisfaction. "That does not mean he is there now. Do you have the name?"

"Lieutenant-Colonel William Baxter."

Jennings reached for the telephone and then paused. "If we arranged it he would know; it would be the last place he would stay."

Ramsey said, "I've come in on this late and only because I was slightly involved at the time the membership was arranged. Would I be right in saying that he was hiding from Rollins and his mob?"

Jennings inclined his head. "That's true; at first. But things have changed and he knows we would like to trace his hideout, so it begins not to make too much sense."

Ramsey shook his head. "He never knew we fixed his membership. He was dealing with Thomas Ewing. Ewing wouldn't tell him how it was fixed and Jackson would probably be furious if he ever found out we did it; he hates our guts."

Jennings thought for a while, then said, "Let's see." He lifted the phone.

"Glenn? How are you, mate? Haven't seen you since I went bananas with a gun in New Jersey. I hope you still have Cirrillo safely tucked away."

"The last I heard was he was walking around on a frame. I've no sympathy. What are you into that makes you call me?"

"How close are you to the Washington Archives?"

"Goddamm it, you certainly pick your cases. What do you want to know?"

"A classified list under Record Group 389."

"Just where the hell did you get that from? If it's classified I probably won't be able to get near it."

"The number is quoted in our own press. My guess, though, is that neither your Government nor ours will want it declassified. Ever. Do you think you can get a peek at it?"

"If I'm going to Washington I can try, but that might be some time away. I don't rate my chances, Jacko."

"Okay. If I give you one single item to look for would that help?"

"I'd still have to dig out the whole file and I'd still have to get up there. There's never anything easy with you."

"Okay. Plan B. Have you a close buddy on the spot who would do it for you? Just the one item? For HM Government?"

"Bull."

"For the Queen, then?"

Patton laughed. "You don't change do you? I'll give it my best shot for Princess Di but will promise nothing. I suppose you want it now?"

"Life and death."

"Yeah! Your life and my death. I'll do what I can. Now give me the item."

When Jacko hung up he had a better idea of why Jennings wanted to keep a close eye on him. It began to make sense.

On impulse, he drove down to South London. He just managed to beat the rush hour and parked his car near to the spot he had used before. It was dark by the time he reached the grocer's shop Dine had stood outside to view the house opposite.

Jacko wondered if he was doing the right thing. The temptation was to cross the street and ring the bell and grasp the nettle. And yet when it came to it he found he could not do it and the reason was centred round Dine himself. He felt the timing was wrong and convinced himself that he had come down here merely because there was nothing else he could do until the next day. And yet he knew it was likely that some of the answers he needed were available behind that door.

With the shops closed and far fewer people about he felt lonely and for a moment thought this was how Dine must feel when he himself made these calls. He continued to stay there getting wet and realised that his reluctance to call at the house was in some indefinable way an attempt to protect Dine. It was a crazy thought and he exorcised it by walking from the scene and returning to the car to drive off. He was so engrossed with his own reactions that he woke up late to the awareness of being followed.

It was virtually impossible to be sure. His windscreen wipers swished in front of him and his rearview mirror presented a blurred vision of the stream of car lights behind him. Yet the feeling hit him like an intrusion. What now worried him was whether he had been lax enough to miss the possibility on the way down.

There was little he could do about it on the main London Road and he was not sure that he wanted to. There were so many ends missing to his hazily formed ideas that it might be better to let something happen to him. He took no evasive action at all on the way back and when he drove into the underground car park at the Army and Navy he was less sure of himself. No car followed him in and when he went to the entrance he could see no obvious signs of anyone lurking. He went up to his room thinking that events were getting to him; he was chasing a lot of shadows which kept fading away.

He slept badly that night, impatient to get on. In the morning he considered ringing Dine again but decided against it. After breakfast he spent some time in making a few purchases and then drove down to the New Forest. He parked roughly in the same place as before and camouflaged his car in the same way. He wore no disguise but did wear a cloth cap and carried a grip like a plumber's with tools protruding each end.

He kept his head low as he approached the house. He gazed around under the porch; nothing seemed to have changed. The police, having found no bodies, had probably lost interest as nothing had actually been stolen. He rang the bell and

215

turned his back to the door, spinning round only when he heard it open.

A woman faced him and his recollection was slow; he had barely glimpsed her when she had passed him in the car with Sam Walters. It was lucky that she did not know him but she was highly suspicious after recent events.

"Is Sam in?" Jacko asked, casting his gaze over her shoulder.

A flicker of recognition touched her eyes as she heard his voice. She opened her mouth to bawl out when Jacko said reasonably, "Please don't scream. I really don't want to use this."

Lilly Walters stared down at the Browning pointing to her midriff and Jacko thought she was going to faint. He put a hand out to steady her and she sank her teeth deep into it. He managed to subdue a yell and thumped her round the side of the head, not too hard but enough to send her spinning back against the hall wall and for him to pull his bleeding hand from her mouth.

While she was still dizzy he spun her round against the wall and groped for a gag and some twine from the plumber's bag. He gagged her first and then bound her wrists when her legs finally gave way and she sank to the ground. He tied her ankles and was about to pull her down the hall so that he could close the door when Sam Walters called out; "Who is it, Lill?"

The voice was from upstairs which Jacko mounted two at a time, slowing down as he neared the landing. He flattened himself on the stairs as he saw the faintest shadow against the wall behind the banisters.

"Lill!" The alarm in the tone suggested that Walters already guessed there was trouble. Jacko still had his gaze on the shadow and then it slowly receded and he now caught the sound of hurrying footsteps. He dashed up the remaining stairs knowing what would happen next, burst into the bedroom where the telephone was and almost stopped a wildly fired shot which chipped the door frame and struck the wall behind him. Walters had the phone in one hand and a gun in the other.

216

Walters was about to fire again but Jacko was already flat on the floor saying quickly, "Don't try it, Sam. Think of Lill."

Walters hesitated, clearly not comfortable with a gun, saw the steadiness with which Jacko held the Browning, felt the gun waver in his hands, and almost burst into tears from frustration.

"Just drop it in front of you, Sam. I'm not going to hurt you."

Walters dropped the gun and put the phone down slowly. Jacko retrieved the gun and stood up. "Lill put up a good show," he said once he was upright. "She's got a bit of a bruise but is perfectly all right; I had to bind and gag her. Now go downstairs and I'll follow and don't do anything daft. Let's all be sensible."

Walters went down the stairs with Jacko following and he ran to Lill as soon as he saw her on the floor. She was already struggling fiercely and did not stop at sight of Jacko who had little trouble in persuading Walters to behave and to tell him where the garage alarm switch was before he bound and gagged him, and then dragged them, one at a time, into the sitting-room.

He made sure the other rooms were empty, switched off the alarm under the stairs and took his bag out to the garage where he broke the repaired haft off the door as he had before, entered and switched on the light. The car was missing.

He went back to the house with some misgivings. The Walters were home so where was the car? He went into the sitting-room to find that Lill had already managed to roll near to her husband who was still roughly where Jacko had put him. He undid Walters' gag and asked him where the car was. Lill shot a look of warning but Walters had not the same courage as his wife.

"A friend is using it."

"When is it due back?"

"I've no idea." Walters was trying to put on a show in front of Lill knowing he would suffer later if he did not.

Jacko dragged Walters into the small study and closed the door. He produced the Browning. "Now, Lill's not listening.

217

Have you anything to add or do you want a smashed kneecap?"

"It's true. The car has been borrowed."

Jacko detected a change of emphasis. "But not by a friend? Someone is using it? One of Rollins' boys? If so when is he likely to come back?"

"I've no idea. He didn't say. Who are you, anyway? You came here posing as a copper. That's a serious offence."

"It's not one that worries me, Sam. I'll be back."

Jacko left Walters where he was and closed the door behind him. He sprinted to the garage not sure how much time he had. He took the plumber's bag in with him, dropped into the inspection pit and pushed the concrete door which rolled easily on its pivot as it had before. He pulled a flashlight from the bag and shone it inside. He sat back on his haunches and cursed. The cavity was empty.

He went inside to make absolutely sure. Everything had gone and the floor had been brushed so that it appeared that nothing had ever been there. Disappointment welled up; he had taken the risk for nothing. He backed out, closed the slab, and climbed out of the pit.

He went back to the house and straight to Walters who took one look at him and saw trouble. "When did they collect it, Sam?"

"Collect what? What are you on about?"

Jacko squatted in front of Walters and gripped his chin with his bloodied hand. "The rules have just changed, Sam. I can't afford to be reasonable any more. Give me one more crap answer like that and you won't be capable of giving any answers at all. And we don't want anything to happen to Lill do we? When did they take the stuff away?"

Walters was now really scared on two counts. "Do you know what they'll do to me?" he pleaded.

"The same as I'm going to do to you. But I'm here and they are not. You'd better remember that I'm the bloke who took out the best they could offer a few nights ago. Did they tell you that one of them was killed? He's probably pig's swill by now. Get it over quickly, Sam, or I will."

Present fear overcame what might be. "Don't let Lill know for God's sake."

"She'll not know from me, Sam. Get on with it."

Sam's mouth suddenly dried up and the words came with difficulty. "They left about an hour before you arrived. They used a little open-backed truck, the sort fencers and gardeners use, and they took our car."

"Where did they go?"

"They were not likely to tell me that. I've no idea."

"Has everything gone? I mean, the chances are that if they have closed this place down they would have topped you before they left."

If Walters was scared before he now visibly trembled; until now he had not considered the possibility but could see that Jacko was right. "I've no idea where they went. They wouldn't confide in me. I'm just a caretaker."

"But why would they take the car? Wasn't there room on the truck?"

"Plenty as far as I could see. I don't know why."

"Perhaps they left it here to collect later and didn't want you to know, otherwise they would have left it in the garage. Did they say they would return it?"

"Yes, but gave no time." Walters was suddenly thoughtful as one or two things began to make sense and added to his terror.

"Where would they hide it if they did not want to use it straightaway and didn't want you to know what they'd done?"

"God, anywhere around here."

"Where would you hide it, Sam? For God's sake don't waste time. They could return at any minute."

"I saw them go off so I know they went to the end of the track and I'm pretty sure they turned right at the top away from the coast. There are plenty of places they could hide it along there, before they reached the main through road. You would have to look."

Jacko straightened. "I'd like to release you now but I don't trust you and certainly not Lill. If I can I'll come back and untie you. Meanwhile you'll just have to work at it yourself."

219

Jacko ran back to his car and whipped the camouflage off as fast as he could. He drove out of the tree-line and turned right on to the track which led past the approach to Walters' house and continued on, slowing considerably once he was past the house. Jacko felt he was chasing moonbeams again but the taking of the car when they already had transport made no sense; they would not be short of cars. And the fact that the Walters had been left indicated that someone would return or Rollins had changed out of recognition.

The weather was kind to him. The clouds had been lightening for some time but now a weak shaft of sunlight broke through the almost bare branches and he caught the faintest suspicion of reflection. The car had been hidden well but not enough for his trained eyes. He took the BMW off the track and swung it round to face the track again before climbing out.

There was no time for subtlety. He was in full view and had to take the risks. He uncovered the car. All the windows were closed and the doors were locked. Trade plates overhung the normal registration numbers.

Jacko took a jemmy from his bag and approached the boot. Before attempting to force the lock he lay prone and examined underneath for booby traps. He forced the hood open to see if the starter was wired up; he did not bother to close it again.

He examined all along the lines of the boot then lay prone again before forcing the jemmy under the rim. At first he applied force gently, then gradually exerted pressure until the lock snapped. He lay still, head down. Nothing happened so he climbed to his feet to open the boot, sensitive to the slightest resistance. It sprung up and he saw why it had not been left in the garage for Walters to explore. An ammunition box was pushed right to the rear. Because of its height, which might not have allowed the boot to close properly, it had been turned on its side.

Still wary of booby traps, Jacko carefully pulled the box towards him. It was heavy, but not as heavy as he expected. He went back for a hacksaw, sawed through the hafts, and finally gingerly lifted the lid. The box was filled with a single parcel wrapped in brown waterproof paper and tied with cord.

It was no time to relax caution. He ran his fingers all round the paper and could find nothing to alarm him. He tipped the parcel out by upturning the box and he took his time in cutting the cord and carefully unwrapping the paper. Yet another parcel faced him now but in a transparent heavy-duty plastic bag. Before opening the bag he was sure he was looking at a considerable amount of heroin, with a street value he would not attempt to evaluate. He lifted the bag out and carried it to the boot of the BMW. He left Walters' car as it was with the boot open and the ammunition case empty.

He drove back to the Walters house as fast as he could, could see nothing on the track to the house and drove to the front of the house. He knew he was crazy to do this but too many people had already died and he did not want the Walters on his conscience. He pulled up in a skid to turn to face the track, and ran into the house, gun drawn.

Lill had already reached the hall en route to search for her husband but her bonds still held. Lill was too risky a bet to free; she would not let it rest there. Jacko ran into the study and untied Walters as fast as he could. He helped him up and held him against the wall. "Untie Lill, and then get the hell out of here as fast as you can. Are you listening? Your life isn't worth a bean. Hide somewhere in the forest, anywhere, until it's safe to cadge a lift. I'll leave your gun in the porch; you might need it."

Jacko dashed from the room, almost tripped over Lill and then jumped into his car. He threw Walters' gun into the porch and then drove off fast, leaving a cloud of dust and hoping that he had not left it too late.

22

Once he reached the main road Jacko slowed to within the speed limit and tried to calm down. The discovery had come as no real surprise but had needed confirmation. Instead of being elated he felt only a deep disappointment that Dine was tied up in drug-running and yet he supposed he had suspected it for some time. The arms theory had never really convinced him. If every ammunition box contained the same amount of heroin then the total must be enormous and, if that equated with a similar quantity on every name and location on the list, then he had uncovered a network of incredible scope.

Yet he felt little satisfaction and felt strongly that what he had discovered was not the real issue. There were plenty of drug-runners, if not of this magnitude, but it was not what he had been looking for. Jacko felt totally deflated. It was Dine who interested him, Dine who had become almost an obsession with him; Dine the enigma who somehow did not seem to fit into the world of drugs. Clearly he was wrong.

He felt an anti-climax, at the same time knowing that it was anything but over yet. The find merely heightened other unexplained issues like how was MI5 involved? Their interest was not in drugs unless it was part of some political security issue and Jacko could not see one here.

He was not sure when it was that he became conscious of a tail, except that he was on the motorway before he did. This was the second day running he had become convinced he had one and he thought he was getting slack. The Rover had been sitting on his tail for some time.

When he accelerated slowly the Rover moved with him. There was no attempt to catch him but when he moved into the fast lane to overtake another car the Rover also overtook. He felt a sense of irritation more than anything. If it was an attempt to intimidate him then the driver should learn something from Li Chai in Hong Kong.

Jacko took the next turning off which led to a group of villages he had never heard of, and slowed right down. The Rover followed and there was nothing behind it on the slip road.

Jacko was going so slow now that the Rover driver was forced to overtake him but as he tried to Jacko accelerated and swung right across to block the Rover which veered away in a skid in order to miss him. The two cars pulled up and Jacko climbed out to run over to the other car half off the road. By now he was convinced it was not Rollins' crowd who were following him.

"What the bloody hell are you doing, you crazy fool? You could have killed us." It was the passenger who was nearest to Jacko who yelled.

"That possibility is still there, matey. You've been following me which means you know where I've been and were so sure of it that you did not have to wait at the spot and chose your point to pick me up on the return."

"You're mad. Bloody loony."

"Go back and tell Jennings that you need to go back to driving school and that you've bodged it. Now release the hood."

"Get stuffed." The driver called across. "I'm going to find a copper. You're blocking the highway, you stupid bastard."

"There's plenty of room to get past." Jacko suddenly produced the Browning and the two men in the car reeled back. "Release the hood."

"No. I've got your number. You won't get away with this. You're a lunatic to wave a gun about like that."

Jacko laughed. "You've had my number for longer than I realised." He fired at the ignition key and the whole dashboard seemed to break. The roar was thunderous in the confines of the car and both men tried to climb over their seats, the driver jumping out the other side. Jacko went back to the BMW and drove off. But he was deeply concerned that they must have followed him from London and it had taken

223

him too long to detect them. It also meant that they knew his starting point.

He continued on, more concerned about Jennings' crowd following than the quantity of drugs he was carrying in the boot. He turned into the next service station, tucking the car round the back, and went inside to ring Ewing at his office.

"Jacko. I'm on my way back to London with a load of heroin in the boot. Must be worth a few hundred grand. It's time we came out in the open to meet. And I think Jennings should be there. His boys have been following me and I had to put their car out of action. I have an idea that their radio survived, though. They must know I'm staying at the Army and Navy."

Ewing said wearily, "Had I known you were there I'd have told you they would know, sooner or later. They fixed it for me at the time."

"Now he tells me. Can we meet at your place? At seven? I can't go back to the club. Don't tell Jennings I'll be there or he'll have a team waiting. There's something bloody odd with their involvement. I don't like it. Thomas, will you just tell him you have to see him urgently. I'll ring again about half-six to make sure he'll be there. Oh, and Thomas, can you put some police cones outside? I want to be sure of parking." He rang off before Ewing could answer.

It was difficult to know where to drive to. The only reasonably safe thing to do was to find somewhere outside London until he had got things sorted out. He found the way back to the motorway again and drove south, opposite to the direction he had been taking. It took him some time to reach Winchester and longer still to find a hotel with parking facilities.

He had no luggage, which the receptionist would think strange and he had a bag full of drugs in the boot of the car which he would have to leave there. He had no intention of handing it over to the police to face the complications which were bound to follow. He signed in under his own name because he had little cash left and would have to settle by credit card; he never used a cash till and had long forgotten the number.

224

There was little he could do until it was time to drive up to London. He had a bath but had no clean clothes with him and felt soiled when he dressed again. He smiled; he had gone soft, almost forgotten the days when he had lain prone in a gulley he had dug with his hands and stayed in it for hours, sometimes days, watching, waiting, the rain pouring down and being almost immune to the conditions and the increasing smell of himself.

The frustration of waiting had always been the worst part; he was trained to it then, could shut his mind to it, but since he had left the service he found it increasingly difficult. He always wanted to get on with the job, and the value of patience sometimes passed him by.

He had plenty to think about but he needed some answers and the whole affair had taken too many directions. He always knew where he stood with men like Rollins. Usually they wanted to kill him and that was clear-cut, something he could face. But when the Security Service came on the scene nobody ever seemed to know what it was they wanted, even people like Ewing. They were a law unto themselves and their work, in their eyes always justifiable, at times crossed some strange boundaries; some would say unacceptable. During his service days he often had to liaise with them, but he was never comfortable even when doing the odd job for them. And here they were again.

He gave himself plenty of time to drive up to London. He had checked to make sure the bag was still in the boot, and could feel the weight of it on the suspension. He took the M3 again, to find it comparatively quiet going north in the early evening. It was already dark and he drove at no more than 70 mph.

He turned into a service station to make his call to Ewing, this time at his home, and said, "I'm calling earlier than I said. Didn't then know where I'd find a billet. Everything okay?"

"He'll be here."

Jacko arrived at Ewing's house at 6 p.m. He double-parked with the engine still running, removed the cones and lined them up on the pavement, climbed back in and parked the car. He was banking on it being too late for wheel-clamping but suspected that Jennings would make his own arrangements with the law to smooth the way. He ran up the steps and rang the bell.

Liz opened the door and gave him a big hug as Ewing appeared behind her. Liz closed the door and the two men shook hands warmly.

"You're very early," said Ewing. "He's not due for another hour."

"It will give me time to check the outside. Meanwhile I'd better bring in the bag."

Ewing was shocked. "I can't have that stuff in here."

"Well I can't leave it in the car and I'm buggered if I'll give it to Jennings. Sorry, Liz." He turned to Ewing's wife, "Slip of the tongue."

Liz smiled. "What's in it? Drugs?"

The following silence suddenly made her realise that she was right. "Oh, my God. What do we do with them?"

"Thomas will know," said Jacko. "It's evidence. The Drug Squad will want it."

"And wonder why they have not been in on it, Jacko. I don't like it. Leave it in the boot until we can sort it out."

Jacko looked from one to the other in some despair. "This will probably turn out to be the greatest drug crackdown in history, certainly in Europe, and all you can say is keep it in the boot. That's bloody marvellous. If you don't take it I'll leave it on the doorstep. I can't hand it to the police until this thing is over, they'll detain me and I can't risk that."

"But this thing is over, surely?"

Jacko was dejected. They were still standing in the hall. "It's far from over. My commission from you was not to look into drugs but how Reginald Dine came across a Sèvres figure belonging to the French, and then we began to look at the man himself. I suspect that drugs are only one of his interests and certainly not the main one. And I sometimes wonder if I've got anywhere at all. I'm going to get it."

Jacko went to the car while Liz and Ewing stood on the top doorstep watching him. He carried the heavy parcel up the steps with difficulty and dumped it in the hall. He undid the outer wrapping to reveal the strong white plastic bag. "That's what heroin looks like. Now try calculating the extent of human misery that lot could cause."

They took the bag into the kitchen and put it under the table. Ewing was not at all happy about it but, until they met Jennings, could see no alternative. When that was done they went into the drawing-room and Liz poured drinks but before Jacko sat down he said, "Is there a street-facing room upstairs I might use for a few minutes?"

"You think Rollins' crowd have followed you here?" Ewing collected his drink from Liz.

"I would be surprised if Rollins knows I'm here. His trouble is that he looks in dirty corners instead of what's on full view. His mind gropes in the dust; it's never seen the sunshine. It would never have occurred to him to watch somewhere like the Army and Navy, especially as he probably knows I was a sergeant."

"Who then?"

"Who knows? May I go up?"

"Turn left at the top of the stairs," said Liz. "The door facing you at the end is a guest bedroom; that faces the street."

Jacko went up knowing he had confused Ewing even further. Ewing liked to keep it simple with simple answers and always had difficulty in believing the depths that some people will sink to. He entered the bedroom and closed the door. The drapes were drawn back but the windows were covered by net curtains. He went to one side and lifted the side of a curtain with a finger. He stood there for some time and heard Ewing call up the stairs asking if he was all right. He ignored the call and crossed over to the other side and did the same. When he returned to the drawing-room Ewing and Liz were seated with drinks.

Jacko drifted over to the chair besides which was his drink.

"Well?" queried Ewing. "Any bogey men?"

"If there are they're not watching you. Cheers. Just like old times." He raised his glass to them.

Jennings rang the bell just as a clock struck seven.

227

Liz said, "I'll let him in then go upstairs and watch television."

Jennings came bustling in, having handed his coat to Liz at the door. He saw Jacko but gave no sign of surprise. "If that's your wife, Mr Ewing, I must congratulate you. She is a super lady."

"Thank you. Call me Thomas. You've already met Jacko, of course."

"Oh, yes. He's the fellow who goes round England toting a gun as if he was still in America, blowing up our cars and frightening the life out of our men who had been detailed to protect him. I suppose that's your BMW outside. You're getting careless."

"Balls," said Jacko with a grin. "If they had told me that I might have believed them. As it was they even denied they were following me. And I only smashed the ignition."

Ewing, who knew nothing of the detail, looked upset. "Do sit down," he said weakly. "What will you drink?"

"A brandy might settle my nerves." Jennings sat down and glared at Jacko in what appeared to be a subdued rage. "You ruined that car," he accused. "They had to get a tow. You really must stop running round shooting everything up. I doubt that you have a licence for the thing."

"It was issued to me by your department about eighteen months ago. You never asked for it back and I never handed it in."

Jennings' features suddenly cracked and he could not resist a smile. He took the drink Ewing handed him. "You certainly know how to trot them out, don't you? What baloney. But you know we would have a job proving it either way." His smile broadened. "You've had that Browning for much longer than that." And then in a completely different tone, "Congratulations, Jacko. You did a great job."

Jacko lowered his drink. "I thought it would choke you to say it."

"Honours are even, gentlemen," Ewing intervened. "Shall we get on with the issue in hand?"

Jacko said, "I really appreciate the thanks but how did you

know? I've only told Thomas here, and he's going to be bloody mad if you've still got his office phone tapped."

Jennings waved a hand of dismissal at the very idea. "We've been involved with this caper for a very long time. It's an ongoing story which arose out of the closures of the arms caches and some of the problems that caused. All the agencies are caught up in it and we've all been beavering away. Now we have some concrete evidence we can make moves to crush the whole enterprise. Action has already been taken."

"Do you mean to say that what I discovered today is the first real evidence you have?"

"Well, you must admit it was well concealed. You did not find it straight away. And we have not your freedom of movement. We have to operate within the law."

Jacko burst out laughing and Ewing had difficulty in subduing a smile. "So you have to admit there are some advantages in gun-toting."

"I could not say so publicly. In less experienced hands there could be real trouble. And you know it. You've been threatening everybody."

"That was because everybody has been threatening me. So where do we go from here?"

"There's nowhere to go. There are over a hundred remaining caches which we must now presume are also used as distribution centres for drugs. We already knew that the big crime syndicates throughout Europe had amalgamated for this project. The arms, in the event, have created a wonderful cover but are still useful in themselves if needed. Did you bring any drugs away with you?"

Jacko had the feeling that Jennings knew full well that he did. "Of course. Otherwise there would be no evidence. But the main load had already been shifted before I got there."

"How much did you get?"

"An ammunition chest full of what I think is heroin. I left the chest there."

"Did they leave it behind? Overlook it?"

"My guess is that a couple of the boys skimmed it off the top to be collected later. I happened to find it."

"What have you done with it?"

"I shall hand it over to the Drug Squad. When I've tidied up."

"I'll relieve you of it. Your job is done."

"I don't think it is. Anyway, it's none of your bloody business."

"Just what the hell do you mean by that? Damn it, aren't you satisfied with what you've done?"

"No, I'm not satisfied. I haven't finished yet. You didn't employ me so you can piss off. You came in on this for your own reasons. And just what the hell has narcotics got to do with MI5?"

"I've just explained. All the intelligence agencies in Europe are involved. And, of course, their respective Drug Squads. This is far too big an issue to leave to one force."

Jacko could feel he had Jennings on the run. "Do the Drug Squad know they're involved? I mean, if so many agencies and specialists are tied up in it why was it one person, an outsider, managed to get the evidence that they couldn't? You're keeping this to yourself, you crafty sod, and I want to know why."

Ewing was listening to this exchange with his head in his hands wishing he could sometimes break from the diplomatic language he was condemned to use, like Jacko did so freely.

Jennings tried to sound reasonable. "Jacko, call me what you like, but we've had your interests at heart once we knew where your enquiries were taking you. We let you have your head and you became a member of the team without realising it. Great stuff. We admire you. We'll even cover some of your expenses. But for you it's over. Mr Ewing, here, will confirm it."

Jacko gazed across at Ewing as Jennings did. He shook his head slowly as a warning for him not to be intimidated into agreeing.

Ewing was in a quandary. All his sympathies lay with Jacko who was right about who had engaged him. But even if he supported him now he knew that if Jennings represented the official line he would have to comply. He compromised. "You might have a prima facie, Peter, but I cannot accept it without confirmation. Preferably in writing from your superiors."

Jennings shrugged. "Well, you won't get anything in writing and I'm surprised you asked. I can ring somebody now, if that will satisfy you."

"No, it wouldn't. You could be ringing anyone; with respect, your profession is no stranger to deception."

"That's the stuff, Thomas. You tell the sly bugger."

Jennings turned to Jacko in fury. "Keep out of this, Jacko, it no longer concerns you. I've told you that your job is over."

"And I've told you to stuff it." Jacko was quietly laughing. "You're beginning to show your true colours, Peter, old boy. I was a bloody hero just now. I knew the truth would stick in your gullet. You'd better treat Thomas with respect or you'll get your fat little arse kicked."

Jennings managed to control his feelings, well aware that Jacko was trying to goad him. He turned back to Ewing. "Would a word from the PM himself satisfy you?"

"Of course. But you don't intend to ring him now, do you?"

"Tomorrow. Meanwhile I'll take custody of the drugs and will give you a receipt."

"I don't know where they are." Ewing had uttered his first lie and failed to feel badly about it; he did not like Jennings' increasing arrogance.

Jennings tried to stare Ewing out but Ewing had now taken his stand and handled it with ease. Jennings lowered his head, gazed briefly at his drink, and was silent for a short while. "You do realise that you are both obstructing the law?"

"Well, you should know all about that," said Jacko who was delighted with Ewing's stand. "I tell you what I'll do. I'll hand it over to the Drug Squad first thing tomorrow. What could be fairer?"

Jennings said patiently, "Why won't you let me take it? You know who I am and my work. So what's the problem?"

"The problem is that it's not here." Jacko was convinced by now that Jennings' men had seen it being taken into the house but that Jennings could not admit to that.

231

"I see. Well I believe it is here." Jennings was controlling his exasperation with credit.

"So you are calling the two of us liars?"

Ewing intervened again. "All you two are achieving is to show just how much you dislike each other." He said to Jennings, "Leave it that you will contact the PM and I'll naturally comply with whatever he says. That seems to me to be perfectly fair. I cannot see the urgency unless you think it will be stolen."

Jennings was beaten and found difficulty in facing it. The power of the department usually made most people very nervous. Not these two, particularly Jacko to whom he now turned. "I'm sorry I was abusive, but you have a way of getting under the skin. Whatever I said to offend, I meant what I said about respecting you. I can see I will have to take this further." He rose. "I do thank you for the drink and the hospitality, Mr Ewing." He turned to Jacko. "Send an account for services rendered to Curzon Street. I'll action it provided it is reasonable. Where are you staying now?"

"The Army and Navy."

"I thought you had left there?"

"No. I'm just wearing different disguises to test your boys." But Jacko was still curious as to why Jennings wanted the drugs, because once he had them there would be no proof that they had ever existed; it would be natural to let the Drug Squad have it for they would be accountable. And that was the problem; men like Jennings were rarely accountable in the public eye.

Liz came down almost as if she had been listening, which she had not, and helped Jennings on with his coat. Jennings made his farewells with good grace but he looked tired when he left, and he did not turn as he went down the steps.

Once the door was closed Liz said, "There goes one unhappy man; what did you do to him?" When neither replied she said she would get some coffee and sandwiches, sensing that they were not yet finished.

"You know why he wants me to send a bill, don't you?"

"So that it will appear that you are accountable to him. That binds you to him."

232

"What's his game?" asked Jacko as they went back into the drawing-room.

"I don't know. But I do know that I lied for you." He reached for the remains of his drink. "And I don't know why I did."

"Because he's up to something. Why does he want me out of it after doing all the dirty work? It's tied up with Dine. He's the one he wants to keep me away from."

Ewing sat quietly reflecting, not too happy with what he had done. "I think he knows we've got it," he said after a while.

"His men would have seen us take it in. He knows all right."

Ewing sat bolt upright. "They've been watching?"

"I think they were waiting for me. I reckon your office is wired up again. They'll still be out there. I saw one of them when he left. They don't trust me. I think I know why but not the real reason behind it. I must see Dine again. He's the key to all Jennings is prattling about. I think the drugs have become a bloody embarrassment to Jennings. Meanwhile I've got to get out of here."

"You could stay the night here," said Liz coming in with the coffee and sandwiches. "I had them prepared already." She put down the tray and waited for Jacko to reply.

"Thanks, Liz. But if they have a full team out, and I suspect they have, they'll still be there in the morning and it's easier to cope with them at night."

Ewing did not like the sound of this. He wanted to believe that apart from Jennings' strange behaviour it really was all over. If Jennings had a team of men outside waiting to follow Jacko then it was far from over and took on a more sinister aspect.

"It's kind of you to offer to put me up but I'd better leave. It's possible they've bugged the car since I've been here. I'll go and check. But first there is something we should do."

Jacko filled a bin bag with soap powder and carried it down to the car, making it appear heavier than it actually was. Ewing helped him put it in the boot and then went up the steps to join Liz who had put on a top coat against the cold.

233

Jacko went round the car with a flashlight while Ewing and Liz remained outside their open front door to keep a watchful eye on things. After a while Jacko found a bug under the base of the boot and crushed it flat with his foot. He ran up the steps, kissed Liz affectionately and gave Ewing a pat on the back.

"Are you sure you'll be all right?" asked Ewing, deeply concerned once the bug had been found.

"I'm used to it," said Jacko. "I don't know what I'm up against because I don't know how important I am to Jennings. There is something he is really scared about to pull a dodge like this. I'll just have to see where it takes me. God bless."

"Take care, Jacko." Liz was holding Ewing's hand tight, unable to hide her deep concern.

Jacko climbed in.

23

Jacko made it easy for them. He was weary and could see no point in a long chase. He drove north to Highbury and they got him in the first deserted stretch. One car raced ahead of him, and one remained on his tail but closed up dangerously so that if he suddenly braked there would be an accident.

As the front car slewed across he was forced to brake and the following car had to swing out to avoid ramming him, and just brushed his fender. But he was sandwiched and he knew they would not waste time. To prevent any help coming his way they stuck blue flashers on their cars to make it look like a police job.

He sat back resignedly and waited for them to come. Two men approached, one either side, and both were armed; Jennings must have warned them about his gun-toting. But Jacko sat placidly and lowered the window before it was tapped. "Is this a hold up?" he asked wearily. "I've no money on me."

"Open the boot or we'll smash it open."

"Oh, Christ. I've nothing in there." But he climbed out and tried to give the impression that he was looking for half a chance just to keep them on their toes. Once he was out they man-handled him and forced him to face the car while they searched him, and were somewhat surprised to find him unarmed.

"Okay. Open it. We know all about you so don't try anything funny."

He went round and unlocked the boot and without hesitation they removed the plastic bag and carried it to the front car. "There's nothing in it but soap powder," he called out just as they climbed into their own cars. Both cars sped away, and he wearily closed the boot and drove off, changing his direction to south. He did not know whether or not they had another detail on him in order to locate where he was staying, but he performed all the usual moves before taking the quickest route back to Winchester. It was very late by the time he arrived there but he still rang Ewing with the brief message of, "It's okay. I'm going to bed."

He rang Georgie early next morning and said, "We've uncovered an international drug ring." He told her because he knew she was tired of reassurances of how soon she would be back at her business and because she had no idea of how things had expanded from the original issue of the Sèvres figure. "There's just one more thing to tidy up. It should not take more than a day or two. I'll sort out compensation for you once you're back. I'm really sorry about all this, Georgie, and believe me I've missed you."

"Does that mean you are now out of danger?"

In fact he was in more danger than ever; Rollins would have found out about the missing drugs and, if the Walters had disappeared without their car, might well blame him. So far as he knew, Rollins still had a contract out on him. How the Security Service rated his well-being was more difficult to assess but he did not fancy his chances against them if he continued on. He had to continue. And that would bring Georgie back into the danger zone. "There was never much danger, Georgie. It was all puff and wind." What he wanted to do was to ask her to find another billet but that would scare her, and as, at the moment, she enjoyed official protection they would know at once where she went.

"Well that's a relief. Oh, I almost forgot. My enquiry agent has come up with a small item. Apparently Michael David Deering had an elder brother who was killed in the Second World War. I don't see how this can help you, though."

Neither could Jacko. To show his interest he said, "Where was he killed?"

"At Caen. His Christian name was Lonnie."

Jacko froze. For a moment he could say nothing and when he did he tried to play it down. "Thanks, Georgie. I'll see what I can make of it. Let your man keep digging."

Jacko went out on to the streets of Winchester and bought himself an electric razor, the best ready-made suit he could find, shoes, shirt, tie and a document case. The only disguise he had was the wig and moustache which were crammed under the dashboard of the BMW, and by now probably ragged. The rest of his belongings were still at the Army and Navy and there was no time to organise for them to be collected.

He bought a morning paper at Reception and had a late breakfast at the hotel, still mulling over his next move. When he had finished his second coffee he flipped through the newspaper and a heading on the third page caught his eye. 'New Forest couple in suicide pact?' There followed an account of a double shotgun killing in the secluded setting of the New Forest. Samuel and Lilly Walters, a quiet couple, who friends say kept themselves to themselves . . .

Jacko lowered the paper. Oh God. The Walters had not moved fast enough but he felt a responsibility; had Lill not been so tough he would have released them both. He read on to discover that, 'it was thought that Walters had bound his wife and then shot her through the head. He had then turned the gun on himself by placing the barrel in his mouth.'

Jacko screwed up the paper knocking over his empty cup. Sam Walters would have been terrified to the end. Jacko realised he must have missed Rollins' men by a fraction. He believed that Walters would have been killed anyway, but discovery of the missing drugs would not have improved his chances. The drugs were one thing Walters' killers could not report back to Rollins unless they could somehow blame him for it.

Jacko felt sick at heart. The Walters were guardians of the drugs but he doubted they ever knew what exactly they guarded apart from arms. They had been small fry and had died because of it.

He went into the foyer and sat reflecting for a few minutes. He needed to contact Glenn Patton at the FBI New York again, but it would have to wait for the evening. Meanwhile he decided to visit South London.

*   *   *

237

For some reason the street where he usually parked was crammed full of cars and he had to roam before he could find a slot and it left him with quite a long walk back. By this time it was nearly midday, the drive over had been packed with tailbacks. When he left the car he was wearing his new suit, wig and moustache, and carried the briefcase.

He reached the street the Parsons lived in and felt all the usual warnings. He was grateful, then, for even a flimsy disguise. He went past the grocer's shop and turned into the doorway he had used before and stood there watching. He just did not like the idea of making a direct call but he knew he would have to.

There was a limit to how long Jacko could wait without someone noticing and remarking upon it. There was also the very serious risk that somewhere here were Jennings' men; they had probably commandeered a room overlooking the house.

He was not sure how long he had been there when a woman came out. She was well dressed, in her late thirties or early forties, carried herself well, and looked vaguely familiar.

On impulse, Jacko waited a short while then followed, keeping to his side of the street. He could not leave it too long but willed her to turn a corner before he made his move. She did, and crossed to his side of the street to do it. He quickened his pace, worried that she might find a cab or have a car parked near by. He was right. By the time he turned the corner she was unlocking the door of an old MG Coupé in splendid condition. She actually had the door open when he called out, "How the devil do you find parking space? I've had to park miles away."

"You have to get here very early," she replied pleasantly but with some reserve.

Jacko could now see she was a striking woman. He had almost reached her as she was about to climb in. He asked, as evenly as he could, "Do you know the Parsons, by any chance? Eric and Annette?"

She had one hand on the low roof of the car and one well clad foot inside, when she stiffened. She gazed at him suspiciously. "Why do you want to know?"

"Because I saw you come out of the house."

She withdrew her foot from inside the car but left the door open. "If you know where they live and want to see them why don't you ring the bell?"

Jacko kept his distance and realised how strange this must sound to her. "Because what I have to say to them might be upsetting and resurrect old, perhaps painful memories. I want to avoid that and would like any help I can get from anyone who might know them. That's why I followed you."

"I don't like the idea of being followed. Why would you want to raise old memories?" Her tone had hardened and she was now clearly uncomfortable.

Jacko plunged in as best he could. "I'm a solicitor. Annette Parsons, *née* Barr, has inherited a little money. Not a fortune, but I see no reason why she should not have it. What I'm looking for is a little guidance before I tell her; the benefactor has been dead for some time and it might come as a shock to her."

The woman stood still for a few seconds and was clearly affected by what he said. Jacko added, "Look, I'm not a kink, a crazy, nor am I trying a new line in chat. Is there somewhere where we can sit down and talk? A café or somewhere like that? Pick your own spot."

"Why on earth would I want to help you? What makes you think I can?"

"Because, unless I've made a terrible mistake, you are Annette Parson's daughter; there is a resemblance."

She stared rigidly for some time and had lost a little colour. "If you see a resemblance you must have seen her." It came out as a suspicious accusation.

"Oh, I have. And I hadn't the courage to approach her."

"That's crazy. What sort of a solicitor are you?"

"One who thinks that while your mother is Annette Parsons, your father was Michael David Deering, killed in Korea. I say that only because I can see no reason for your mother not to tell you, particularly as your father was a brave man."

She suddenly slammed the door and leaned with her back against the car. "God, I can't believe this. What a conversation to have with a stranger in the street."

Jacko could now see that she was very disturbed. "I did ask if we could sit down somewhere."

She turned her head, eyes misted and retorted, "Look at you. A solicitor who wears a toupee badly and looks more like an amiable thug. And I'm expected to fall for this?"

Jacko smiled. "Has the damned thing shifted?" He made an adjustment which made her half-laugh, half-cry. He carefully kept his distance knowing the next few seconds were crucial. "I can't help looking like a thug," he said. "That's why I wear the wig, to soften my image."

She lowered her head, fair hair falling forward. Suddenly she looked up at the lowering sky and then suddenly faced him. "There's a place just round the corner."

She led the way and Jacko called out, "You haven't locked the car."

She turned back while he kept his distance, and locked the car door. "Thank you. You'll be quite safe walking beside me."

Jacko smiled at that, for reasons he would not tell her, but he was pleased. The café was run-of-the-mill and a block away. It was peak hour and they could not find a table so finished up at the counter on high stools. They ordered burgers and milk shakes which neither of them wanted, and Jacko paid from his dwindling cash. "What's your name?" he asked at last.

"Laura Martin. Married, two children. What's yours?"

"Noel Thomas, unmarried, no kids." He handed her a solicitor's card. "Did your father know he had a daughter?"

"We don't know. My mother sent letters but he might already have been killed. It's such a long time ago. You'd better explain this legacy."

Jacko thought quickly. "It's not much more than a thousand pounds but it is possible that there might be more. We can only guess that it stemmed from your father before he died in a Korean POW camp. The Koreans have not been helpful but one or two wills have recently come in from Russia and China who have been sitting on these things for years and years. The new political atmosphere in Russia has helped a bit. But the Chinese have been less helpful and would

240

admit to nothing except to pass on odd 'bits and pieces which have come to light'. So sometimes the name of the would-be recipient is given but not the donor. Meanwhile names have changed, people have married, divorced and married again, and have probably moved several times. It has taken a long time to sort it out. Perhaps you can see why I don't want to approach your mother direct."

Laura was fully recovered now, listening carefully and sometimes sipping her milk shake. "You think she would not want to be reminded of Daddy?"

"Would she? In this way? Is there some way of giving it to her without her knowing?"

"You're the lawyer; you should be able to answer that."

Switching the subject entirely, Jacko said, "Did you know your father won the Military Medal for gallantry?"

"Yes. Mother has the medal in a box. I think you are making a big fuss out of nothing, Mr Thomas. Just go and tell her and pay her the money. It was all a very long time ago. Why all the mystery?" Laura suddenly paused while drinking her milk shake. Her hands shook very slightly and she looked straight in front as if she could not face Jacko. Then the moment passed as if she had shrugged it off and she lowered her glass.

"I'm just a sentimentalist," Jacko replied. "I just don't like upsetting people."

"A lawyer who doesn't like upsetting people? You didn't mind upsetting me." And then, eyeing him quizzically, "Are you telling me everything? Is there something you are hiding?"

"Only inconsequential. During our extensive enquiries we discovered that your father had an elder brother who was killed in World War Two."

"Yes. Lonnie. Towards the end of the war. That seems to be the pattern of the family; Daddy was killed towards the end of the Korean War."

"Did they like each other? Brothers don't always get on."

"I can only tell you what my mother has told me over the years. The two brothers were very close; peas in a pod except for the difference in ages. You've disappointed me,

241

Mr Thomas. I thought you had much more to tell me. Why am I left with the feeling that you have learned more from me than I have from you?"

"Your mother is coming into a little money; you've learned that. Would you be good enough to let me have your address in case I need to contact you?"

Laura frowned. "I don't wholly trust you. If you want to write, send it care of Mother."

"Will you trust me more when your mother has received her money?"

"I don't know. There's more to you than meets the eye."

"I don't intend to hurt you or your mother in any shape or form, Laura. Believe me."

Laura got off the stool. "I find that easier to believe than some of the other stuff you've been spinning." She glanced at the card. "Perhaps I'll be contacting you. May I go now?"

Jacko slipped down from the stool and gave a wry grin. "Have I been holding you prisoner?" He held her by the elbow to the door and she trusted him that much by not resisting.

"No," she replied. "I'm just wondering what your real game is."

"Your father would have been proud of you," he said spontaneously.

"How can you possibly know that?"

"Well, I would be if I was your father, but in age I'm more likely to be your younger brother." He grabbed her hand as she tried to strike him in the side. "Is my wig on straight?"

She reached up and made an adjustment. "Now it is. You don't need one."

"You'd be surprised just how much I do."

"I'm beginning to think I wouldn't. Do I get to hear the full story one day? The truth?"

He stared down at her and noticed how clear and steady her eyes were. "I will try to make a point of it. Don't make me do it through your mother; give me a telephone number."

Laura produced a pen and scribbled the number down on the back of his hand. "No paper," she explained. "That does not mean I trust you but merely that I would like to hear the rest some time. Will my mother really get some

242

money? She's very proud but I give her what she will accept."

"Yes. She really will receive some. It's nice meeting you, Laura."

On the way back to Winchester he could not make up his mind whether meeting her had been good or bad luck. He had held certain things back and perhaps he might have learned more from her mother. At the same time he was glad he had met her. He had gone as far as he could; it was time to meet Dine. But first he must contact Glenn Patton again and hope he had done the research he wanted.

He hung about the hotel, having booked the call and it seemed hours before Patton came through. The two men knew each other sufficiently well to skip the niceties. "How did you make out?" asked Jacko flatly.

"It's a very sensitive area. You've scored in one respect. The list is classified and successive United States and British Governments have repeatedly requested that it never be declassified. It's a can of worms created by the Cold War in the early 1950s. Some in Russia but the one that would interest you is the POW Compound in the Fu Hsing Road, Canton. It is controlled by the South China Military Area HQ. There is still despatch No. 1716 from our Consulate-General in Hong Kong on file. No-one wants to take the lid off, Jacko. Watch your step."

When Jacko hung up he had filled the gap and now knew why M15 were involved; they were holding down the lid Patton had referred to.

Jacko rang Dine who answered in a voice he did not recognise. "We've got to meet. It's urgent."

"I know how urgent it is, Jacko. It will not be easy."

"I suppose you are surrounded by the Security Service?"

"Oh, they've been around for a long time. I suppose you initially thought they were after you? That came later. Have you any suggestions?"

Jacko thought Dine's voice sounded weaker, even resigned, which distressed him. "Press the panic button at exactly eight o'clock. Let the whole bloody street hear the alarm."

"Do you know what you are doing?"

"No. Just do it, Reg. Trust me. Right now I'm all you've got."

"Oh, I've known that for some time. Anything else?"

"You don't sound well. It worries me."

"It's just the strain. It's been with me for a very long time."

"Take it easy and do as I say. Eight o'clock on the dot and don't let anyone in. Nobody except me." He hung up abruptly.

Again he had to wait. He stripped the Browning, not because it needed it but to fill in time. He made sure the magazines were full, one in the butt and two spares, and went down for a tomato juice at the bar. If ever there was a time to keep sober this was it. They would rather kill Dine than let him get to him again and he belatedly realised that Dine had been a threatened species for some time.

When it was time to go he drove off giving himself plenty of time in hand. He was driving against the traffic and delays were minimal while he passed the massive tailbacks coming out the other way from the London area.

He reached the Chelsea Embankment just before seven o'clock but did not drive along it so that the BMW would not be seen there. He parked where he could but well away from the house and strode slowly back to the end of the embankment without actually entering the street. It all appeared so normal; street lights, house lights, a spattering of people, cars pulling up or driving through. He reasoned that Security personnel would be sitting in parked cars with heads down.

Jacko, wearing his only available disguise, had the Browning tucked into his hip pocket and the BMW's mobile phone in the briefcase he carried. He retreated from the corner, not wanting to be seen by anyone. He checked the time. There was still fifteen minutes to go. It would seem an eternity. It was strange that waiting so often went with silence and that every small sound became an increasing intrusion.

Ten minutes to go. He was tempted to peer round the corner but managed to refrain.

At five minutes to eight he pulled out the phone, dialled

999, asked for the police and spoke precisely; "There is a break-in on the Chelsea Embankment and there are a lot of strange men hanging around in cars watching it. I heard a scream too, you'd better be quick." He cut off before they could ask for his name or address.

Jacko knew that Dine's alarm was connected with the nearest police station and the moment it sounded his call would be taken seriously. The alarm rang out two minutes later.

It was as if a fire engine had suddenly appeared. The sound in the quiet street shut out everything else. Even the Security men were startled and two stepped from their cars giving away their location.

The police sirens sounded inside three minutes and suddenly the place was alive with blue flashers. Three police cars double-parked, then a sergeant ran up the steps of Dine's house and rang the bell while others stayed at the bottom of the steps and scanned the upper house. One of the Security men ran up the steps to join the sergeant, flashed an identity and said, "I think you'll find this is a false alarm, Sergeant. We have the house under surveillance. Could you call your men off?"

The sergeant resented the interference and replied crisply, "No, sir, I can't. It's not just the alarm, we had a phone call too."

"You can see nothing is happening, for God's sake."

Just then there was an almighty yell as though somebody was suffering terribly and a light went out. Jacko chose the moment to put in an appearance. He walked briskly to the house, was stopped by a policeman at the foot of the steps until Jacko identified himself as the occupant's solicitor and had an appointment. He ran up the steps. The Security man said, "Who are you?"

Jacko ignored him and introduced himself to the sergeant making the same explanation as he had to the constable. The sergeant was banging on the door at the same time dispersing his men, some going round to the next street. Jacko turned to the Security man and asked loudly, "Aren't you that actor fellow? The one who goes round embarrassing people with stupid pranks? Did you set off the alarm?"

245

Just then the door opened and a distressed Dine stood there and demanded to know what was going on. Then he spotted Jacko and said, "Right on time. Do come in."

The sergeant went in with him and the Security man tried to follow but Jacko blocked him deftly and gave him a push that sent him stumbling outside. He closed the door quickly.

The exasperated sergeant said, "Would you mind explaining what the hell is going on, sir? Are you being burgled or not?"

"It's a false alarm, Sergeant. It was set off by my cook. And I always get confused about how to turn it off." He held up the keys.

Jacko took them from him. "Where's the box?"

"Under the stairs."

Jacko went off as the sergeant said, "But there was a telephone call."

Dine looked surprised. "Not from here. Probably made by one of those strange fellows who have been hanging around."

Jacko bawled out from under the stairs, "I think they are actors looking for real material." At that moment the alarm stopped ringing and the silence was painful. Jacko came back with the keys and said to Dine, "I'm sorry to hustle you but I've brought a copy of the will for you to see."

The sergeant said, "But there was an almighty yell inside the house."

"That was me. I'm so sorry. I'd been dozing when the alarm went off. That was bad enough but when I heard the commotion downstairs and saw all those blue lights flashing I was sure an army was breaking in. I was still only half awake. I must say I feel an utter fool." Dine placed a friendly hand on the sergeant's shoulder. "I'm so sorry. I'll put a sizeable donation into the Police Fund."

"So it was all a mistake?"

"I'm afraid so."

"Then I suggest you learn a little more about handling your alarms, sir."

"Fair comment. I will, of course."

Jacko opened the door for the sergeant to leave, and it

was Jacko who made sure that no M15 man was going to enter. He had achieved what he had set out to do. He had got into the house it was intended he should be prevented from entering. The two men shook hands and went upstairs to the drawing-room.

"I had to play it by ear," Dine complained.

"I know you did. So did I. I know the police hate being told what to do by the Security Service. Well, it worked and I need a drink."

While Dine poured them he said, "You're in, but how are we going to get out?"

Jacko whipped off his moustache and wig. "I thought you might have worked something out."

Dine smiled weakly. "Perhaps I have."

Jacko took his drink and when he was seated opposite Dine, he raised his glass and toasted, "Here's to Michael David Deering, MM."

24

"How long have you known?" asked Dine.

"A few hours. I had my suspicions. I knew you had served some time; you kept using remarks like, 'marking time, firing line', that sort of thing. But it took some effort to find anything about your marriage and service career. And even then it took me a long time to work out that Reg Dine is an anagram of Deering. Georgie Roberts had to use an enquiry agent to dig up the fact that you had a brother called Lonnie. As you named your son after him it was obvious that you and your brother were close. That sort of wrapped up most of it. But before I pass judgement, what the hell happened?"

Dine began a story he had told no-one before. "I was captured in Korea in '53, four months before Armistice Day. We were bundled into POW camps and treated pretty badly. After the Armistice most of the boys were repatriated home. But for some reason, probably because that was the nature of the Communists at the time, they were full of hatred and contempt for us, some of us were held back. From information I've received since, there were over 150 British and Commonwealth troops unaccounted for and God knows how many Americans. Some were transported to Russia, and, with a few others, I finished up in China."

"The POW Compound on the Fu Hsing Road, Canton."

Dine inclined his head in acknowledgement. "You have done your homework. Although, at first, we were taken to Tungshan, and later to Canton. I spent fourteen years there, Jacko. Fourteen years of misery and brainwashing and of total hopelessness. They talked enough of the Middle East hostages; nobody was allowed to talk about us. I later discovered that they tried to get us back at first, and probably tried hard, particularly the Americans, but these were Stalinist days and his methods reflected through the Communist world."

Dine was reliving the whole soul-destroying episode and was finding it difficult to recount. "Some of the poor sods are still there, elderly now, and will die there. Good mates suspended for ever in limbo. The fortunate are the ones who have already died. Once successive governments, both here and in the USA, got nowhere with their efforts, they decided it was best to take the Communist line that all who had not been returned were dead. When a decision like that is made it's political suicide to go back on it. A curtain was drawn over the whole sordid business. It was better that way."

Dine suddenly finished his drink and went to pour himself another. He took a bottle of whisky and a carafe of water and placed them beside Jacko. When he was reseated he stared into space and dragged out the agony of a life he wanted to forget.

"I escaped from Canton in December 1967 but it was well over a year before I managed to get out of China to Macao. The Chinese wanted me back before I could expose their lies, so to stay free I had to live like an animal, on scraps, anything I could find. I became an expert scavenger. I was a European, but by that time I spoke both Mandarin and Cantonese like a native. There was no way I could live honestly and it was no problem, in those circumstances, to turn to crime. It was the only chance of survival. Believe me, Jacko, I would rather have killed myself than go back to the POW Compound.

"At first it was petty crime, plain stealing just to live, but as it continued I made contacts into bigger stuff, and finally as a carrier for drugs. I had no problem of conscience at all. I actually started to make enough money to buy food. And then some clear-thinking drug baron saw how useful I could be on the other side of the 'bamboo curtain'. It was he who finally got me across the estuary into Macao. He had a huge network of runners, petty crooks, pushers. Even the Communists couldn't stop them but I often wondered if they wanted to. Drugs into the West was okay by them; it brought in money and spread degradation where they wanted it to spread most."

Sweat was trickling down Dine's face as he related his escape; he could still feel the fear of it, smell the stench of rough living, followed by the wonderful, unbelievable sensation of freedom once he reached Macao, stepping ashore in the dark from a leaking sampan.

"It was easier to build up a background in Macao. In no time at all I was making big money. The biggest problem around that time were the Communists, orchestrated from mainland China, who were beginning to cut up rough. They later did the same in Hong Kong but were not so effective. So I still had to play it cagily. That was one of the reasons I went to Hong Kong to live. I had a few friends, you might call them the Triads but that was not a name so publicly known at that time, working out a solid family history for me; a combination of digging up suitable parents from the actual past, and corrupting certain minor officials. If they could not be bribed they would be intimidated but there was no problem. In-between making money I studied, knowing that I would have to give the right impression to the colonials. I started some solid enterprises. But there is no way back from the drug scene except six feet down, and only that after some physical inconvenience."

Dine rose again, clearly restless. He walked over to one of the windows and peered through the netting. He returned to his chair, looked over at Jacko as if seeing him for the first time, then picked up the thread.

"At that time I probably carried at least as much information about Far Eastern drug cartels, contacts, networks in China and out, as any man. It was something to trade with once I decided to go home to the UK.

"I was married at twenty-one and presumably still had a wife. But she had become a misted memory, Jacko. Brainwashing does that to you; I still suffer from it. Whatever life she had made for herself, there was no way I was going to disrupt it by coming back from the dead after so many years. By the time it was safe enough for me to return to England it was 1981; twenty-eight years after I was captured. But the

250

moment I was home I began to worry about her. I had to find out how she was without her knowing. I tried to shake it off and did so for a few years but it gradually became an obsession. I had to know."

Jacko reached out to pour himself another drink. "That was when the Security Service began to worry about you. They thought you might blow the whole thing."

Dine smiled his acknowledgement. "That's good guessing, Jacko. They were never sure of me when I applied to come here, but saw my uses. They must have done a lot of digging of their own, but they could never prove anything and I knew some quite important people by then. They quietly threatened and could have made life difficult; MI5 collaborated with MI6, who used my Far Eastern network for their own reasons, and it gave them useful contacts in China. They ostensibly joined the drug scene, operating through me, of course. Once I started to keep an eye on Annette, they got very nervous indeed. They might have coped with that but then you came on the scene and they were running scared."

"I know," said Jacko. "It was those stupid bastards who snatched Georgie."

"They were, and still are afraid that you will find out what they think they know, and thereby cock up the whole business. I think they might be resigned to losing their China circuit but they could not let it be known that I was an escaped POW of the Korean War and that others were still there. That would be disastrous for them and the Americans; a tremendous political embarrassment. We're all dead, for God's sake; records show it. If you found out then they had a double danger."

Jacko looked surprised. "You don't think they intend to top you?"

"It would solve their problems, wouldn't it? I can blow the lid off a national disgrace and the Americans would be livid; they have far more out there than us and have most of the names including ours. Even with you still around they could laugh your story away. You could never prove it. I can. It suits me not to but they are too unsure now, to take chances."

"What about the drugs?"

251

"If they have any they will get the police to hang the whole thing on Rollins. I made contact with him before I left Hong Kong and he was already into the British side of the arms caches. Quite a clever move for him, once he had coerced Simon Wherewell. The idea to use the caches as drug distribution centres was mine. More local distribution was done through the clubs and leisure centres belonging to Charles Jason."

Jacko said, "They tried to take the drugs I lifted from the New Forest which will now be handed over to the Drug Squad. I suppose they did not want the police to have them until they had sorted out the business with you and perhaps not even then. They are afraid to go public on it particularly as you say they are involved, if only for other motives. But it wouldn't look good, would it?" Jacko suddenly laughed. "I thought you were trying to top me, you sod."

Dine grinned widely for the first time. "There were some pretty drastic warnings, but once I had checked on you, you were never in danger from me as you should have learned from Hong Kong. It was Rollins who did the killings, Rollins who panicked, Rollins who got rid of people who were seldom a real danger to him, and it was Rollins who made the dangerous attacks on you. I tried to stop him, but you see, he saw that as his part of the business."

"They will still be out there," said Jacko, as if Dine needed reminding.

"I know. Did you ever meet Annette?"

"No. I saw her. I saw you watching her. You were pretty worked up or you might have spotted me." Jacko paused, thinking carefully before saying, "I met your daughter, Laura, though."

"What!" Dine sank back in confusion. He rubbed his eyes. "I did not know she existed until lately. But I never even saw her. She doesn't know . . ."

"No. You'd be proud of her. Your sort of guts. Good looking. Married with two kids. She resembles you although I told her she looked like her mother. That clinched it for me. I told her I am a solicitor and have a small legacy for her mother

252

from some obscure source. I'll pay it out myself; I won't let them down."

"There's no need. We've got to get out of here and you'll have to trust me." Dine suddenly straightened himself. "I'm going to disappear. I've been preparing for some time. Wherever I've been I've always had an escape plan ready and I have one now. But it will mean I will have to disappear for some time. Meanwhile, Jacko, I want your word that you will do certain things for me."

"If it's within my scope, of course I will."

"Don't concern your insurance company with the Ferrari. I shall replace it for you, and other out-of-pocket expenses. Don't try to argue; I know you are well off but I'm loaded with the filthy stuff. I want you to look after Lonnie. He won't want for life but it will have to be administered. Your girlfriend can handle the legal side but a power of attorney for you has been drawn up and signed. There will be a provision for Annette and Laura; they'll be puzzled but they'll be okay. There will be more than adequate funds for fees and I think I've thought everything through."

"Just how long are you going away for?"

"It's bound to be a few years. I might have to build up another background. I won't be able to administrate these issues if I'm to be untraceable."

"What am I to tell Lonnie?"

"I've written a special letter to him." Dine went to a bureau and produced a thick package, carefully wrapped up. "Get your girlfriend to go through the papers. Everything is in there. Everything. Put it in your briefcase. Those monkeys out there still think you are a lawyer; nice touch that."

Jacko put the package away. "So what happens now?"

"Our best chance of safety is in separation. I can't take you with me, Jacko, and even if I could you wouldn't come. You've got your own life. As for me, I am and always will be in limbo. I've got used to it." He paused. "Come on. Put that stupid wig and moustache back on and say goodbye."

Jacko rose. "How are you getting out?"

"They'll try to wring it out of you if I tell you. It's very simple really. The best plans always are. But I need you as a distraction, so this is what you do." Dine went back to the window and peered through again. As it was dark outside, apart from street lights, Jacko wondered what he expected to see.

Dine continued. "Go downstairs and open the front door. Leave it open and stand in the open doorway. I want the hall light full on. You will hear three spaced shots. Do you think they will hear them, through the open door?"

"They should do. It will depend on where they are fired from. What's the idea?"

"Once they hear the shots they'll dash in. It is important that they do. If they don't, come back in and close the door and we'll have to start again. Is that pretty clear?"

"All except where you are going to spirit yourself after they've come in."

Dine offered a secret little smile. "These are old houses, hold a lot of secrets." He crossed over to shake Jacko's hand. "If only we could have met in different circumstances. I shall miss you. Oh, one more thing. Details of the drug operation and the arms caches are all in there, and the main operators, like Rollins and Jason. I'm going to start clean. There are separate copies for the Drug Squad and the Anti-Terrorist Squad. Do not give anything to MI5 or MI6. And the Sèvres, by the way, is on its way back to Paris." He paused, this time a little awkwardly, and then said, "I'll try to get in touch some time."

Now it was time to leave Jacko was reluctant. They shook hands again. "You sure you'll be all right?"

"I'm good at this sort of thing. I've had a lot of practice. Don't worry."

Jacko went down the stairs, hesitated in the hall, looked back up but there was no sign of Dine. He crossed the hall, opened the front door, looked back once more, and stepped on to the porch, leaving the door wide open. Nothing stirred opposite him. Then there was a single pistol shot which echoed down the stairs and out into the street.

Two men appeared from the cars and ran lightly across the road as Dine had predicted. Jacko turned back to face the hall but the men raced past him. Only then did Jacko realise he had been duped by his own kind of talk. He had believed Dine. The coldness which now seized him told him he should not have done. He sank slowly to the top step, put his case between his feet and his head in his hands, sick at heart. He knew for a certainty that Dine had at last escaped from limbo. And he had done it in part to free Jacko himself who now had nothing without the man to prove it all.

One of the security men came running out again and bawled to someone to radio for an ambulance. Jacko rose slowly, legs leaden, mind numbed, and slowly walked away, almost unaware that he was moving.

And then, through the depression, almost as if Reg Dine himself had planted the thought, he decided to collect the Renoir from Len Tiler, and give it to Georgie.